Katelyn

A BOOK SENSE WINTER CHILDREN

AN EDGAR AWARD NOMINEE

AN E.B. WHITE AWARD NOMINEE

AN NYPL BOOK FOR THE TEEN AGE

A NAPPA GOLD BOOK

AN ABC BEST BOOK FOR CHILDREN

"Engaging." —*Kirkus Reviews*

"Likely to acquire a cult following."
—*Publishers Weekly*

Praise for

THE NAME OF THIS BOOK IS SECRET

"Equal parts snarky and delightful."
—*Booklist*

"Entertaining for both parents and children."
—*Arizona Parenting*

"Smart and suspenseful."
—*The Buffalo News*

"One of those super fun mystery/ adventures . . . an engaging read."
—Bookloons.com

"Playful voice, engaging characters, and unusual plot . . . a delight to read."
—Kidreads.com

THE NAME OF THIS BOOK IS

secret

By Pseudonymous Bosch

Illustrations by Gilbert Ford

LITTLE, BROWN AND COMPANY
New York ⋅⋅ Boston

LITTLE, BROWN AND COMPANY
(THEY'RE NEITHER LITTLE NOR BROWN, BUT THAT'S ANOTHER STORY)
HACHETTE BOOK GROUP USA
237 PARK AVENUE, NEW YORK, NY 10017
VISIT OUR WEB SITE AT WWW.LB-KIDS.COM

FIRST PAPERBACK EDITION: SEPTEMBER 2008
FIRST PUBLISHED IN HARDCOVER IN OCTOBER 2007
BY LITTLE, BROWN AND COMPANY

PRINTED IN THE UNITED STATES OF AMERICA

RRD-C

10 9 8 7 6 5 4 3 2 1

Library of Congress Cataloging-in-Publication Data

Bosch, Pseudonymous.
  The name of this book is secret / by Pseudonymous Bosch; illustrated by Gilbert Ford.—1st ed.
    p. cm.
  Summary: Two eleven-year-old misfits try to solve the mystery of a dead magician and stop the evil Dr. L and Ms. Mauvais, who are searching for the secret of immortality.
  HC ISBN 978-0-316-11366-3 / PB ISBN 978-0-316-11369-4
  [1. Adventure and adventurers—Fiction. 2. Immortality—Fiction. 3. Synesthesia—Fiction.] I. Ford, Gilbert, ill. II. Title.
  PZ7.B6484992Nam 2007
  [Fic]—dc22   2007021909

FOR W.P. MAY

THE NAME OF THIS BOOK IS SECRET

WARNING:
DO NOT READ BEYOND THIS PAGE

Good.

Now I know I can trust you.

You're curious. You're brave. And you're not afraid to lead a life of crime.

But let's get something straight: if, despite my warning, you insist on reading this book, you can't hold me responsible for the consequences.

And, make no bones about it, this is a very dangerous book.

No, it won't blow up in your face. Or bite your head off. Or tear you limb from limb.

It probably won't injure you at all. Unless somebody throws it at you, which is a possibility that should never be discounted.

Generally speaking, books don't cause much harm. Except when you read them, that is. Then they cause all kinds of problems.

Books can, for example, give you ideas. I don't know if you've ever had an idea before, but, if you have, you know how much trouble an idea can get you into.

Books can also provoke emotions. And emotions sometimes are even more troublesome than ideas. Emotions have led people to do all sorts of things they later regret — like, oh, throwing a book at someone else.

But the main reason this book is so dangerous is that it concerns a secret.

A *big* secret.

It's funny the way secrets work. If you don't know about a secret, it doesn't bother you. You go about your business without a care in the world.

La la la, you sing. Everything's fine and dandy. (Maybe you don't actually sing "la la la," but you know what I mean.)

But as soon as you hear about the secret, it starts to nag at you. *What is this secret?* you wonder. *Why am I not supposed to know about it? Why is it so important?*

Suddenly, you're dying to know what the secret is.

You beg. You plead. You threaten. You cajole. You promise never to tell anyone else. You try anything and everything. You dig into the secret-keeper's belongings. You pull his or her hair. And when that doesn't work, you pull your own.

Not knowing a secret is just about the worst thing in the world.

No, I can think of one thing worse.

Knowing a secret.

Read on, if you must.

But, remember, I warned you.

XXX XXXX X XXXX, XXXXX XXX X XXX XXX X XXXX. Xxxx xxxx xxxx x xxxxx xxxx xx Xxxxxxx. Xxxx xxxxx xxxxx Xxxxxxxxx xxx Xxx-Xxxxxx. Xxxxx xxxxx xxxxxxxx xxxxx xxx. Xxxxx'x xxxxxxxxxxxxx, xx x xxxxxxxxx.

Xxxxxx xxxxxxxx xxxxxxx x Xxxx xx xxxxxx xxx. Xxxx x xxxxxxx. Xxxxxx xxxxxxxx xxxxxx xx Xxxxxx Xxxxxxxxxxxxxxx? Xxxxxxxxxxxxx. Xxxxxxxxxxxx. X xxxx xxxx xxxx xxxxx xxx xx xxxxx. Xxxxxxx xxxxxx, xxxxxxx xxxxxxxx x xxxxxxxxxx. Xxxxx xxxxx. Xxxxx.

Xxxxxxx xx, xxxx xxxxx, xxxxx xx xxx.

Xxxx'x?, xxx xxx.

Xxxx xxxxxxxxxxx xxxxxxx'x . . . Xxxxx xxxxxxxx Xxxxxxxxx xxxxxx xxxxxxxxxx xxx xxxxxxxxxxx xx, xxxxxxxx xxxxxxxx xxxxxxxxxx xxxxxx xxxx xxxx x xxxxxxxxxxx . . . Xxxxx xxxxxxxx'x xx xxxxx xxx xxxx xxxx xxx Xxxx.

"Xxxx," Xxxxxxxxx xxxxx, "Xxx xxxxxx?"

"Xx!" Xxx-Xxxxxx xxxx.

Xxxxxx xxxxxxxx xxxxxxx; x xxxx xx xxxxxx xxx. Xxxx x xxxxxxx. Xxxxxx xxxxxxxx Xxxxx'x xx xxxxxx, xxxxxxxxxxxxxxx? Xxxx xxxxxxxxx. Xxxxxxxxxxx. (Xxxxxx xxx xxx xxxxxxx xxxx xxxxxx.) Xxxx, Xxx-Xxxxxx xxxxxxxx xxxx xxxxx xx x x xxxxxx xx xxxx. Xxxxxxx xxxxxxxxxxxxx xxxxxxxx x xxxxxxxxxx. Xxxxx xxxxx, Xxxxx. Xxxx x xxxx, xxxxx.

Xxxxxxx, xx xxxxxxxx xxxxx. Xxxxx xx xxxxx, xxxx xxxx x xxxxx xxx xxxx. Xxxxxxxxx, Xxxxxx xxxxxxxxxxxx xxxxxxxxxxxx xxx, xxxxx xxxxxx xxxxxxxxxx xxxx xxxx xxxxxxxxxx xxxxxx xxxx xxxx x xxxxx xxxxxx . . .

XxxxxxxxxxxxxxXxxxxxxxxxxxx,xxxxxxxxxxxxxxxx? Xxxx xxxxxxxxx. Xxxxxxxxxxx? Xxx xxxx xxx xxx xxxxxxx xxxx xxxxxx. Xxxx, xxxxxxxx xxxx xxxxx xx x x xxxxxx xx xxxx. (Xxxxxxx xxxxxxxxxxxxx xxxxxxxx x xxxxxxxxxx.) X xxxxxx xxxx Xxxxx xx xxxxx xxx x xxxxxxxx.

"Xxxx," Xxxx xxxx, "Xxxxxxxx!!!!"

Xxxxxxxx xx x xxxxxxxx x Xxx-Xxxxxx xxx, xxxxx xxx xxxx x xxxxxx xxx xxxxx xx xxxxxxxxxxxx.

Xxxx, xxxx, xxx xxxxxx, xxxx xxxx xxxxxxx.

Xxxxxx xxxxxxxx xxxxxxx x xxxx xx Xxxxxx xxx. Xxxx x xxxxxxx. Xxxxxx xxxxxxxx xxxxxx xx xxxxxx xxxxxxxxxxxxxxxx? Xxxxxxxxxxxxx. X xxxxxxxxxx. X xxxxxx xxxxxx, Xxx-Xxxxxx xxxxxxxx x xxxxxxxxxx. Xxxxx xxxxx! Xxxxx!

Xxxx Xxxxx xxxxxx x xxxxxxxx.

X xxxxxx xxx x xxxxxxx x xxxx xxxx, Xxxxxxxxx xxx Xxx-Xxxxxx xxxx x xxxxxx xxx x xxxxx xx xxxx xxxxxxxx.

Xxx xxx xxxxx.

X xxxxx.

Xxxx?

Xxx, Xxxx.

Xxx xx xxxxxx xxx xxxxx . . .

CHAPTER ONE AND A HALF

Apologia* Apologia
logia Apologia Apologia
ologia Apologia Apologia
ogia Apologia Apologia
pologia Apo

* AN APOLOGIA, IF YOU'RE WONDERING, IS
NOT A VARIETY OF INSECT. NEITHER IS IT A TYPE OF
CANCEROUS TUMOR. IT'S AN APOLOGY. IN OTHER WORDS,
IT'S NOT WORTH THE PAPER IT'S WRITTEN ON.

'm sorry I couldn't let you read Chapter One.

That was where you would have learned the names of the characters in this story. You also would have learned where it takes place. And when. You would have learned all the things you usually learn at the beginning of a book.

Unfortunately, I can't tell you any of those things.

Yes, this is a story *about* a secret. But it's also a *secret story.*

I shouldn't even be telling you that I shouldn't be telling you the story. That's how much of a secret it is.

Not only can't I tell you the names of the people involved, I can't even tell you what they've done or why.

I can't tell you what kind of pets they have. Or how many annoying little brothers. Or how many bossy big sisters. Or whether they like their ice cream plain or with mix-ins.

I can't tell you about their schools or their friends or their favorite television shows. Or if they ride skateboards. Or if they are champion chess players. Or if they compete in fencing competitions. Or even if they wear braces.

In short, I can't tell you anything that would help you identify the people involved in this story if you were to meet them at your orthodontist's office.

(Teeth, as you may know from watching television, are very useful when detectives are identifying cadavers.)

This is for your own protection as well as mine. And for the protection of your friends. And even of your enemies. (You know, those ones you say you want to kill but in the end you'd rather keep alive.)

Still, you must find my silence very frustrating.

How can you follow a story if you don't know whom it's about? *Somebody* has got to be getting lost in the woods, or slaying dragons, or traveling in time, or whatever it is that happens in the story.

I'll tell you what — I'll make you a deal.

To help you follow my story, I'm going to break my own rule — already! — and I'm going to give my characters names and faces. But remember these aren't their *real* names and faces. They're more like code names or cover identities, like a spy or a criminal would have.

If you don't like a name I choose, change it. If I write "*Tim* loved to pick his nose," and you prefer the name Tom to Tim, then read the line as "*Tom* loved to pick his nose." I won't take offense. You can do that with all the names in this book if you like.

Or keep my names. It's up to you.

Now, just as it's hard to read a story without

knowing whom the story's about, it's also hard to read a story without knowing where the story takes place. Even if you were reading about extraterrestrials from another dimension, you'd want to imagine something about their surroundings. Like that they lived in a murky green miasma. Or in some place really hot.

Although the real location of this story will have to remain a mystery, to make it easier for all of us, why don't we say the story takes place in *a place you know very well?*

We'll call it Your Hometown.

When you read about the town the characters live in, just think of the town you live in. Is the town big or little? By the sea or by a lake? Or is your town all asphalt and shopping malls? You tell me.

When you read about the characters' school, think of Your School. Is it in an old one-room schoolhouse or in a bunch of double wide mobile homes? You decide.

When they go home, imagine they live on Your Street, maybe even in a house right across from yours.

Who knows, maybe Your Street is where the story really takes place. I wouldn't tell you if it was. But I couldn't tell you for certain that it's not.

In return for all the freedom I'm giving you, I ask

only one favor: if I ever slip and reveal something that I shouldn't — and I will! — please forget what I've said as soon as possible.

In fact, when you're reading this book, it's a good idea to forget everything you read as soon as you read it. If you're one of those people who can read with their eyes closed, I urge you to do so. And, if you're blind and reading this in braille, keep your hands off the page!

Why do I write under such awful circumstances? Wouldn't it be better to scrap this book altogether and do something else?

Oh, I could give you all kinds of reasons.

I could tell you that I write this book so you will learn from the mistakes of others. I could tell you that, as dangerous as writing this book is, it would be even more dangerous not to write it.

But the real reason is nothing so glorious. It's very simple.

I can't keep a secret. Never could.

I hope you have better luck.

CHAPTER TWO

A WEDNESDAY

True, I cannot tell you the year this story begins, or even the month. But I see no harm in telling you the day.

It was a Wednesday.

A humble, unremarkable day. The middle child in the weekday family. A Wednesday has to work hard to be noticed. Most people let each one pass without comment.

But not the heroine of our story. She is the kind of girl who notices things that others don't.

Meet Cassandra.

Wednesday is her favorite day. She believes it's just when you least expect something earth-shattering to happen that it does.

According to Greek myth, the original Cassandra was a princess of ancient Troy. She was very beautiful, and Apollo, god of the sun, fell in love with her.

When she rejected him, Apollo became so angry he placed a curse on her: he gave her the power to predict the future, but he also ensured that nobody would believe her predictions. Imagine knowing that your whole world was about to be destroyed by a tornado or typhoon, and then having nobody believe you when you told them. What misery!

Unlike the Cassandra of myth, the girl who figures in our story is not a prophet. She cannot see into the future. Nor has she been cursed by a god, at least not to my knowledge. But she resembles a prophet in that she is always predicting disaster. Earthquakes, hurricanes, plagues — she is an expert in all things terrible and she sees evidence of them everywhere.

That is why I am calling her Cassandra — or Cass, for short.

As you know, I cannot describe Cass in detail. But this much I will tell you: from the outside, Cass looks like a typical eleven-year-old. Her major distinguishing feature is that she has rather large, pointy ears. And before you tell me that I shouldn't have told you about the ears, let me explain that she almost always covers her ears with her hair or with a hat. So chances are you will never see them.

While she may look like other girls, Cass is in other respects a very un-average sort of person. She doesn't play games involving fortune-telling or jump rope or strings of any kind. She doesn't even watch television very often. She doesn't own a single pair of soft suede boots lined with fleece. She wouldn't even want a pair, unless they were waterproof and could protect her in a snowstorm.

As you can tell, Cass is very practical; she has no time for trivial matters.

Her motto: *Be Prepared.*

Her mission: to make sure that she and her friends and family survive all the disasters that befall them. Cass is a *survivalist.*

These are things Cass carries in her backpack every day:

Flashlight

Compass

Silver Mylar space blanket — surprisingly warm if you haven't tried one; also has useful reflective properties

Box of juice — usually grape, doubles as ink in a pinch

Bubble gum — for its sticking value, and because chewing helps her concentrate

Cass's patented "super-chip" trail mix — chocolate chips, peanut-butter chips, banana chips, potato chips (and no raisins, ever!)

Topographic maps — of all the closest desert and mountain areas, as well as of Micronesia and the Galápagos Islands

Rope

Tool kit

First-aid kit

Dust mask

Extra pair of socks and shoes — in case
of flash floods and other wet conditions
Matches — technically not allowed at school
Plastic knife — because a jackknife is
really not allowed
Schoolbooks and homework — when
she remembers, which is not very often
(she keeps forgetting to put schoolwork
on her supplies checklist)

On the evidence of the items in her backpack, you might guess that Cass had led a very adventurous life. But you would be wrong. The truth is, up until the time this story begins, none of the disasters she predicted had befallen her. There'd been no earthquakes at school — none strong enough to shatter a window, anyway. The mildew in her mother's shower turned out to be just that — not the killer mold Cass predicted. And that child spinning around on the grass did not have mad cow disease — he was just having a good time.

Cass didn't exactly mind that her predictions hadn't come true. After all, she didn't *wish* for disaster. But she couldn't help wishing people took her concerns more seriously.

Instead, everyone was always reminding her about the boy who cried wolf. Naturally, *they* took that story to mean the boy shouldn't have cried wolf when there weren't any. But Cass knew the true moral of the story: that the boy was right, there really *were* wolves around, and they'd get you in the end if you didn't watch out.

Better to cry wolf over and over than never to cry wolf at all.

Of all the people in the world, only two paid attention to Cass's predictions: Grandpa Larry and Grandpa Wayne.

Larry and Wayne weren't Cass's original, biological grandfathers. They were her *substitute* grandfathers. Larry had been Cass's mother's history teacher in high school, and they'd remained friends ever since. Since neither of Cass's original grandfathers were around, Cass's mother asked Larry and Wayne to fill in.

Larry and Wayne lived around the corner from Cass in an old abandoned fire station. The bottom floor, where the fire engines had been kept, they had converted to an antiques store and warehouse. Their living quarters were upstairs, where in the old days the firemen had slept between fires.

Every Wednesday after school, Cass was supposed to work in their shop until her mother called to say dinner was ready. But, in truth, very little work ever got done at the fire station.

"You're just in time for tea," Grandpa Larry would say whenever she visited.

Grandpa Larry wasn't British, but he'd spent time in England when he was in the army and he'd developed a serious tea habit. Cass thought Larry's elaborate tea rituals were a little silly, but she loved the cookies Larry made (he called them "biscuits") and the stories he told while their tea was brewing. By now, Cass suspected that most of his stories were exaggerated, if not entirely made up, but they always included useful information — like how to put up a tent in a sandstorm or how to milk a camel.

On the particular Wednesday that this story begins, Larry was showing Cass how to make a compass by placing a cork in a bowl of water.* The compass was almost complete, and the cork just about to point north, when her grandfathers' basset hound, Sebastian, started barking so noisily that the water shook out of the edge of the bowl.

Sebastian was blind, and now that he was growing old he was very nearly deaf as well. But he had the keenest sense of smell in town — everyone called him "Sebastian, the Seeing-Nose Dog" — and he always knew when visitors were about to enter the shop.

"Fire drill!" called Grandpa Wayne from down

*For Grandpa Larry's compass recipe, turn to the appendix. That's at the end of the book, by the way, not in your body.

below, which was their code for when a customer
had arrived.

"Guess the compass will have to wait," grumbled
Grandpa Larry. "Now get down. Smoke rises, so the
best way to keep breathing is to stay low to the
ground."

He and Cass crouched down and pulled their
shirts over their noses, as if the room were filling
with smoke. Larry pointed to the station's old brass
fire pole: "Ladies first."

Cass eagerly grabbed the pole and stepped out
into the opening in the floor.

"Wait," said Larry. "Promise not to tell your
mother?"

"Promise," said Cass, already starting to slide.

Despite the fact that it was their job, Cass's grandfathers couldn't bear to sell anything; they loved all their things too much.

As a result, their store was crammed so tight it was like a huge maze with walls of furniture. Every surface was covered with stuff they'd collected — from old clown paintings to mechanical monkeys to broken typewriters to things you couldn't describe if you tried.

By the time Larry and Cass had navigated their way through, the front door was opening to reveal a short pair of legs staggering under the weight of an enormous cardboard box.

As soon as he saw the box, Larry rushed to the doorway and threw his arms across it, barring the way.

"No, no, no! Bad Gloria!" he said sternly, as if he were addressing a dog and not a person under a box. "I told you last time, no more things. Look around. We're stuffed to the gills."

"At least let me put this down for a minute," complained the voice of the unseen woman.

Taking pity on her, Larry grabbed hold of the box and placed it on the threshold. A small round woman in a bright yellow suit scowled at him. This was Gloria Fortune.

"Don't you even want to hear where it comes from?" she asked, still red-faced and breathing hard under her tall beehive hairdo. "Such fascinating things . . . Well, never mind!" she said brightly. "Is there a Dumpster in back?"

Larry almost choked. "No! I mean, yes, there's a Dumpster, but . . . you're not . . . you wouldn't . . . throw the box away?" he asked, as if Gloria were threatening murder.

Gloria smiled slyly as she twisted a curl of hair that had sprung loose. "Sorry, Larry. You're my last resort. *I* certainly don't have any room."

Larry hesitated. "In that case—why don't you come inside for a cup of tea, and I'll just take a peek, before you do anything rash —"

Gloria grinned victoriously. "You won't regret it," she said, entering the store.

Sheepishly, Larry picked up the box and followed her back inside.

"Sorry," he whispered to Cass. "This should only take a second, er, minute, er, five, er, ten . . . twenty minutes at the most. . . ."

Gloria, as Cass learned over her third—or was it her fourth?—cup of tea, was a real estate agent, a "probate specialist," meaning that she sold houses after their owners passed away. She was, in effect, a real estate agent for the dead.

Gloria loved to gossip, and Larry was always ready to listen to ghoulish tales about her dead clients. (Wayne, who was a retired auto mechanic, always left to go fix something when Gloria was around.) As for the box of stuff she had just brought, it came from the home of a "strange and reclusive man — some kind of magician or something. What I call a real old coot," Gloria said.

"Watch it, Gloria," said Grandpa Larry. "Some of us are pretty cootish ourselves!"

The magician, Gloria continued obliviously, had died very suddenly several months earlier in a kitchen fire, the source of which was never determined. He had no known relations or survivors. "Not a single friend left, poor man."

Because the magician's house was so "off the beaten path" his death might never have been discovered had not his gardener investigated the terrible smell emanating from the kitchen.

Cass nodded knowingly at this bit of information. "The smell of decomposing flesh can be very strong," she said, trying to show she was familiar with cases of this kind (although, I hasten to point out, her knowledge of corpses was not yet firsthand).

"True," sniffed Gloria. "But actually what the gardener was smelling was something else. Sulfurous, he described it. Like *huevos podridos.*"

"That means 'rotten eggs' in Spanish," said Cass, who was studying the language at school.

"I thought it meant Talky Girls," said Gloria pointedly.

Cass considered it wise not to say anything more, and she excused herself to do some homework, pretending she was no longer interested in the story of the dead magician. But she continued to listen, or, as you might call it, eavesdrop, while Gloria finished telling her story.

In fact, almost nothing of the magician's body was left — smelly or otherwise. The fire had been so intense that only a few of his teeth remained. (See, I warned you about teeth.) Curiously, while the magician's entire kitchen was incinerated, the rest of the house was left unscathed, as if the fire had gone out as quickly as it had started.

According to Gloria, the source of the noxious aroma was never found, and traces of it still lingered. She hoped it wouldn't hamper the sale of the house, which was going to be difficult enough thanks to the house's "quirky and offbeat" character.

Gloria pronounced these words as if they were

slightly distasteful, but Cass, not knowing precisely what they meant, thought they sounded just grand. She decided if she ever bought a house she would want to buy one just like the magician's.

After Gloria left, Wayne rejoined the others to rifle through the magician's belongings. Mostly, the contents of the box were disappointing. What Gloria had described as a "contraption for mixing potions" turned out to be an ordinary kitchen mixer. And what she had guessed was "something to make objects disappear" was in fact a piece of exercise equipment.

They thought they'd extracted everything they could, when Sebastian started barking excitedly. The blind dog circled the box, sniffing it, like there was something inside he really wanted. Or something inside he was really scared of. Or both.

Cass pushed aside the last remaining bits of newspaper at the bottom and saw something they'd missed earlier: another box. Sebastian's barks grew louder as she pulled it out.

The box was flat, about the size and shape of a briefcase, and fitted with brass hinges and fastenings. It was made of a darkish, reddish, stripy type of wood, and it was carved with a design of swirling vines and flowers surrounding an uplifted face. The face was shown in profile inhaling what looked like curling smoke.

"Rosewood," Wayne said, taking the box from Cass so that he could examine it more closely. "Too large for a cigar box. . . . Maybe a cutlery case?"

Larry nodded. "Probably . . . Art Nouveau design. About a hundred years old. French?"* He took the box from Wayne and held it up to look at the bottom. "No markings. Looks like one of a kind."

"Can I open it?" Cass asked. She knew from experience they could go on for hours if she didn't stop them.

Wayne nudged Larry, and Larry handed her the box. "Go ahead," he said, although, no doubt, he would have liked to open it himself.

With a substitute grandfather peering over each shoulder, Cass carefully sprang the latch and raised the lid. From their gasps, Cass could tell they'd never seen anything like it before. She certainly hadn't.

The interior of the box was upholstered in lustrous purple velvet. Nestled in the velvet, and arranged in four concentric semicircles, were dozens of sparkling crystal vials. Most of these vials (Cass later counted ninety-nine of them) contained liquids in a variety of colors: lavender water, amber oil, alcohol

---

*Art Nouveau means "new art" in French, but as you can see from the box it's actually a very old style. If you ever go to Paris, and I hope you do, you will notice that some of the metro entrances are made to look like vines growing out of the sidewalk — an Art Nouveau jungle.

in an alarming shade of green. Other vials were filled with powders of various degrees of fineness; others with flower petals, leaves, herbs and spices, shards of wood and bark, even dirt. One vial held a single strand of hair.

"What is this, some kind of chemistry set?" Cass wondered aloud.

"Hmm, could be," said Larry. "Did you know that in England pharmacists are called chemists?"

Touching the velvet for the first time, Cass noticed something that had been hidden by a fold: a small brass plaque on which someone had engraved the words:

The Symphony of Smells

"'The Symphony of Smells'?"

"Maybe it's a perfume-making kit," suggested Wayne.

Cass pulled out a vial and opened it. A sharp citrus aroma was released into the air.

"Lemon?" she guessed.

She handed the vial to Wayne and pulled out another. They spent the next few minutes opening vials, and guessing the scents they contained: mint, lime, root beer ("sassafras," Larry called it), wet wool, old socks, freshly mown grass.

"I think it's a kind of smelling game," said Cass, who was enjoying herself immensely. "To train your nose. Like if you were a detective. So you would know what you were smelling in an emergency. Or at the scene of a crime."

"Whatever it is, my nose is getting very tired," said Larry.

"Just one more," said Cass, picking up a vial from the end of the second row. There was a hairline crack in the vial, and it was nearly empty, save for a light dusting of yellow powder. She opened it — and recognized the smell immediately.

It was the smell of *huevos podridos*. Rotten eggs.

CHAPTER THREE

and now introducing... Max-Ernest

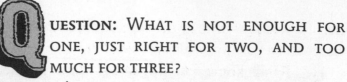**UESTION:** WHAT IS NOT ENOUGH FOR ONE, JUST RIGHT FOR TWO, AND TOO MUCH FOR THREE?

ANSWER: A SECRET.

Max-Ernest, eleven-year-old aspiring stand-up co-median, had read the joke — really a riddle, if you want to get technical — in one of his seventeen joke books, and now he was trying it on each of his twenty-six classmates in turn.

None of his classmates laughed. Or even smiled.

Most of them were so tired of his jokes that they didn't bother to respond at all. Those who did said things on the order of "Uh huh" and "Whatever" and "That's stupid" and "No more jokes — it's so annoying, Max-Ernest!" and "Why can't you just have one name like a normal person?"

You or I would probably burst into tears if our jokes met with such negative reactions, but Max-Ernest was used to it. He never let what other people said upset him.

He was going to be the funniest and best stand-up comedian of all time. He just needed to practice.

Max-Ernest looked around the school yard for a student who hadn't heard his joke yet. There was only one. She was squatting by the edge of the soccer field, a baseball cap on the ground beside her.

He didn't know her personally because they didn't have any classes together. But he recognized her on the basis of a certain physical feature: her big, pointy ears.

Since I've already made the mistake of describing Cass's most identifiable trait (yes, her ears! I thought she never exposed them, but I guess I was wrong), I may as well describe our other hero, Max-Ernest, for you. But remember what I said about forgetting what I said? Try to erase the image of Max-Ernest from your head as fast as you can — for your own safety.

Aside from his small size, the first thing you would have noticed about Max-Ernest was his hair. Each strand stood on end, as though he were a cartoon character who had just stuck his finger in an electrical socket.

His hairstyle was not a fashion choice; it was a philosophical one. Max-Ernest cut every hair on his head the exact same length because he didn't like to favor one hair over another. Hairs may be made of dead cells, he reasoned, but they're still growing things, and each one deserves to be treated fairly. (If you think this point of view is a bit odd or eccentric, well, I'd have to agree.)

That hair is dead but still growing is what is known as a paradox: something that seems impossible but is nonetheless true. Max-Ernest was very fond of paradoxes, as he was of all kinds of riddles and puzzles and word games.

Max-Ernest also liked math. And history. And science. And just about any subject you can think of.

Despite his diminutive stature, Max-Ernest attracted attention wherever he went. He couldn't help it. As you will soon discover yourself, Max-Ernest was a talker. A big talker. He talked all the time. Even in his sleep.

His "condition," as his parents called it, was so extreme that they'd taken him to numerous experts in hopes of finding a diagnosis.

The first expert said he had attention deficit disorder. The second expert said the first was out of order. One expert said he was autistic, another that he was artistic. One said he had Tourette's syndrome. One said he had Asperger's syndrome. And one said the problem was that his parents had Munchausen syndrome.

Still another said all he needed was a good old-fashioned spanking.

They gave him pills to take and exercises to practice. But the more ways people tried to cure him, the worse the problem got. Instead of stopping his talking, each cure gave him a new thing to talk about.

In the end, the experts weren't able to agree on a name for Max-Ernest's condition any more than his parents had been able to agree on a name for *him*.

HOW MAX-ERNEST BECAME MAX-ERNEST
A Short Story

Max-Ernest was a preemie. That is, he was born prematurely — about six weeks earlier than expected.

Prior to his entering the world, his parents hadn't done anything to prepare for his arrival. They had no stroller, no crib, no annoying musical toys, no baby wipes, no box of diapers. There were still plenty of pointy, dangerous things around the house.

And they had no name for their baby.

As the lump of shriveled pink flesh that would become Max-Ernest lay in the hospital incubator, like a small chicken (or maybe rabbit?) roasting in a glass oven, his parents argued about what to call him.

His mother wanted to name him after her father, Max, but his father wanted to name him after *his* father, Ernest. Neither parent would budge. Max-Ernest's mother declared she would rather her child have no name at all than have a crusty old name like Ernest. His father swore that he'd rather have no child at all than that his child have a meager, mini little name like Max.

Being only a few days old, Max-Ernest was unable to tell his parents which name he preferred. But that didn't stop them. When he cried, Max-Ernest's mother took it as evidence that he hated the name Ernest and wanted the name Max. When he spit up on his chin, his father said it was a sign that he hated the name Max and wanted the name Ernest.

Finally, a nurse threatened to put their child up for adoption if they didn't reach a decision. So Max-Ernest's parents decided to split the difference and put both names on his birth certificate. But the argument left them so bitter and angry that they got a divorce as soon as they left the hospital with their baby.

Now eleven years old, Max-Ernest has

been able to speak quite clearly for a long time. But whenever his parents ask him which name he prefers, as they do every year on his birthday, he goes mute. He knows that to choose one *name* over the other is actually to choose one *parent* over the other, and, like most children, he'd rather do anything than do *that*.

Thus Max-Ernest has two names to this very day and very likely will keep them for the rest of his life. The End.

At the exact moment Max-Ernest eyed her from across the school yard, Cassandra was digging in the mud with her bare hands. Dirt kept getting under her fingernails, and she muttered to herself that she should be wearing protective gloves. It wasn't like her to be so unprepared.

She glanced a few feet away to a spot under the bleachers, where a small gray furry thing was lying in the grass: a dead mouse.

Sure, maybe the mouse had died of natural causes, Cass thought. But then why was she smelling rotten eggs again? What if the mouse had died from the same thing as the magician? What if the whole town were built over a toxic waste dump? If she didn't do something about it, everybody she knew would perish!

Or should she let them? Maybe they didn't deserve to live.

If you haven't guessed already, Cass was having a bad day.

That morning, she had told her school's principal, Mrs. Johnson, that she had reason to suspect their school was built on top of a toxic waste site. Cass made the sensible suggestion that Mrs. Johnson evacuate the school and order an excavation of the grounds.

Mrs. Johnson, who was a real stickler ("a principal with principles," she called herself), gave Cass a stern look. "What's the magic word, Cassandra? Whether you're asking for an evacuation or a glass of water?"

"*Please* evacuate the school," said Cass impatiently.

"That's better. But the answer is still 'No.' What did I tell you about the boy who cried wolf?"

From there, the day only got worse:

"You look like you need a Smoochie."

Amber caught Cass on her way out of the principal's office and there was no escape. There was never any escape from Amber.

Amber was the nicest girl in school, and the third prettiest.*

Amber's only fault, and it was more like a charming habit, was that she was "totally addicted," as she put it, to a particular brand of lip balm called Sweet 'n Sassy Lip Smoochies by Romi and Montana. (Romi and Montana Skelton, otherwise known as the Skelton Sisters, were teen heiresses and television stars who controlled their own cosmetics empire; Amber "totally worshipped" them.) Every week, Amber got a new, differently flavored Smoochie, and she gave the previous week's away. Most kids in school considered it a great honor to receive Amber's half-used Smoochies, and they dangled them from their necks like Olympic medals. Cass, on the other hand, knew the only reason Amber gave her so many was that Amber felt sorry for her.

Cass *hated* people feeling sorry for her.

Each time she accepted a Smoochie, she promised herself she would refuse the next one, but Amber always managed to catch Cass when her guard was down. Before she knew it, Cass would find herself mumbling her thanks and shoving another Smoochie deep into her pocket.

That morning, Amber was accompanied by Veronica, the second prettiest girl in school (and not

---

*Nobody knew how these ratings had been established; they were simply facts, like gravity or Mrs. Johnson's hats.

even the fourth or fifth nicest). After Veronica gushed about how sweet Amber was for giving Cass her Watermelon-Superburst Smoochie (as if it were an extra-good good deed to give it to Cass as opposed to someone else), Cass tried to enlist their support in uncovering the toxic waste. She figured if she got Amber and Veronica on her side, the whole school would rally to the cause.

Cass told them she knew there was toxic waste because the grass on the soccer field had turned yellow. And because all the dogs in the neighborhood acted nervous and pricked up their ears when they came near the school.

But all Amber said was, "Wow, you're really smart, Cass." And she left with Veronica, never bothering to answer Cass's plea for help.

When they thought Cass was out of earshot, Veronica started giggling. "That's why she has those ears. To pick up danger sounds. Like a dog."

"Don't be so mean, V," Cass heard Amber say.

But she heard Amber giggling, too.

Covering her mouth with her shirt collar, and her hands with her cuffs, Cass started digging with renewed vigor. She wasn't going to let Mrs. Johnson or Amber or anyone else stop her. And, later, when they all thanked her for saving their lives and begged her forgiveness — well, she'd decide what to do then.

Suddenly, she heard a voice behind her head.

"Hi, you're Cassandra. I'm Max-Ernest. We don't know each other. But I know who you are and you probably know who I am. Well, you definitely do now. But I mean you probably knew before because everybody here knows who everybody is. Even if they've never met. Isn't that weird how you can know somebody and not know somebody at the same time? How 'bout that?"

Cass looked up to see a short — a mean person might say "puny" — kid looking down at her. It was true, she did know his name was Max-Ernest — but only because she'd heard other kids complaining about him. She could already see why he irritated them so much.

"So, you wanna hear a joke?" Max-Ernest asked.

Cass put her hat back on her head. "If it's about my ears, I've heard them all before," she said in a not very encouraging tone.

Max-Ernest swallowed nervously. "Actually, I think your ears are cool. They make you look like an elf. I mean, in a good way. Well, I think it's good because elves are my favorite fictional humanoids. Well, favorite after orcs. Not that I would want to meet an orc. Besides, you don't look anything like an orc. Or maybe I should quit while I'm ahead, right?"

He paused for a quick breath. When she didn't take the opportunity to yell at him, he continued,

"Hey, do you think I talk too much? Everybody does. I don't mean everybody talks too much, I mean everybody thinks I talk too much. Even my parents. They think I have a condition. My parents are psychologists. That means they're doctors who cure people by talking. But my problem is talking and they don't know how to cure me! How 'bout that?"

Cass didn't know what to say, so she asked, "What was your joke?"

"Oh, I almost forgot! What is not enough for one, just right for two, and too much for three?"

"What?"

"A secret."

She didn't laugh any more than anyone else had. "I don't get it."

"Well," Max-Ernest explained patiently, "you can't have a secret between yourself and yourself. You need someone else to have a secret with. That's two people. But it's not really a secret anymore if three people know it."

Cass thought about this. "But that doesn't make

any sense. One person can have a secret. Three people can have a secret. It doesn't matter how many people have a secret, as long as they don't tell anybody else."

Max-Ernest stared at her in surprise.

He was used to being ridiculed and teased and spat at and having his lunch stolen. But never before had anyone told him he didn't make sense. He prided himself on his logical mind.

"No, no, you're wrong!" he sputtered. "If you have a secret from somebody, they're still two people!"

Cass shrugged. "Well, anyways, it doesn't matter, because it's not funny if you have to explain it."

"What do you mean? Why?"

"I don't know, because you just have to get a joke. It's not like a logical thing."

"So then how do you know if a joke is funny?" Max-Ernest asked, extremely confused.

"You just do. Maybe you just don't have a very good sense of humor," Cass said helpfully.

"Oh."

For the first time since she'd met him, Max-Ernest seemed at a loss for words. He looked so sad and defeated that Cass took pity on him.

"Or maybe you just haven't found the right joke yet," she added.

"Yeah, maybe."

She didn't know he had been trying out a new joke every day for months.

He was silent for another second. But only a second. Then he pointed to the hole in the ground. "So, what are you looking for? Buried treasure? Because buried treasure isn't just in books, you know. There's real buried treasure. Like in shipwrecks. Did you know the *Titanic* was —"

"I'm looking for toxic waste," Cass said, cutting him off before he could go off on a tangent about the *Titanic.*

Max-Ernest nodded knowingly. "Yeah, I heard they always put schools over toxic waste dumps. Because the land is really cheap. And then they don't tell anyone. And then everyone gets sick. You want help? Hey, they have rubber gloves in the science lab. Maybe we should get some. Exposure to toxic waste might give us a skin rash."

Cass smiled. Maybe Max-Ernest wasn't so bad after all.

CHAPTER FOUR

A MESSAGE FOR THE WINDS

fter her experience with Amber and Veronica, Cass had vowed never to discuss her predictions with anyone again. But she made an exception for Max-Ernest because he seemed so knowledgeable about toxic waste. By the time they returned to the soccer field with the laboratory gloves, Cass had told him all about the dead magician, the dead mouse, and the mysterious sulfur smell.

Max-Ernest scrunched his nose. "It doesn't smell like rotten eggs to me. Are you sure it's the same smell?"

He suggested they take out the vial from the Symphony of Smells and compare it to the scent of the soccer field. Cass was slightly annoyed that she hadn't thought of this herself. Nonetheless, she pulled the wooden box out of her backpack to show him.*

When she opened the small dusty vial and took a whiff she had to agree it didn't smell much like the soccer field. Perhaps she had jumped to conclusions too quickly.

Max-Ernest put his face to the ground and sniffed. "I think the grass smells more like you-know-what—"

"No, what?"

"You know, number two!" said Max-Ernest, turning red.

---

*WHY WAS THE SYMPHONY OF SMELLS IN HER BACKPACK AND NOT IN THE SHOP WHERE IT BELONGED? I'M AFRAID I CAN'T EXPLAIN WITHOUT PUTTING CASS IN A RATHER NEGATIVE LIGHT. BUT — HYPOTHETICALLY — WOULD IT BE SUCH A BAD THING TO TAKE IT IF SHE REALLY THOUGHT SHE WAS SAVING LIVES?

Cass rolled her eyes. But when she sniffed the ground herself, she had to agree he was right.

Then she noticed something she hadn't seen earlier: only three feet from the mouse, there was a pile of fertilizer. What they were smelling was manure!

And there was something else: a box with a picture of a rat inside a red circle with a slash through it. Rat poison. That's what had killed the mouse. She decided it wasn't necessary to point this out to Max-Ernest. If he noticed it himself, fine. If he didn't, well, he didn't. No sense making him cocky.

Anyway, it didn't mean there wasn't toxic waste. Not necessarily.

Meanwhile, Max-Ernest had begun inspecting the Symphony of Smells more closely. "Did you see that the back comes off?" he asked.

Cass hadn't noticed, but she didn't say so. She wasn't sure how many more of Max-Ernest's discoveries she could take.

Max-Ernest pulled a velvet panel away from the inside of the box's lid and a bunch of papers slid out onto the ground.

Cass started looking through them. "Beethoven ... Mozart ... Franz Liszt ... Who's that?"

"Beethoven and Mozart are classical music

composers, like from a long time ago," said Max-Ernest. "Maybe Franz Liszt is, too."

"I know who Beethoven and Mozart are! I just didn't know who Liszt was," said Cass. "Anyway, these look like recipes . . . See? Symphony Number 9 — juniper, chocolate, allspice . . . Sonata Number 12 — mint, rosemary, lavender . . . I guess they're like smell versions of the music? Like scratch and sniff?"

"I seriously doubt that. How could there be a smell version of music?" asked Max-Ernest, who, as you know, was always very logical. "Music is made of sound."

"I know! I don't mean it's really music. It's just a cool idea, like, I don't know . . . elves and orcs. Here, look —"

She held up a hand-drawn chart, and started reading aloud. "First violin: ginger. Viola: maple. Cello: vanilla."

"It's an orchestra?"

"Right — the Symphony of Smells. Here's oboe. That's what I play. It's licorice."

"Huh," said Max-Ernest, turning over the oboe-licorice connection in his head. "Why do you think it's licorice? Do you like licorice?"

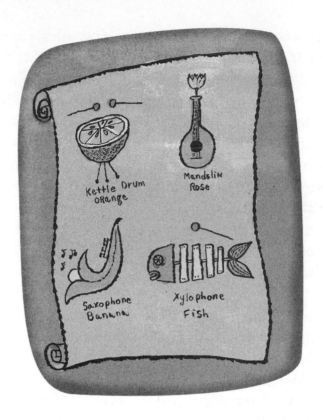

"Not the black kind. But I don't really like oboe either."

"I still don't see how a smell is supposed to be music," said Max-Ernest.

"Maybe we should play one," said Cass, pointing to the sheet music. "Or smell it, I mean."

Using the chart to locate their "musical instruments," they tried smelling Beethoven, then Mozart, then a symphony by Franz Liszt. All the music smelled good, except for the Liszt, but eventually even Cass had to admit she couldn't tell what was especially musical about it.

As they put the music back in the case, a tattered piece of paper fell out and started blowing around in the breeze. Cass caught the paper just before it landed in the manure. It was smudged and wrinkled and singed around the edges, but she could still make out the words written on it.

"A message for the winds," she read aloud. *"In order to spell it, you must first smell it."* Below this note, the names of four instruments had been written, one beneath the other:

Clarinet
Flute
Oboe
Bassoon

"You think it's some kind of coded message?" Cass asked.

Max-Ernest nodded. "Definitely! You can tell by

the instructions. I'll bet all we have to do is turn the instruments into smells."

Using the chart, they wrote the name of the matching scent next to each instrument name. And this is what they came up with:

Heliotrope
Echinacea
Licorice
Peanut butter

Excited, they took the appropriate vials out of the case and smelled them in order. Then they looked at each other expectantly, as if they'd just cast a spell and they were waiting for a ghost or vision to appear.

Nothing happened.

They tried smelling all the scents at once, but that only served to confuse their noses further.

"I guess our noses aren't strong enough," said Max-Ernest.

"Or maybe it wasn't really a coded message after all," Cass said, putting the paper back into the box.

Max-Ernest pulled the paper back out, staring at it. "You know how it says, '*first* smell it'?" he asked.

"Uh huh . . . ?"

"Well, look at all the first letters: Heliotrope. Echinacea. Licorice. Peanut butter. H — E — L — P. It spells 'help'!"

"You're right!" said Cass, impressed despite herself. "But you got one thing wrong."

"What?"

"It doesn't *spell* 'help,' it *smells* 'help'!"

Max-Ernest laughed. Then it was his turn to be annoyed. Why was it funny when *she* made a joke?

"Hey, Max-Ernest," said Cass suddenly.

"Yeah?"

"What if it's real?"

"What do you mean?"

"The message. You think it's from the magician? Look at the edge of the paper — it looks like it was in a fire. What if he really wanted help?"

Their eyes locked, the very same chill tingling both their spines.

"Well, it wouldn't be the best way to get help, would it?" asked Max-Ernest, a little more slowly than usual. "I mean, he could have just called someone — like the police. Or the fire department. But I guess maybe if he didn't want everyone to know. Like if it was only for a certain person —"

"Whoever it was for, we're the ones who read it," Cass pointed out. "That means *we* have to help him."

"But he's dead!"

"Not for sure . . ."

"That's true," said Max-Ernest, considering. "And, even if he is, I guess it might be good to find out—"

"Shh!" Cass put her finger to her lips, stopping him mid-sentence. "Look at Benjamin Blake—"

A pale boy with big staring eyes—Benjamin Blake—stood downwind of them, nose in the air, concentrating hard.

"You think he's smelling the licorice or the peanut butter?" whispered Cass.

"How could you tell?" Max-Ernest whispered back.

"I don't know—how could you tell anything about Benjamin Blake?"

Benjamin Blake was a continual source of confusion to Cass, indeed to all his classmates. If they'd included him in their ratings, they might have rated him *spaciest* or *weirdest*. But what was weirdest of all was how grown-ups fawned on him.

Benjamin had recently won a big art prize. None of the other students could believe it; judging by the artwork hanging in the school hallway, he couldn't even draw a straight line. Nonetheless, there was a picture of him in the newspaper, and Mrs. Johnson had made an announcement over the PA as if the prize were some huge historical event. Benjamin got to paint a mural in their town's City Hall, and he even got to go to Washington, DC, for an awards ceremony. After that, all his teachers treated him like he was a movie star or he'd been elected president.

When Benjamin realized Cass and Max-Ernest were looking at him, he blushed and mumbled something under his breath.

"What did he say?" asked Cass. "Something about a herd of buffalo?"

"I think he said he heard an oboe," said Max-Ernest.

"You're joking, right?"

Max-Ernest shook his head "no."

"That's weird. He must have been spying when we read the list. I can't believe someone so spacey could be so nosy."

For a second, it looked like Benjamin wanted to say something more. But when Cass slammed shut the Symphony of Smells case, he turned and walked away.

CHAPTER FIVE

LYING

As much as they differed from each other, Cass and Max-Ernest had one thing in common: neither was a liar. This was unfortunate. As I'm sure you know from experience, lying is an important skill to have.

It is extremely important, for example, when you want to visit the site of a mysterious disappearance and possible murder, and you don't think your parents will let you go if they know what you're up to.

Cass decided to practice by lying about something little.

On Friday nights, her mom always brought home takeout from Thai Village, their neighborhood Thai restaurant. Thai food was Cass's favorite; she especially liked pad thai noodles (except for the egg part) and beef satay with peanut sauce. That Friday night, as she carefully nibbled on her beef satay, Cass said, "So, I learned in Ms. Stohl's class today why satay comes on a stick."

"Cass, I thought we had an agreement about your backpack," said Cass's mother, who either hadn't heard what Cass had said or was ignoring it. "You notice I haven't said anything about that new hole in the left knee of your jean."

The agreement was that if Cass stopped wearing her backpack inside the house, Cass's mother would stop bugging her about the condition of her clothing. Normally, Cass would have pointed out that by saying she wasn't saying anything about the hole her mother was saying something about it anyway. However, tonight Cass had a lie to tell, so she didn't argue.

Instead, Cass put her backpack on the floor and tried again. "So you know why satay comes on a stick?"

"No, I don't," said her mother. "Why?"

"Because they don't have plates in Thailand," said Cass.

This wasn't true. In fact, they do have plates in Thailand. Moreover, Ms. Stohl hadn't even discussed Thailand that day.

Although insignificant, it was the first lie Cass had ever told her mother and she could feel her heart pounding in her chest — and her blood rushing to her ears.

Her mother didn't seem to notice. "Really? They must have some plates," she said. "What about pad thai?"

"Well, they have bowls. And big plates for serving things," Cass added, in case her lie was too extreme. "But no regular plates."

"Well, I guess we better take your plate away

then," her mother joked. "And you can eat off the table. You might like that."

"Ha-ha. Very funny, Mel," said Cass, relieved that her mother seemed ready to believe her without asking any more questions. (Cass's mother was named Melanie, but everybody called her Mel — even Cass when she wanted to make a point or just wanted to sound adult.)

Since her practice lie had gone so well, Cass decided to go ahead and try the real one. She started by telling her mother the truth, because she figured if half of what she said was true then she was only half lying.*

"I have to go over to Max-Ernest's house tomorrow," she said. "He's this guy from school. You never heard me talk about him before because he's in Mr. Golding's, not Ms. Stohl's. Also he's kind of hyper."

That much was true. Then came the lying part. "We have to do this science project," she said quickly. "It's like one of those make your own volcano experiments, but you have to build the mountain part first. Everybody is matched up with somebody from the other class and we're supposed to collaborate on it."

Cass could tell her mother was only half listening. "Tomorrow?" she asked.

"It's due on Monday."

---

*I CAN'T SAY I AGREE WITH CASS'S REASONING, MORALLY SPEAKING. ON THE OTHER HAND, MIXING SOME TRUTH INTO A LIE IS ALWAYS AN EFFECTIVE TECHNIQUE.

"Oh, well, if you're going to be gone, maybe I'll go to yoga. I can take you on the way."

"He lives really close. I can walk."

"You don't have to. I can take you."

The conversation wasn't going the way it was supposed to go. If her mother took her, her mother would want to meet Max-Ernest's parents and discuss what their kids were going to do for the day. Cass's plan would be foiled.

"Cass, your ears are turning red — are you upset about something?"

"No, well, I don't know —"

It was time to take out what are called "the big guns" — those special arguments you hold in reserve for emergencies. Cass screwed up her nerve and began:

"It's just — remember you said you were going to stop being so overprotective? You said it was only because you felt bad that you had to work so much of the time, and you couldn't always be there yourself, and that was why you wanted people to be watching me all the time, but you agreed it wasn't fair that I should feel like I was in jail just because you were working? And now it's like I'm a prisoner again! And it's not even when you're working. . . . Besides, I'll take Sebastian and he'll protect me. I already asked Larry and Wayne and they said I could have him on Saturday."

"That blind old dog? Who's going to protect *him*?"

"He can see — he just does it with his nose. He's a Seeing-Nose Dog, remember?"

"OK, OK, if you really want to walk you can walk. Just . . . be careful, okay? No disasters!"

And that was that. Cass felt a twinge of guilt at deceiving her mother and employing emotional black-mail to boot, but she managed to stifle it quickly. All in all, her first experience with lying had gone pretty smoothly — even if her ears had almost given her away.

For Max-Ernest, lying proved more difficult. Although the part that his parents didn't believe happened to be the truth.

"You have a new friend?" his mother asked.

"Since when do girls talk to you?" asked his father.

They weren't trying to be as mean as they sounded. It was just that they were so surprised; Max-Ernest had never had a friend before.

The only thing that convinced them the situation had changed was the appearance of Cass herself.

When she arrived on Saturday morning with Sebastian, Cass immediately noticed something strange about Max-Ernest's house. Indeed, it would be hard not to notice, even from a distance. The house was split down the middle. Half the house was white and geometric-looking; a real estate agent like Gloria Fortune would say it had a "sleek and modern" design. The other half was dark and wooden; Gloria would probably describe it as "warm and rustic." The modern side was Max-Ernest's mother's side. The woodsy side was his father's.

When the door opened for her, Cass saw that the split personality continued on the inside. Neither parent was supposed to cross into the other parent's side of the house — something Cass figured out when she tried to shake Max-Ernest's father's hand while she was standing in Max-Ernest's mother's half of the entry hall. Cass almost fell over because she was expecting him to reach out his hand and he didn't.

"Hello, Cass, I've heard so much about you," he said, smiling, but not moving from his side of the entry.

"Cass, welcome! Max-Ernest has told me so much about you," said Max-Ernest's mother, as if his father hadn't just said the same thing.

For her, apparently, Max-Ernest's father did not exist. And vice versa. It was an odd arrangement, to say the least.

When Cass commented that she'd never seen a house like theirs before, Max-Ernest explained that although his parents were divorced, they believed every child should be raised with two parents in the house. In fact, it was the only thing his parents agreed on. As a result, they lived together — but they kept every aspect of their lives separate, including the décor of their home.

"Oh, well, I only have one parent — my mom," said Cass. "So our house only has one style." She was about to add that she liked it just fine that way, but then she decided against it; she didn't want to pick a fight when she and Max-Ernest were about to embark on an important secret mission.

Despite their strangeness, Cass found Max-Ernest's parents quite nice. They were obviously very excited to meet their son's first-ever friend and they treated her like visiting royalty. They let her take Sebastian inside, each of them immediately giving him a bowl of water (much to the confusion of the blind dog, who was used to being given only one bowl of water at a time). And they didn't even make a fuss when Cass refused to take off her backpack.

"I'm a survivalist," Cass explained. "I have to keep it on at all times."

"Terrific," said Max-Ernest's mother. "It's important to be prepared for emergencies."

"That's great," said Max-Ernest's father. "Emergency preparation is important."

Each parent insisted on making breakfast for Cass: Max-Ernest's father offered pancakes. Then his mother offered waffles. Then each offered what the other had offered. Cass had already eaten, but she knew it would be rude not to accept anything. So she asked for toast, thinking that would be fastest. In a flash, Max-Ernest's mother handed her a piece of toasted French bread with plenty of butter. Almost as quickly, Max-Ernest's father gave her a piece of toasted whole wheat bread with raspberry preserves.

Before Cass could finish a single piece of toast, let alone both pieces, Max-Ernest said they had to go. Cass was ready with a story about how they were going to the park to collect materials for their science project, but Max-Ernest's parents were so thrilled that he had a friend that it didn't even occur to them to ask where the kids were going.

"What happened to your dad?" asked Max-Ernest, after the door had closed behind them.

"What do you mean? Who says something happened?" asked Cass, walking quickly away from Max-Ernest's house.

"Well, you said you only had a mom."

"Yeah, so?"

"So you never had a dad?"

Cass hesitated, avoiding Max-Ernest's eyes.

"Well, actually, I did," she said after a moment. "He died when I was three — he was electrocuted."

"Electrocuted? Wow!" said Max-Ernest, clearly very impressed. "Like in an electric chair? Did he kill someone?"

"No! It was from lightning, dummy. He was camping. There was a storm. And he was tying his food to a tree branch — you know, so bears couldn't get it? — and then suddenly a lightning bolt hit the tree."

"Oh. I guess that was bad luck, huh?"

"Yeah, pretty much. Anyway, it's kind of a secret. I mean, not a secret secret. Just — I don't like to talk about it."

"Why? If he didn't kill anybody or anything, what's the big deal?"

"I just don't like people feeling sorry for me and stuff. I mean, I hardly even remember him."

"Okay, I won't talk it about then. But —"

"No buts. We have to call to find out where the magician's house is. C'mon —"

Without saying anything more, she headed toward the phone booth down the road, Sebastian at her heels and Max-Ernest straggling behind.

CHAPTER SIX

The Magician's House

magician's house is impossible to find. At least that is what Cass was beginning to think.

"Are you *sure* this is the right street?" she asked.

"How could I be sure? I've never been here before," Max-Ernest pointed out.

"Do you *think* it's the right street then?"

"Well, the sign said—"

Wait! Stop! Hold on!

I just realized I was about to reveal the name of the magician's street. That would have been a serious mistake. It's one thing for Cass and Max-Ernest to make the ill-fated journey themselves; I could never live with myself if you placed yourself in the same danger they did.

Let me begin again. This time, I promise to pay attention:

A magician's house is impossible to find. At least that is what Cass was beginning to think.

"Are you *sure* this is the right street?" she asked.

"How could I be sure? I've never been here before," Max-Ernest pointed out.

"Do you *think* it's the right street then?"

(Now watch this: I've come up with a very novel way of hiding the street name. I'm going to leave it blank.)

"Well, the sign said ____ Road," Max-Ernest continued. "And the address that real estate lady gave us was on ____ Road. But maybe she guessed we weren't really grown-ups when we called, and she gave us the wrong street on purpose. Or maybe somebody put the wrong street sign up. Or maybe there are two ____ Roads. Or maybe the magician moved. Before he was dead, I mean. And for some reason, they still had his old address. And they were trying to sell the wrong house. But then, I guess this would still be the right street for *that* house—"

"Forget it! Let's just go a little farther."

"How far is a lit—"

"Aargh! Why do I even bother talking to you?"

Cass was becoming very impatient with Max-Ernest's strictly logical way of thinking. He reminded her of the artificial intelligence program she had tried at school; he only gave you the answer you wanted if you asked the right way. The difference was: you could turn off the artificial intelligence program. Turning off Max-Ernest was not an option.

They had been walking along a winding street of the sort that creeps upward without you quite realizing it, and by now they were high up on a heavily wooded hill. They hadn't passed any houses for about forty minutes, and none were visible ahead.

Even Sebastian seemed tired. Like most elderly bassets, he had a bad back, and it was a long trip for him. He kept barking in a way that sounded an awful lot like the words "When are we going to get there?"

Just when Cass was on the verge of giving up, Sebastian started tugging on his leash.

"I think he smells something. Maybe the house is around that curve," Cass said. "If it's not, we'll turn around."

"You mean this curve or that—?"

She gave Max-Ernest a warning look and he stopped in the middle of his question.

As soon as they rounded the curve that Cass had indicated they ran into a big **FOR SALE** sign attached to a roadblock on the side of the street. The sign was bright yellow and decorated with balloons so you couldn't miss it if you tried. Under the words

there was a picture of Gloria smiling toothily. A big arrow pointed to a pathway that otherwise would not have been visible, it was so overgrown.

After a short but thorny walk, they reached a clearing that must have served for the magician as a front yard. Cass stared. Max-Ernest stared. (Sebastian would have stared, too, but he was blind.) They couldn't believe they were standing in front of the right house. Was *this* what a "quirky and offbeat" house looked like? It looked so *normal*. Nothing about the house suggested a magician might have lived there. It was just a plain white cottage with black shutters. The only thing that distinguished the magician's house from any other was that it was very, very small; it looked like it had all of one room.

They tried peeking in the windows but the curtains were closed. Screwing up her courage, Cass knocked on the door.

Nobody answered.

"We're going to have to break in," she said, doing her best to sound as if she did this kind of thing all the time.

"Really?" asked Max-Ernest, alarmed. He hadn't considered the possibility of a break-in.

"How else are we going to get inside?" asked Cass, taking a screwdriver out of her backpack. "Anyway, it's not really breaking in because we're helping the magician, and it's his house."

"I'm not sure that makes any sense—"

"C'mon. Let's see if we can get any of these windows open."

Trying not to let him see how nervous she was, Cass started pulling on the windows, looking for the loosest one.

Max-Ernest hesitated at the door. On a whim, he tried the doorknob. It turned.

"Hey, it's open!" he said.

"Well, why didn't you say so?" asked Cass, relieved but also a little frustrated that she wouldn't have the chance to practice her window-prying technique.

As soon as they stepped inside, they realized the house wasn't quite as normal as it had seemed. Instead of a living room, or even an entry hall, they were standing in a tiny, wood-paneled room about the size and shape of a coat closet. There were no windows, or even any doors, other than the one they had come through.

"You think there's some kind of secret door?" asked Cass, examining the wood paneling. There didn't seem to be any hidden knobs or hinges.

"It doesn't look like it," said Max-Ernest. "Hey—"

Without warning, a breeze had shut the door behind them. And now another door was sliding shut in front of it. They were trapped.

"Now what?" said Max-Ernest.

"I don't know, I've never been stuck like this," Cass reluctantly admitted.

Then she noticed the two buttons sticking out of a panel in the corner of the room. "Look, it's an elevator!"

Cass pressed one button, then the other. Nothing happened. "How do you think we start it?" she asked.

Max-Ernest pointed to a small sign above a speaker. It said, *What's the magic word?*

"Abracadabra!" said Cass.

Nothing happened.

"Open sesame!" said Max-Ernest.

Nothing happened.

"Hocus pocus!" said Cass.

Nothing happened.

"Simon says, go down!" said Max-Ernest.

Nothing happened.

"Wait, I've got it," said Cass. "I know the magic word." She looked directly at the speaker and very carefully pronounced the word "Please."

As if it heard her, the elevator groaned, and started to descend. Silently, Cass thanked Mrs. Johnson for being such a stickler.

"I hate manners," said Max-Ernest.

"I think it's supposed to be funny," said Cass. "You know like people always say 'What's the magic word?' But this time it's really magic."

"It's not really magic, it's electronic. It's voice-activated."

"I know! It's just a joke."

"Oh, right. Ha!" said Max-Ernest, not really getting it.

When they got out of the elevator they found themselves in a typical, average, everyday sort of house. It had a living room and a dining room. It had a bedroom and a bathroom. It had a laundry room and a kitchen. It had all the things most houses have. With one small but critical difference: the magician's house was entirely underground.

It was also empty.

"Gloria must have gotten rid of everything. She's that real estate agent," whispered Cass.

"Why are you whispering?" whispered Max-Ernest.

"I don't know. . . . Hello? Anyone here?" Cass asked, still not very loud. No answer. She repeated her question, forcing herself to shout. But all she got in response was a louder echo.

There wasn't a single book or picture or piece of furniture or anything personal of any sort left in the house. Nonetheless, as they walked around, Cass could feel the personality of the dead magician. The floorboards were worn in the places he had walked over and over. The closets showed his handprints. And the wood-paneled walls seemed to have a special sheen where his shoulders had rubbed against them.

"I think he was a nice man," said Cass.

"How can you tell?" asked Max-Ernest.

"I just can."

"That doesn't make any sense."

The only place that didn't show any sign of the magician was the kitchen, where everything was either brand-new or newly painted. You would never know that anyone had used the kitchen before, let alone that there had been a fire. Sebastian, however, seemed to find the kitchen particularly interesting. He kept raising his head and sniffing, as if the room was haunted by aromas of the past.

Cass tried to sniff in the same direction. "I think I smell it—do you?"

"What? The paint?" asked Max-Ernest.

"The sulfur smell!"

"Oh, yeah. Maybe. Well, not really. But my nose is kind of stuffy. I have a deviated septum."

"Is there anything you don't have?" asked Cass sarcastically. "C'mon. There's nothing in here. Maybe there's a clue somewhere else in the house."

"What kind of clue are we looking for again?"

"I'll know it when I see it."

As they reentered the living room, the dog broke loose from Cass's grip and lumbered over to a corner bookshelf.

"What's he growling at?" Max-Ernest asked nervously.

"Probably just a bug."

"You think it's one of those magic bookcases and there's a secret room behind it?"

"Those are just in movies," said Cass confidently.

They looked under the shelf but they couldn't see anything.

When they stood up, Cass looked curiously at Max-Ernest. He was bouncing on his feet and clenching his hands.

"I think I . . . I've got to go to the bathroom," he stammered.

"Well, then go."

"You think it's okay?"

"Yeah, why not? You know, if there's a nuclear

war and we're all living in an underground bunker, you can't be so embarrassed about it. Everybody's got to go sometimes."

Cass waited as Max-Ernest shut himself into the bathroom. She tried not to listen, but every sound in the magician's house was magnified. Besides, boys always peed loudly.

Finally, she heard the toilet flush.

Then she heard two screams. One sounded like Max-Ernest. The other sounded like no one — no one human, that is — at all.

F or about a second and a half, Cass stood frozen. Then she ran.

When she reached the bathroom, the door was opening and a scrawny old cat darted out. (It was the cat, Cass realized with relief, who was the source of that second scream.)

Max-Ernest was standing by the toilet, panting and pointing. Next to him, the wall had opened up, revealing a large hidden room.

"It just . . . happened when I flushed," he said. "There was some kind of hidden door."

Determined not to let herself be scared by another cat or any other pet, Cass boldly stepped into the opening. Max-Ernest followed cautiously.

The hidden room was dominated by a big wooden desk and was crammed top to bottom with the magician's things.

"His workroom!" said Cass, who was instantly reminded of her grandfathers' antiques store and therefore felt very comfortable. "I guess Gloria doesn't know about it—that's why there's still so much stuff. There's got to be something for us in here."

Max-Ernest, who was still not recovered from the shock, pointed to the empty bowl of cat food and not-so-empty litter box. "You think that cat's been in here since the magician died?"

Cass nodded. "Okay, you start at one end. I'll start at the other."

"So, then, you have to admit, I was right, there *was* a secret room. How about that?"

Cass didn't answer. She just started combing through boxes.

"It stinks," Max-Ernest grumbled. But he started looking around all the same.

They were half amazed and half disappointed by what they found. There were none of the objects you usually see in a magician's workroom: no magic wands, no boxes for sawing women in half, no top hats for hiding rabbits, no bits of trickery or fakery of any kind.

Instead, there were the kinds of things you see more often in the study of a mad professor: there was a broken brass scale and an enormous magnifying glass covered with dust; there was a microscope holding an empty slide, a telescope pointed at a spot in the ceiling, and even a stethoscope draped over the desk chair; there was a taxidermy ferret, a collection of rocks and crystals, all of which had some kind of incandescent, luminescent, or opalescent quality, and hundreds of butterflies pinned to cardboard with their wings frozen in a last attempt at flight; and there were books and papers everywhere.

But there was nothing magical. Or sulfurous. Or in any way lethal.

Sebastian, meanwhile, was sniffing around a drawer underneath the magician's desk. Following his lead, Cass opened the drawer and pulled out a large, leather-bound notebook.

"What's that?" asked Max-Ernest.

Cass put her finger to her lips. Sebastian had moved away from the desk toward the outside wall and was twitching nervously — a sure sign of danger.

The sound of the elevator moving echoed through the house.

Max-Ernest opened his mouth to say something but Cass immediately clamped her hand over his mouth and held tight. He looked furious but he couldn't remove her hand no matter how hard he tried; she was too strong.

Then they heard the elevator door open and a voice — unmistakably Gloria's — ring out from it. She was so loud and shrill they could hear every word.

"Newlyweds, you say? How wonderful! You make such a striking couple! You know, I do have some aboveground homes to show that might be more to your taste. . . . Oh, you've always wanted an underground house? Marvelous!"

Cass pointed with her free hand to a small grate

that looked out into the corner of the library where Sebastian had been growling earlier. (It must have been the cat that made him growl.) She and Max-Ernest watched through the grate as Gloria stepped out of the elevator and walked toward them.

Thankfully, Sebastian remained quiet. It was as though he knew they didn't want to be found.

"You know I had a feeling about this house," Gloria continued, "that the right couple would just fall in love with it. So romantic, isn't it, Dr. . . . ?"

"Dr. L," said a deep voice with one of those elusive accents you can't quite identify no matter how hard you try.

"Oh, L what?" asked Gloria.

"Just L," he responded in the smug tone of someone who's just won an argument.

"I see," said Gloria, who clearly did not see at all. "And that makes you Mrs. . . ."

"It's *Ms.* Mauvais," answered a woman, evidently Ms. Mauvais, her voice tinkling in a way that should have sounded light and musical but instead sounded icy and unpleasant.

"Oh, so then you didn't take your husband's name, or rather, I mean his initial?"

"Apparently not," said Ms. Mauvais, as she and

Dr. L finally came into view towering above the short real estate agent.

Cass pressed her face against the grate to get a better look at these newlywed house-hunters.

Gloria was not exaggerating when she said they made a "striking couple."

Dr. L was tall and tan and had the whitest teeth Cass had ever seen. He wore a gray suit with a silver tie, and he had silver hair that looked like it had been blowing in a wind; and yet his hair never moved. Despite the color of his hair, he didn't have any wrinkles on his face. He was so handsome that he seemed far away even when he was close.

If anything, Ms. Mauvais was even more dazzling, and not just because she was dripping with gold jewelry. She was almost as tall as Dr. L and she had a teeny-tiny waist — like a Barbie doll brought to life. She had blond Barbie hair that swooped up from her forehead forming a perfect golden helmet, not a strand out of place. She had blue Barbie eyes that were big and round and sparkling and never seemed to blink. Her skin, too, was smooth and flawless like a doll's. No part of her face ever moved, even when she spoke.

It was as if she and Dr. L had taken photographs of themselves at just the perfect moments when they looked their absolute best, and then they had cast a spell so that they would look like their photographs forever.

One other thing was strange about them: they both wore gloves on their hands. Even though the day was really warm.

They were terrifying. At least to Cass.

Max-Ernest, on the other hand, was transfixed. "That's the prettiest woman I've ever seen," he whispered when Cass finally released her hand.

"Are you crazy?" Cass whispered back. "She looks like a zombie. They both do."

Ms. Mauvais was looking toward them, something like a quizzical expression on her face. For a second, they thought she'd heard them, but perhaps this was how she always looked. Then she turned back toward Gloria.

"I see you've cleared out all of the previous occupant's belongings," said Ms. Mauvais. "A magician, did you say he was?"

"Yes, well, no, I don't think I mentioned it. Or rather I must have!" Gloria laughed. "How else would you know?"

"How else, indeed," said Ms. Mauvais, while surreptitiously eyeing Dr. L. "He must have had many interesting things. Could you tell much about the magician from his belongings?"

"Oh, no," said Gloria. "It was just a lot of junk. . . . Wouldn't you like to see the other rooms?"

"So where is this 'junk' now?" Ms. Mauvais persisted, ignoring Gloria's suggestion.

"Oh, I gave it all away."

"I see. And whom did you give it to?" continued Ms. Mauvais, as casually as if she were asking about the weather.

When she heard this last question, Cass found herself shaking her head "no," silently willing Gloria not to answer. For some reason—maybe it was the way Sebastian was reacting to them, or was it just the sound of their voices?—she didn't think Dr. L and Ms. Mauvais were really house-hunting. She wasn't even sure they were newlyweds at all. What she was sure of was that she didn't want them ever to go anywhere near her grandfathers' antiques store.

"Oh, I can't remember. I think I threw it all away," said Gloria, perhaps thinking the same thing.

Cass breathed a sigh of relief.

Dr. L took a step toward Gloria. "So this magician of yours, he didn't leave any papers or files that would tell us something about him?"

Gloria shook her head nervously and took a step backward. "No, nothing like that."

Dr. L looked piercingly at her, like a prosecutor interrogating a witness. "A leather notebook perhaps? Think hard."

When Max-Ernest heard this, he coughed and flung back his head, knocking over a pile of boxes.

It's hard to say what happened in the commotion that followed. This much Cass would remember later: when she and Max-Ernest and Sebastian exited the bathroom, she looked directly at Dr. L and Ms Mauvais and she said, "I think the notebook you're looking for is in there."

As the two stunned grown-ups scrambled into the bathroom, Cass shut the door on them and headed toward the elevator. Gloria stared at them in surprise.

"What are you kids doing here?!" she asked sharply. "You're trespassing. This is private property. . . . Hey, I know you," she added, looking at Cass. "You're that pesky little girl from Larry and Wayne's."

"Run!" shouted Cass, pushing Sebastian toward the open elevator.

"Come back here right now!" shouted Gloria. "And what's that in your hand?!"

"Um, up!" Cass said, as soon as they were inside the elevator.

Nothing happened.

"I mean, please!" The elevator started to move.

"Stop! Thief!" shouted Gloria, waddling up to the elevator, but she was too late.

As for Dr. L and Ms. Mauvais, they managed to get out of the magician's study just in time to see the elevator closing on Cass and Max-Ernest.

And to see Cass clutching the magician's notebook tight in her hand.

've also decided not to repeat the terrible threats that Dr. L and Ms. Mauvais screamed when they realized that Cass was holding the magician's notebook because it would only give you nightmares. Neither will I describe how that creepy couple searched the neighborhood for over an hour while Cass and Max-Ernest hid terrified in the bushes — although I will tell you there was an especially scary moment when Dr. L and Ms. Mauvais were standing only inches from Cass and Max-Ernest.

Sebastian almost gave them away by growling at the magician's cat, who happened to be skulking nearby. But then the cat bolted. Which caused Ms. Mauvais to jump back in fright. Which caused Dr. L to laugh at her. (His laugh was as strangely accented as his voice.) Which caused Ms. Mauvais to call him nasty names. Which caused them both to turn away from the bushes.

In the end, suffice it to say, our heroes acted very bravely, or at least very patiently, and they outwaited their pursuers. I am also happy to report that neither Cass nor Max-Ernest ever considered giving up the notebook — although neither could have said exactly why if you'd asked them.

When they reached Max-Ernest's house, his parents were naturally distressed to see their son's clothes torn and soiled, not to mention the scratches all over his arms and legs. But they were so unused to the situation that they didn't know how to react.

"Is this how kids always look after they go out?" asked his mother.

"Kids will be kids, er, won't they, kids?" asked his father.

"Yes, Mom. That's right, Dad," said Max-Ernest, making sure to answer each parent separately.

Cass left Sebastian with his two bowls of water, then followed Max-Ernest upstairs. As soon as Max-Ernest closed his bedroom door — his room was carefully positioned so that it was divided equally between each parent's half of the house — Cass sat down on the floor and pulled the notebook out of her backpack. "What do you think could be in here that they want so badly?"

"Paper? That's what's usually in a notebook," Max-Ernest pointed out.

Cass rolled her eyes. "Um, I think it's probably something the magician wrote. Duh."

She opened the notebook on the floor and flipped through the pages so they both could see what was inside.

"That's all?" said Max-Ernest.

Cass shrugged. She had to agree it was a bit of a letdown. All the pages were blank, except the first.

Cass read the lines scrawled across it:

Please be SILENT and LISTEN.
I am the SCHOOLMASTER
and you are in THE CLASSROOM.
Just like ELEVEN PLUS TWO equals
TWELVE PLUS ONE,
And even a FUNERAL can be REAL FUN,
You will find my DICTIONARY
is quite INDICATORY.
If you want to read my story, just look . . .
THEN UNREAD.

Cass scrunched up her face. "How do you 'unread' a story?"

"Uh, I think . . . I don't know," Max-Ernest admitted. "I guess it means 'not read'? Or maybe 'forget what you read'?"

"The book is blank. We can't read it anyway."

"How do you know? Maybe it's just hidden somewhere. Or maybe it's in invisible ink. Or maybe the poem is really another secret code, and if we crack it, it will tell us where the story is."

Cass thought about this for a second. "Well, I don't think it's a very good poem, if it's even a poem. But maybe you're right about the code part. With all that school stuff and the numbers, do you think maybe we're supposed to do math?"

"Too easy," Max-Ernest said confidently. "Everyone knows eleven plus two equals twelve plus one. The whole point of a secret code is that it's hard to figure out."

"I know what a secret code is! What about the funeral? Why's he saying a funeral can be fun?" Cass asked, studying the notebook. "That's kind of weird. Or do you think it's 'cause 'fun' rhymes with 'one'?"

"That's the only rhyme. There would be more if that was the reason."

Cass handed him the notebook, annoyed.

"You look at it then. What makes you the secret code expert anyway? How many have you figured out?"

"You mean like real secret codes?"

Cass nodded.

"You mean like besides the one in the Symphony of Smells?"

Cass nodded.

"Um, well, none," admitted Max-Ernest. "But I've read about a lot of them."

"So you don't really know anything about secret

codes then," declared Cass, who believed you had to experience things to know about them.

She looked over at Max-Ernest to see if he would contradict her but he wasn't paying attention to her anymore. He was staring at the notebook.

"It's so obvious!" he said. "I can't believe I didn't see it before."

"What?"

"Look how all the capitalized words look the same. LISTEN and SILENT . . . SCHOOLMASTER and THE CLASSROOM . . . DICTIONARY and INDICATORY . . ."

"Yeah . . . ?"

"They're anagrams!"

"Right," said Cass nodding. Then she asked, "What's an anagram?"

"It's when two words have all the same letters but in a different order. Then when one word spells another one backward it's a kind of mirror writing called a palindr—"

Cass cut him off before he could start another lecture. "Okay, I get it. They're all anagrams."

"Even the numbers," Max-Ernest continued. "ELEVEN PLUS TWO is like TWELVE PLUS ONE. Only two capitalized words don't have an anagram—"

"THEN UNREAD!" finished Cass, growing excited.

"We have to figure out an anagram for THEN UN-READ."

Max-Ernest found a piece of paper and they started trying different letter combinations (Cass had done this before with her grandfathers when they played Boggle and Scrabble):

THE DEAR NUN
RAN THE DUNE
EAT RUDE NNH
RED NUT HE NA
TREE HAD NUN

And so on. Most combinations were total gibberish. And none worked when you tried to put them into the magician's sentence. They thought they might have it with HUNT A DEER or HEAT UNDER, but then they realized both combinations were missing an N. All the while, Max-Ernest kept talking to himself.

"Can't you keep you mouth closed for even a second?" said Cass.

"But I think I've got it," said Max-Ernest, trying to talk through his teeth.

"What?"

"It's UNDERNEATH!" exclaimed Max-Ernest, giving up on keeping his mouth closed because he was much too excited. "If you want to read my book, just look UNDERNEATH. How 'bout that?"

Cass nodded. "Yeah, that must be it! Like underneath the ground, I guess. Do you think he buried it somewhere?"

They didn't have any time to discuss the matter further because Cass's mother had arrived to take Cass and Sebastian home. Despite having to leave Max-Ernest's just after they decoded the magician's secret message, Cass was very glad to see her mom. It had been a long and scary day and a hug had rarely felt so good. But there was sadness in the hug, too. More than anything, Cass wanted to tell her mother everything that had happened at the magician's house. But she couldn't.

There were two good reasons not to tell:

1. She had lied about her plans for the day and her mother would be angry and possibly ground her.
2. Her mother would worry about her safety and wouldn't let her investigate further, grounded or not.

As you might have guessed, Cass's mother wasn't as easy to put off as Max-Ernest's parents when it came to the condition of her child's clothing. But Cass told a story about chasing the blind dog through the park that was so long and involved that her mother gave up trying to understand and just said she was glad Cass was OK and the state of her clothing wasn't important.

Cass knew her mother well enough to know when something was on her mind. Sure enough, her mother didn't get out of the car when they got home. Instead, she turned and looked at Cass and said she had something to tell her.

At first, Cass thought her mother was going to tell her something really terrible, like that she was getting married or dying of some rare fungus. How could she have not seen this coming? She, Cassandra, the one who predicted everything! And her mom had fallen in love and she hadn't even known?

As it turned out, the news wasn't so terrible. Her mother was going away on a business trip to Hawaii. The insurance company she worked for was sending her to a conference on "risk assessment" (which sounded kind of interesting) in Honolulu; and she was going to stay an extra couple days so she could spend a little "downtime" (which sounded boring) on the beach. Grandpa Larry and Grandpa Wayne had agreed to let Cass stay with them while her mother was away.

Cass couldn't have been more surprised if her

mother had announced she was flying to the moon. She hardly ever traveled — and she *never* traveled without Cass.

No doubt, her mother was *interested* in traveling; you could even say it was a hobby of sorts. She was famous for her collection of travel guides, and her friends always asked for her help planning their trips. From the best beaches in Costa Rica to the coziest cabins in Colorado, no matter where you were going Cass's mother had a book on the subject. She had guides to trekking in Nepal even though she'd never gone on a single hike in her life, and maps for helicopter skiing in Canada even though she was afraid of flying *and* she didn't like the snow.

To Cass, nothing was more torturous than hearing about all these fabulous places she would never get to see. To her mother, books were better than travel. "Who needs to go somewhere when you can read about it," her mother liked to say. "You don't even have to wait in line at the airport!"

Now, finally, her mother had decided to take a vacation — or at least to add a vacation onto a work trip. And Cass wasn't invited?

"I know it doesn't seem fair," her mother said, "but it's just not practical. Next time, you'll come — I promise."

Once she got over the shock, Cass assured her mother that the Hawaiian work-plus-vacation trip was no problem. "I'll be okay," she said. "Anyways, I like staying with Grandpa Larry and Grandpa Wayne. Because they let me do whatever I want. Just kidding!"

"Thank you for being so mature and understanding," said her mother, hugging Cass for the third time in as many minutes.

Her mother might not have been so grateful had she known what Cass was thinking while they were hugging. The reason Cass was being so mature and understanding was that she had come to the conclusion that the timing of her mother's trip was perfect.

In reality, she hadn't been kidding when she said her grandfathers let her do whatever she wanted. With her mother gone, it would be much easier to go back to the magician's house and start digging. And then to solve the mystery of his death. And then to save the rest of the world from suffering the same fate. And then to have everybody know what a hero she was and that her predictions were real and that she wasn't just crying wolf.

CHAPTER NINE

a tight leash

Unfortunately, Cass's mother seemed to think that her absence meant Cass should have less freedom rather than more.

A week after she broke the news about her trip, even though she was late for the airport, her mother spent twenty minutes listing all the things Cass wasn't allowed to do while she was gone. Including sliding down the fire pole and riding in the back of Wayne's pickup truck.

Cass's mother pushed a credit card into Cass's hand. "For emergencies," she said. "But there better not be any!" Then she turned toward Cass's substitute grandfathers (and now substitute guardians). "Remember, she's not as adult as she seems—she's still our little girl."

Which was just about the most infuriating thing her mother could say.

"Don't worry—we'll keep her on a tight leash," said Grandpa Larry.

Which made Cass even madder.

"Yeah, Sebastian has a few extras," joked Grandpa Wayne.

Which was so unfunny it wasn't funny.

Apparently, keeping Cass on a tight leash meant dragging her around with them wherever they went.

As soon as her mother left, Grandpa Larry and Grandpa Wayne started filling all her out-of-school time with trips to flea markets and swap meets and garage sales and auto parts junkyards. They said they were "just checking out the competition," but Cass noticed they never left anywhere empty-handed. After two days with them, Cass never wanted to see another old or broken thing for the rest of her life.

Still, the field trips were a relief compared to the time she spent in the shop. Whenever she was at the fire station, Cass worried that Gloria might show up and tell her grandfathers about seeing Cass at the magician's house. What had Gloria called her—a trespasser and a thief? Hearing those words would be enough to get her grandfathers to call her mother. And to get her mother to cancel the rest of her trip. And to get Cass in pretty much the biggest trouble she'd ever been in.

Unable to bear the suspense any longer, Cass asked her grandfathers if they'd heard anything from Gloria.

"Oh, don't you worry, she always comes back," said Grandpa Wayne, completely misinterpreting Cass's concern. "And I'm sure she'll have plenty of loot! Maybe she'll even have a new adding machine for us! Wouldn't that be cool?"

Cass wasn't sure what could be less cool than a new adding machine unless it was the way Grandpa Wayne said the word "cool." In any case, his answer did not reassure her.

But Gloria stayed away that day. And the next. And the next. Gradually, Cass's anxiety about Gloria *re*appearing was replaced by a new anxiety: an anxiety about Gloria *dis*appearing. What if Dr. L and Ms. Mauvais had done something to her? Was that why Gloria hadn't dropped by the shop? The more Cass thought about it, the more certain Cass became that Gloria had met some terrible fate. The magician's house was so remote, Gloria's body might rot there for years and nobody would know.

When the next Saturday arrived, Cass's grandfathers announced that it was time for them to take their once-a-year inventory. Each and every single thing in the store had to be counted. Cass could only imagine what this would be like. The store was so disorganized that it would take an entire year to catalog its contents — and then it would be time for the next year's inventory! She couldn't ask for a better opportunity to return to the magician's house and resume her investigation.

As if she were just trying to be helpful, she offered

to take Sebastian for a walk while her grandfathers were working. They accepted on condition that she not stay away too long. Cass knew they'd lose track of time as soon as they got started on the inventory so she readily agreed. She even promised to clean up after the dog. (Being blind, Sebastian had a tendency to go about his "business" in inconvenient places.)

There was one thing she had to do before she left: in case her grandfathers were more efficient about taking inventory than she imagined, Cass stealthily removed the Symphony of Smells from her backpack and slipped it back onto the shelf where Grandpa Larry had last stored it. Probably, they wouldn't look, but it was better to be careful. Besides, her backpack was heavy enough as it was. The magician's notebook, of course, she kept. No way was she leaving that.

Then she said a loud good-bye and headed out with Sebastian.

The morning was sunny and windy, which was one of Cass's favorite weather combinations, and she was happy and excited about the day ahead of her. (She also liked it when the weather was sunny and rainy at the same time, which is when you're most likely to see a rainbow. However, mud would have made it difficult to dig, so it was a good thing it wasn't raining.)

Mentally, Cass went over her list of supplies — she took her own inventory, so to speak — until she was satisfied she had everything she needed, from a collapsible shovel to extra plastic bags for picking up dog poop. In no time at all, Cass felt confident, she and Max-Ernest would find whatever it was the magician had buried in the ground. She only hoped they didn't find the magician — or Gloria — buried along with it!

When she reached Max-Ernest's house, Cass hit a snag.

Max-Ernest was standing in the driveway, flipping a coin in the air. On one side of him, his mother sat in her car. On the other side of him, his father sat in *his* car.

"Okay, heads I go with Mom, tails I go with Dad," he was saying as Cass walked up to him. (This was the way Max-Ernest made many decisions concerning his parents. So he didn't have to pick a favorite.)

The coin fell to the ground before he could grab it.

"Oh, darn! You made me mess up," he said to Cass.

"Well, that's okay because you're not going with either of your parents. You're going with me," said Cass. "We're going back to the magician's house," she added in a whisper.

"We can't. I'm going to a new doctor," Max-Ernest whispered back.

"Tell them it's important."

"But he thinks he knows what my condition is. I have to go!"

"Well, then I'll just have to go the magician's house without you," said Cass, very displeased with this turn of events.

"You'd go without me?" asked Max-Ernest in alarm.

"Don't worry, I know how to handle myself," said Cass, which was a line she had once heard in a movie.

"That's not what I meant," said Max-Ernest. "I thought we were partners. You said we were collaborating."

Cass immediately bristled at this suggestion. "I never said that! That was just something to tell our parents. We're not even really building that volcano. I'm a survivalist, remember? I don't count on anybody but myself."

"Oh. Well, I've never counted on anybody either."

Something about the way he said this — maybe it was the fact that tears were welling in his eyes — made Cass think twice. Although Cass liked to think of herself as a fearless adventurer, she also wanted to be fair-minded. Technically, it was true, she had never agreed to collaborate with Max-Ernest on the investigation. But she had acted like they were collaborators, and it amounted to the same thing. Almost.

Maybe he was right: she shouldn't go without him.

After a few seconds of intense, whispered negotiation, they agreed to go back to the magician's house Monday after school. Even if it meant having to skip an oboe lesson (Cass) and a Mathletes meeting (Max-Ernest). Disappointed but resigned, Cass turned around and headed back to the firehouse.

When she got there, she let Sebastian off his leash and opened the big red front door. Usually, Sebastian would run in at this point and head for the kitchen in search of food. This time, Sebastian hesitated at the door, refusing to enter when Cass tried to nudge him in.

"What's wrong? Don't you want your breakfast? You know, food . . . eat . . ."

Cass waited until he finally entered the store, but he kept growling and turning his head this way and that, as if trying to catch an elusive scent.

Cass looked inside. Everything was the way it was when she left. It didn't look as though her grandfathers had made any headway on the inventory.

"Grandpa Larry? Grandpa Wayne?"

Nobody answered.

Cass couldn't remember the firehouse ever being so silent.

She called their names again.

Something was wrong.

Her instincts told her to turn around and leave as fast as she could.* But what if her grandfathers were bound and gagged and locked in a closet and she could have saved them but she didn't? Or what if they were lying in the kitchen in a pool of blood breathing their last breaths and she could have been there to hear their dying wishes but she wasn't? Or what if . . .

Instead of entering quietly, Cass made a lot of noise as she walked in. She talked loudly to Sebastian. She banged on furniture. She figured if the bad guys heard her, maybe they'd sneak out to avoid being seen. It was better than surprising them and having them knock her unconscious in a moment of panic.

For about ten tense minutes Cass searched the firehouse. She had never realized how many hiding places there were in her grandfathers' store, how many wardrobes to climb into and tables to climb under. Even so, it looked like her strategy had worked. The bad guys had left when they heard her. Or else

---

*WHICH IS EXACTLY WHAT SHE SHOULD HAVE DONE. AND WHAT YOU AND I SHOULD DO IF WE EVER FIND OURSELVES IN HER SITUATION.

they'd already left. Or else they'd never been there. Her grandfathers were not tied up in a closet. There was no blood on the kitchen floor. Everything seemed to be okay.

Except for the fact that her grandfathers were missing.

Then she heard a loud bang. It sounded like gunfire.

CHAPTER
TEN

An Awful
Accusation

Cass held her breath, unable to move. Had someone been shot?

"Cass, what's wrong? You're white as a sheet!"

Grandpa Larry entered, followed by Grandpa Wayne, their arms full of new purchases.

What she'd heard wasn't gunfire, only the front door.

"I — I thought something happened."

"Didn't you see our note?" asked Grandpa Larry. "There was a garage sale down the street. We couldn't resist."

"What's with Sebastian?" asked Grandpa Wayne. "He looks worse than you."

"He's . . . I don't know," admitted Cass. "He's been acting weird all day."

Only then did Cass notice where Sebastian was standing: right next to the shelf where they stored the Symphony of Smells. Cass blinked in surprise. It was gone!

Grandpa Larry followed her eyes. "What happened to the Symphony of Smells? Did you take it down?"

"No! I mean, yes. But I put it back."

"Well, where is it? I thought we agreed we'd only look at it together," said Grandpa Larry, giving her a very slightly reproachful glance.

"Um, it should be there."

This was perfectly true, but somehow it sounded like Cass was lying—even to herself.

"It wouldn't be with your things, by any chance? Like in your book bag?" asked Grandpa Wayne.

She shook her head, blushing furiously.

"You know, your ears are telling a different story," said Grandpa Larry.

She couldn't believe it—her grandfathers were accusing her of stealing! Usually, they were the only ones who trusted her. And the worst thing was she couldn't open the bag to prove the Symphony of Smells wasn't inside—they would see the magician's notebook.

No, the very worst worst thing was that they were right—she *had* stolen the Symphony of Smells. But she admitted that she had. And she'd put it back. Which made it borrowing, not stealing. So why did she feel so ashamed? It was all so unfair!

"Just try and think where you might have put it," said Grandpa Larry. "I know you thought it was a game, but it's very rare and valuable."

"She knows that," said Grandpa Wayne. "I'm sure she'll find it, and put it right back where it was."

Nobody mentioned the Symphony of Smells to her again that day, but Cass could tell her grandfathers were thinking about it. At one point, she heard them talking in low voices, speculating that she had broken some of the vials and that she felt too guilty to say anything. If only!

As far as Cass was concerned, there could only be one explanation for the Symphony of Smells' disappearance: Dr. L and Ms. Mauvais had been there. Their scent must have been what upset Sebastian.

For a brief, mad moment, Cass considered telling her grandfathers everything that happened at the magician's house, and how she was sure the Symphony of Smells had been stolen by Dr. L and Ms. Mauvais. But she knew it would sound like she was making up the story just to exonerate herself. Once she solved the mystery of what happened to the magician, maybe then she could confide in them — and maybe then they would trust her again.*

Cass hardly admitted it to herself but she was beginning to wish her mother hadn't left town.

Before she left, her mother had given Cass her first cell phone, something Cass had wanted for years. "So we won't really be apart," her mother said. Just like she promised, her mother called every night at nine p.m. sharp to say good night (even though they both knew Cass never went to sleep before mid-

*SHOULD SHE HAVE CONFESSED ALL? I WILL LET YOU, READER, BE THE JUDGE — AS EXPERIENCED AS I KNOW YOU ARE AT PLOTTING AND SCHEMING AND GETTING IN AND OUT OF SCRAPES. GROWN-UPS CAN BE USEFUL AT TIMES — MONEY AND CAR RIDES COME TO MIND. BUT THEY ALSO HAVE A HABIT OF GETTING IN THE WAY WHEN YOU WANT TO DO SOMETHING THEY DON'T APPROVE OF.

night). But Cass felt so much pressure to act like everything was fine that their conversations only made her feel more alone.

It was a new sensation — missing her mom. And she didn't like it.

That night, she told her mother she was too sleepy to talk.

"So, Larry and Wayne are really running you ragged, huh?" asked her mother.

Cass forced a laugh she didn't feel. "Yeah, totally ragged."

After she said a rather abrupt good-bye and turned off her cell phone, Grandpa Larry came into her room. She figured he was going to ask her about the Symphony of Smells again, but what he said was:

"Hurry, they're hot."

He placed a plate of chocolate chip cookies and a glass of milk beside her bed.

"You better eat them really quickly if you want to burn your tongue and get chocolate all over your fingers."

Cass laughed and bit into a cookie. It was warm and soft and the chocolate was still melted which was, as Grandpa Larry well knew, just how Cass liked her cookies.

As she swallowed the last bite, she held up her chocolate-covered hand to show him.

"Hmm. I don't know, your other hand still looks pretty clean," he said sternly.

Cass felt a little silly, but she obediently grabbed a cookie with her other hand and ate it even more quickly than the first.

"Good. Now, make sure you smear chocolate all over your glass. I want evidence!"

While Cass drank the glass of milk—soothing her burned tongue—Grandpa Larry moved her backpack aside, and sat down on the edge of her bed. Then he proceeded to tell her a story.

A year earlier, if someone had baked Cass cookies and tried to tell her a bedtime story, she might have been insulted and felt she was being treated like a little child. Now, she was just old enough to enjoy again the cozy comforts of a bedtime story. (Trust me, the older you get the more appealing the idea of a bedtime story becomes; and the rarer the chance to hear one.)

I won't repeat Grandpa Larry's entire story here because it is what some people call off-topic, but I will try to give you a sense of its general outlines: the story was about a time Larry got separated from his platoon during his stint in the army. The story involved a reed that Larry had pulled out of the ground where it was growing next to a pond. In a single day, Larry used the reed as an underwater breathing device, a fishing pole, a wind instrument, a weapon, and a straw. When the reed snapped in two, he was convinced his luck had run out. Without the use of his magic reed, he told himself, he would perish.

As it turned out, however, the sound of the reed breaking had alerted one of his comrades to his presence, and he was reunited with his platoon moments later.

"So you see, breaking the reed wasn't the end of the world, just the end of the reed. And the end of this story. Not to mention the end of these cookies," finished Grandpa Larry, taking the last cookie for himself.

Before Cass could respond, Grandpa Wayne, who had been listening from the doorway, stepped into the room.

"I don't understand," he said. "There were plenty more uses for that reed, even after you broke it. You could have made splints. Toothpicks. Chopsticks. A flute. Or at least a piccolo . . . I'm surprised at you, Larry. What happened to your imagination?"

"That's not the point, Wayne, and you know it!" said Larry in one of the crossest tones Cass had ever heard him use. "Cass, listen, it doesn't matter about the Symphony of Smells. Whatever happened, it's just . . . a thing. I know you know we like things. And the Symphony of Smells was a nice thing. But, well, if it's gone, it's gone."

"Right. We can always make a new one," said Grandpa Wayne, at last catching the message of Larry's story. "In fact, I have an old set of test tubes I found, and I've been wondering what to do with them. We could start collecting scents to put in the tubes—"

"What we're trying to say is that human beings are more important than things," said Larry, interrupting Wayne.

"At least, *Cass* is more important," Wayne qualified.

"Cass, your appearance in our lives has been the greatest gift we could have asked for," Larry continued, as if Wayne hadn't spoken. "No matter how many boxes Gloria delivers to our doorstep, nothing inside them could match you. We love you very much."

As he said this, he put his arms around Cass, and Cass snuggled gratefully against him. "I love you, too," she said.

But she never said a word about what happened to the Symphony of Smells. Or about anything else.

*   *   *

Moments later, after her grandfathers had bid her good night, Cass picked up her backpack and placed it again by her pillow.

Just in case.

CHAPTER ELEVEN

The MAGICIAN'S NOTEBOOK

For most people, Monday mornings are a source of dread. Although Cass was unconventional in many ways, including her attitude toward most days of the week, she, too, often felt a sense of doom on Monday mornings, when she faced the prospect of the long school week ahead.

But on this Monday morning, on the school bus, Cass could hardly think about school. She was too excited.

That afternoon the investigation would resume.

Slipping down low in her seat, out of view of the other student passengers, she pulled the magician's notebook out of her backpack and examined it in her hands. The notebook was larger than the common, school variety, and it was flatter. It had no rings and was more like a binder than what you usually think of as a notebook. The leather cover was brown and shiny and embossed, Cass noticed now, with a familiar Art Nouveau design: the same swirling vines and flowers that decorated the Symphony of Smells. But Cass was certain the notebook was not nearly as old. The magician must have had it made to match. Maybe, when her investigation was over, she could ask her grandfathers about that.

As she flipped through the pages of the notebook, she accidentally discovered something about them: all the pages were *double pages,* folded over on themselves. After a little fiddling, she released the pages from their binding and they opened up like an accordion.

She stared in amazement.

Unwittingly, she had figured out what "UNDERNEATH" meant. The answer wasn't buried underground; it had been right in front of them all along. The magician's story was written on the reverse sides of the notebook pages — *underneath* them.

The rest of the bus ride was pure torture. All she could think about was what was written on the undersides of the notebook pages. She wanted nothing more than to start reading but she knew that wouldn't be fair to Max-Ernest. As annoying as he was, she reminded herself, they were collaborators. She had to wait.

Hoping to catch Max-Ernest before he went to class, Cass started looking for him as soon as she got to school. Unfortunately, she couldn't walk very fast; something was standing in the middle of the hallway, impeding traffic.

When she got closer, she saw that that something was Benjamin Blake.

Oblivious to the crowd of students around him, Benjamin stared at the paintings on the wall, as though he couldn't quite believe they were real. The funny thing was: the paintings were his. As was the plaque next to them, declaring him the winner of the Young Leonardos Contest. As were the congratulatory letters from the mayor and the governor. As was — well, you get the idea.

As Cass tried to pass him, Benjamin mumbled unintelligibly; it sounded like he said, "I smell a hint — dip your ice cream."

"I don't have any ice cream — does it look like I do?" responded Cass, who hated mumbling even when she wasn't in a hurry. "By the way, in case you haven't noticed, you're in everybody's way. Besides, you probably shouldn't stand in front of your paintings like that. It looks kind of conceited."

Benjamin reddened — and rushed off in the direction Cass had come from. Cass continued down the hall, knowing she had been a little insensitive — it wasn't Benjamin's fault he was the way he was — but she didn't have time to worry about his feelings. She had to find Max-Ernest.

She hadn't made it much farther when her path was blocked by Mrs. Johnson, who was talking to some other grown-ups and showing them around the school. Cass was about to push past them when she stopped cold, her heart beating a mile a minute.

It was *them.* She was positive. She recognized their hair. And the gloves on their hands.

At *her* school.

Cass hung back a few feet, shielding her face with her backpack in case Dr. L or Ms. Mauvais turned around.

"Well, I guess that's all the questions we have," Ms. Mauvais was saying in her terrible tinkle. "We're glad to see you have such talented students and staff."

"Thank you so much for your time," added Dr. L in his recognizably unrecognizable accent. "You're very generous."

"Not at all," said Ms. Johnson, beaming at them. "It's wonderful to see such involved and concerned parents. I'm sure your son will be very happy at our school."

Their *son?* thought Cass. What son?

Dr. L turned, so Cass had to duck out of sight. When she looked again, they were gone. And Mrs. Johnson was walking toward her.

Cass waited for the principal, then started walking alongside her. Mrs. Johnson was a fast walker. It was hard to keep up.

"Those people—did they ask about me?"

"Cassandra, when you want to speak to me, you

should say 'excuse me, Mrs. Johnson.' Then wait until you have my attention."

"Excuse me, Mrs. Johnson. Do I have your attention now?"

"Yes, you do. And, no, they did not ask about you. Why would they? They're parents of a prospective student. They were asking about our art program."

"Then they were lying," said Cass fiercely. "They're horrible. I don't even think they're really parents."

"Cassandra! What an awful thing to say about people you don't even know."

"Did you notice how they were wearing gloves even though it's hot out?"

"Some people consider it polite to wear gloves in company. Personally, I think it's a very refined habit. I may just start wearing them myself." Mrs. Johnson looked hard at Cass from underneath her large turquoise hat. "Is this all because I wouldn't order that evacuation you wanted? You know, if I shut down the school every time you thought something was wrong nobody here would ever get an education!"

"Yeah, I'm sorry, Mrs. Johnson. Bye."

Cass left Mrs. Johnson shaking her head and hurried down the hall. But it was too late. They were gone.

*　　*　　*

Cass spent a good ten minutes—at least five of those minutes being past the beginning of first period—searching the school inside and out. To no avail. Not only couldn't she find Dr. L and Ms. Mauvais, she couldn't even find Max-Ernest.

Just as she was trying to figure out what excuse she could give her teacher for being late, she happened to look through the school's back gate—

Across the street, Dr. L. and Ms. Mauvais were slipping into a waiting limousine. The limousine was painted a blue so dark it was almost black, and decorated with tiny, jewel-like stars. Emblazoned in gold across the door were the image of a rising sun and the words:

The whole vehicle shimmered so brilliantly it looked enchanted.

As the limousine drove out of sight, a boy's face was briefly visible, staring out the back window.

Cass stared back, imagining for a second that she had caught the boy's eye. Why did he look so familiar? Was Ms. Johnson right? Was that their son? Was it possible they really were parents? Cass dismissed the idea as soon as it popped into her head. She remembered the awful things they had screamed at her and Max-Ernest. No parent would ever say those things to a kid. No *real* parent.

By a lucky coincidence, Cass and Max-Ernest both had study hall that morning after first period. As soon as she saw him, Cass pulled Max-Ernest over to the desk that occupied the most private corner of the school library.

Speaking so fast that all her words blurred together, she filled him in on how "theSymphonyof-SmellswasstolenfromthefirehouseonSaturdayandIknow ithadtobeMs.MauvaisandDr.LbecauseSebastianwent totallycrazyandthentheyshowedupatourschoolthis morning,canyoubelieveit?,withMrs.Johnsontakinga tour!ShesaidtheywereparentsandthenIsawthemleave withaboyinthebackofthislimousinethathadthe nameMidnightSunonit!"

Most people wouldn't have been able to understand

her. Max-Ernest was such a fast talker himself he had no trouble.

"They have a kid? I don't believe it," he said.

"Exactly! That's what I'm saying," said Cass, slowing down only because she had exhausted herself. "I think the parent thing was just a lie, you know, a cover story, so they could look for us. But then who was the kid in the limousine? . . . Hey, I almost forgot. I figured out what 'UNDERNEATH' means — it means underneath the pages. All the writing is in the notebook, it's just hidden!"

"Wow. Did you read it?"

"No, I waited for you."

Cass didn't say "I waited because we're collaborators." And Max-Ernest didn't say "Thanks, that means a lot to me." But each could tell what the other was thinking.

"You know," Cass said after a moment. "You don't always talk so much. Every once in a while, you're quiet. Like now."

"You're right," said Max-Ernest, amazed. "And I wasn't even trying. How 'bout that?"

"So what did that new doctor say your condition was, anyway?"

"He said he wouldn't know for sure as long as my

parents were living together, because my family situation was too stressful."

"Really? So are your parents going to stop living together?"

"No, they just got into a big fight about it. But at least they were talking to each other!"

Cass and Max-Ernest had to be quiet for a minute because they got a warning look from the librarian, but when the librarian left — study hall always operated on the honor system — they wasted no time in opening the notebook.

They could now see that, far from being blank, the entire notebook was full of the magician's handwriting; it was just that the notebook was inside out, or rather outside in. Judging by the slant of the letters, he had written very fast. Whatever he was writing about must have been very important.

While Max-Ernest leaned in close, Cass read to him in a whisper, her face growing increasingly grave with every sentence.

Dear Reader,
   If you are reading these words,
I know about you two things.

You are brave enough to hold in your hands this notebook, a notebook for which all over the world the villains are searching. And you are clever enough to decipher a riddle, the riddle on the other side of these pages.

Both these qualities you will need in the days ahead.

My life is in danger. For this reason, I write.

No, I do not fear the death — I am an old man and I have survived worse things — but I do not want to die without I first make right an ancient wrong.

Do you know the expression, The ignorance is the bliss? Think on it well. Some secrets are not meant to be known — but once known you can never forget them.

If certain people discover you have learned the things I am about to tell you — Let me just say this, that it is the safest for you to stop reading now and to leave this notebook far away from the place you call home. If instead you keep

reading, please, I beg you, repeat to no
one my story.

Here Cass put the notebook down and looked at
Max-Ernest. He was still being unusually quiet.

"Well?" Cass prompted him.

"Well, what?" Max-Ernest asked.

"Well, should I keep reading?"

"He has a weird way of writing," Max-Ernest
said, as if in answer to her question. "I think maybe
he's foreign."

"That means, no, you don't want me to keep
reading?"

"No, it doesn't mean 'no.'"

"So then it means 'yes'?"

"Yes. I guess."

"Oh. Well, I think I should keep reading, too,"
said Cass. "I just thought, you know, if you thought
it was too dangerous—"

"I'm not scared!" said Max-Ernest. "I just think
he sounds foreign."

"I'm not scared, either."

"So keep reading then."

"OK, then, I will."

Cass picked up the notebook again and coughed

just the way Grandpa Larry did before he started a story—for some reason, her throat felt dry—and then she began to read—

Although I am reluctant for obvious reasons, I think I must also continue recording the magician's story. You see, the magician's story goes straight to the heart of mine. It is not too much to say my story would not exist without his.

You and I, then, will read over the shoulders of Max-Ernest and Cass. Before we do, I suggest you take a break. If you need to go to the bathroom, this is a good time. If you're sleepy, go to bed and save the next chapter for tomorrow. For the magician's story, you must have all your wits about you. No wandering minds allowed.

Are you ready? Rested? Alert?

Or did you just skip ahead because you couldn't wait?

If so, I'd like to point out that reading by flashlight under a blanket is always a good way to tackle the most difficult and dangerous parts of a book. I'd also suggest you have a snack handy. Or some gum to chew. Otherwise you might find yourself biting your fingernails until they bleed.

OK. Have all your reading supplies at hand?

Here it is, then, the magician's story in his own words:

La Storia della Mia Vita
"The Story of My Life"
by
Pietro Bergamo

Never trust a magician. We use words only to divert your attention. Look at my pretty scarf, we say, so you do not see our sleight of hand when the rabbit disappears.

But I write now as a man, not a magician, and I promise my story is true. How I wish it were not! For it is the story of the tragedy of my childhood, and of a terrible secret that has brought nothing but the misery and the death.

My brother, Luciano, and I, we were born in a small town in Italy, in the time between the Wars.

We were twins — what they call in English the "fraternal" twins, not the identical twins. A distinction that is very useless, I think. Yes, if you looked at us closely, there were many differences between us — like the birthmark on the back of Luciano's neck that resembled so perfectly a crescent moon. But Luciano and I, we were identical in our hearts.

When we turned nine years old, our lives, as they say, turned upside down. A terrible man rose to power in Italy, and our whole family it was in danger.* Our parents, they were being watched, but they managed to find the passage for Luciano and me on a boat to America. They promised to join us as soon as they could, but we knew that would not be very soon. Or maybe ever.

It was an awful thing to leave our home at such a young age, but at least we had each other. During the time we were making the crossing of the Atlantic Ocean, we never left each other's sides. As a parting gift, our father, he had given

---

*THIS TERRIBLE MAN WAS THE ITALIAN DICTATOR BENITO MUSSOLINI. AS A CHILD, MUSSOLINI WAS EXPELLED FROM SCHOOL FOR STABBING AN-OTHER STUDENT AND FOR THROWING A POT OF INK AT HIS TEACHER. HIS PERSONALITY NEVER IMPROVED BUT HIS LUCK SURE DID. HE WENT ON TO RULE ITALY WITH AN "IRON FIST," MAKING EVERYONE IN THE COUN-TRY — INCLUDING ALL THE TEACHERS — SWEAR THEIR LOYALTY AND OBEY HIM WITHOUT QUESTION.

to us an old book of the magic tricks, and we spent all our days practicing the card tricks and amusing the crew on the boat. Every night, as we went to sleep, we fantasized about our new lives in America, and how we would become world-famous magicians.

Our mother, she had a cousin in Kansas City. We were very excited to be going there because we had heard the story of the Wizard of Oz and we knew Kansas was full of the tornadoes and the adventure. What we did not know (until it was too late) was that her part of Kansas City was in Missouri, over sixty miles far from the capital of Kansas, Topeka, where we happened to get off the train.

It was the nighttime and we were cold and tired and we'd been wandering through the streets of Topeka for several hours when we saw a marvelous spectacle lit up in front of us: a circus.

Alas, having no money, we could not enter the circus tent, the Big Top, as it is called.** But we found a flap in the tent through which we could watch the horses galloping, the clowns juggling, and even a mangy old tiger jumping through a hoop of fire.

A LITTLE-KNOWN FACT ABOUT MUSSOLINI IS THAT HE WAS ALSO A NOVELIST. TO ME, THIS MAKES PERFECT SENSE. THE WRITER OF A NOVEL IS LIKE THE DICTATOR OF THE NOVEL; HE MAKES ALL HIS CHARACTERS DO EXACTLY WHAT HE WANTS THEM TO DO, AND SAY EXACTLY WHAT HE WANTS THEM TO SAY. BUT PLEASE DON'T DRAW ANY CONCLUSIONS ABOUT THE

What most impressed us was the Ringmaster, so magnificent in his top hat and tails. We didn't speak much English but we could tell what he was saying by the tone of his voice, and by the screams and the cheers of the crowd. At one point, I could have sworn he saw us and he winked at us. It was like as if he knew us and, although we were outside and we had not paid for the tickets, we were the most important audience members of all.

When the show ended, we followed with the rest of the circus audience out into the Midway. This was an old-fashioned traveling circus with all the great sideshow attractions like a fire-eating strong man, a fat lady with a beard (which we later learned was fake), and a "fakir" (actually a white man dressed up to look like an Indian swami). Being amateur magicians, we wanted to look inside all the booths, but the carnival workers — the carnies — they were watching us like as if they were the hawks.

We had such a great hunger that the smell of all the cotton candy and the popcorn and the peanuts was almost too much to suffer. Then we spied a food cart that had been left unattended. A row of red candy apples glistened under a string

KIND OF PEOPLE WHO WRITE NOVELS. AFTER ALL, NOT *ALL* NOVELISTS ARE POWER-HUNGRY MADMEN — SOME ARE POWER-HUNGRY MAD*WOMEN*.
**CIRCUS PEOPLE HAVE A LANGUAGE ALL THEIR OWN. I'VE COLLECTED A FEW WORDS IN THE APPENDIX — JUST IN CASE YOU DECIDE TO RUN AWAY AND JOIN THE CIRCUS YOURSELF.

of lights, ripe for the taking. Quickly, we each grabbed an apple and darted into the shadows behind the cages of the animals. What luck!

But as soon as we sank our teeth in, those apples they were ripped out of our hands. Shocked, we looked up to see grinning down at us a tough old carny. He was missing most of his teeth and, believe me, that grin was a scary thing to see.

"Nice of you to help feed the animals," he said, tossing our apples into the cage of the tiger.

"Oh, no," he laughed as we watched the tiger swat aside our apples like a cat with the yarn. "She don't like apples. Them apples is just to give her the smell. The smell of human, I mean."

As he said this, he gripped us by the scruffs of our necks, and he made a big show of sniffing us like as if we were the dinner. Then he dragged us toward the door of the cage of the tiger. We screamed and we struggled, but it was useless, his grip was so strong.

By now, we were crying and pleading for our lives in Italian. We thought truly we had reached the end.

"Good-bye," I said to Luciano.

"No, not good-bye, just arrivederci," he said,

looking up toward the sky. "We will be together always."

"Yes, together always," I said, trying to be as brave as he was. I touched my finger to the crescent moon of his birthmark and I closed my eyes.

"Let go of them, Sammy!"

It was the Ringmaster walking toward us. "Don't worry, boys. That old tiger don't got any more teeth than Sammy does. She couldn't hurt a fly!"

Eyes twinkling, he said we should know better than to run away like that with the stolen goods.

"When you steal something, you should walk away slowly," he instructed us. "Otherwise you attract attention."

As a punishment for our poor attempt at thievery, the Ringmaster ordered us to help Sammy clean the cages of the animals. Very relieved to be alive, we worked so hard that even Sammy was happy with us.

The next morning, exhausted but also exhilarated, we were sitting outside the Ringmaster's trailer with his three-year-old daughter while inside his wife prepared the breakfast. To pass the *time, we took out our deck of cards and practiced the tricks — which the Ringmaster's daughter seemed to find extremely amusing. We did not know it but the Ringmaster he was watching us from the trailer. When we finished, he applauded.*

"Lucy knows a good trick when she sees it," he said, pointing to his daughter. "We try out all our acts on her."

After Luciano and I we ate all the bacon and the flapjacks (why is it that the food always tastes so much better in the outside?) the Ringmaster instructed to us to help his crew pack up the tents. He never asked from where we came or to where we were going. He just assumed that we would be traveling with the circus — and so did we.

If you're one of the lucky (or is it the un-lucky?) people that are meant for the life of the circus, it is as natural as the migrating is for the geese, or as the hibernating is for the bear.

After reading that last sentence, Cass closed the magician's notebook. She had to stop reading not because the story had ended but because the bell had rung. Actually, it had started ringing around the time Pietro and his brother were being fed to the tiger and if Cass and Max-Ernest didn't move very quickly they were going to be late for their next classes.

Max-Ernest, in an unusually rebellious mood, suggested they skip their classes altogether and continue reading, but Cass pointed out that they might attract unwanted attention that way. After all, neither of them was in the habit of ditching class. So they reluctantly agreed to postpone reading until lunch, when they would remeet behind the gym.

*OF COURSE, I DON'T REALLY BELIEVE THAT THE NUMBER THIRTEEN IS
BAD LUCK — BUT UNDER THE CIRCUMSTANCES, WHY NOT PLAY IT SAFE?

When lunch hour arrived, Cass was so anxious to get back to the magician's notebook that she didn't notice the police cars and fire trucks parked in front of the school.

Can you imagine—Cass missing what may well have been the first real disaster in her school's history? What can I say—even a survivalist gets distracted sometimes.

I promise we'll return to those police cars and whatever terrible event it is that they foreshadow. But let's stay with Cass for the moment; I'm sure you're almost as anxious to get back to the notebook as she was.

In case for some reason you had to stop reading earlier when she did—if, say, some mean person caught you reading this book when you were supposed to be doing your schoolwork, or when you were supposed to be outside "enjoying the sun"—I remind you that Pietro and his brother, after accidentally stumbling on the circus, have now become a part of it.

As soon as Max-Ernest joined her behind the gym, Cass jumped right back in and started reading aloud:

After a few weeks in which we did every job from cleaning up the elephant dung to acting as the shills, the Ringmaster let us put together our own circus act. The act included not only the card tricks but also the mind reading — this was perfect for us because we knew each other so well and practically we had been in the telepathic communication all of our lives.

Also, and this will become important to my tale, we both had the condition that is called the "synesthesia" — the confusion of the senses.*

For people who have the synesthesia, the sounds and the colors and even the smells are all mixed up in our heads.

When I hear the sound of scraping metal, I see a streak of bright yellow-green light. Screeching tires are orange-red. Most bells are blue, although when I see the blue, I don't hear the bells, I smell the soap.

There was even a certain woman who needed only to say one word and I would see a dark gray cloud and then feel like I was drowning in the coldest lake on the Earth — but I am getting ahead of myself. She appears a little later in my history. If only she never appeared at all!

What was the most helpful for our act was that, for me and for Luciano, the numbers and the letters they all had the colors. For example, the number 1 was green, 2 was purple, and 3

*IF YOU WANT TO KNOW HOW TO PRONOUNCE SYNESTHESIA, IT SOUNDS LIKE ANESTHESIA, BUT WITH SIN AT THE BEGINNING.

was yellow. At the same time, the letter X was red, Y was gray, and Z was turquoise.*

I can recall the day my brother and I first realized that other people did not see the letters the way we saw them. We were seven years old and a friend from the neighborhood she was drawing with us. She kept writing her name over and over and we kept telling her she was using the wrong colors. I am ashamed to say we were not very nice about it. Our friend started crying so loudly that our mother had to come and tell us that our friend could use whatever colors she chose.

In the circus, it was very easy for us to have conversations with each other in the color code. If I asked a girl in the audience what day her birthday was, I could tell Luciano the date simply by waving at him a few colored scarves. He would pretend to concentrate really hard, then he would shout out her birthday like it had come to him in the trance. In this way, we seemed like very convincing psychics.

Over time, our act grew into something very splendid. The Ringmaster's wife, she made for us the satin capes and the turbans, and Sammy, who was now our friend, he helped us to create some magical effects with the music and the

---

*SEEING LETTERS IN COLOR IS SOMETIMES CALLED *AUDITION CO-LORÉE* — COLORED HEARING.

smoke and the lights of many colors. But it was after a mysterious gift arrived that our act truly came to life — and also came to the end.

One afternoon, a local boy, he brought to us a large package wrapped in brown paper. He said a beautiful lady had paid to him a buck to deliver it to us — a fortune of money in those days.

As soon as he left, we ripped open the package. At first, we had no idea at what we were looking, or why it had been given to us. It was a wooden case, very old, containing dozens of the glass vials. Was it some kind of chemistry kit? For what purpose was it?

Only when we saw a small brass plaque that read "The Symphony of Smells" did we have the inkling. Could it be true? Were there other people in the world who experienced the music and the smells together? How fantastic!

After a few days of the experiments, we discovered we could make stronger the scents by making a fire and pouring in just a little bit from the vials. The smoke it turned many colors, and the aromas they filled the air. We added also a little of the gunpowder — enough to make the sparks together with the smoke and the smells. It was very exciting to see.

Luciano and I, we practiced every day until we were able to communicate with the smelly smoke — "smell signals" we called it. Imagine — now I could tell Luciano the name of somebody's cat just by releasing the scent of mustard into the air! Truly our act was now "the feast for all the senses."

The Ringmaster, he liked it so much he bought for us a special tent with a big banner announcing "The Amazing Bergamo Brothers and Their Symphony of Smells." Everywhere we went he put up the posters advertising our act. And the crowds, they lined up again and again.

It had been a year since we'd joined the circus and we were once again in Kansas. There was an article about our act in the newspaper and we wondered if perhaps our mother's cousin would come to see us. Who knew — maybe our parents had already come from Italy and they would come, too!

During the show, I searched the audience, but I saw nobody special. Except, that is, for a woman who stepped into our tent toward the end of our show — and made me forget all about my parents.

This woman, she was so beautiful she seemed to make the whole world stand still. She had

blue eyes and a waist so tiny she should have herself been a circus attraction. She had long blond
hair, and she wore long, elegant gloves that
reached up to her elbows. Gold jewelry glittered
on her everywhere.

Truly she is a Golden Lady, I thought.

Afterward, I saw her standing by the entrance of our tent. When the rest of the crowd
had left, she smiled and told my brother and me
how much she enjoyed our show.

"Did you like your present?" she asked. "It
seems you've put it to good use."

"What present?" I asked.

"Why the Symphony of Smells, of course! It's quite a treasure, you know. It was made by a French doctor many years ago. A scientist by training. But he was a great lover of the arts."

Before we could thank her for the gift, the Golden Lady, she said she had a proposition for us. Could she take us to the dinner to discuss it?

Since we had never been to a restaurant before, her offer was very exciting and my brother eagerly accepted it. I, however, did not want to go. I had no real reason to be suspicious — and yet, as soon as I heard her speak, I knew she was not what she seemed.

Yes, as you may have guessed, the Golden Lady was the woman whose voice made me feel like as if I was drowning. I shiver now, just to think about it.

I tried to make the excuses, reminding my brother of all the chores we had to do. He kept saying our chores should wait. What was wrong with me? Here this nice woman was offering to take us to a real restaurant! And it went on like that. I think he was more than a little bit in love with her.

Finally, the Golden Lady she suggested that Luciano go to the dinner while I stayed behind.

"If I can't have both brothers, can't I at least have one?" she asked, as if she was the child and we were the toys in the toy store.

I could see that Luciano was nervous about being separated from me for the first time in our lives, but we were too much angry at each other to argue against the idea. My brother, he left without saying the good-bye.

I stayed up all the night waiting for Luciano, imagining all the terrible things that could happen to him. When he had not returned by the morning, I searched the roads, looking for the signs of an accident. Then I searched the circus grounds, thinking maybe he was hiding from me because of the anger.

My brother, he was nowhere.

When I found the Ringmaster inside his trailer he looked very surprised to see me, as if I were a ghost or I had just sprouted the antlers. But he recovered quickly and started barking the orders at me. It was almost time to go. What was I doing lollygagging around? When I tried to tell to him about Luciano being taken away, he said he was too busy to worry about my brother.

The Ringmaster, he always acted impatient like this, but he said something else which confused me. "Anyway, she seemed like such a nice lady," he said under his breath. "I'm sure your brother won't come to any harm."

How would he know? I wondered. Had he met the Golden Lady?

As he spoke, I noticed him pick up something from the table. It was a pile of the cash and he played with it in a very nervous way. I was still young but I'd been around long enough to comprehend what meant the money.

Nowadays, it would be a very shocking thing to sell a pair of ten-year-old twins to a stranger. This was the circus. My brother and I, we were some carnival attractions, no better than the trained monkeys. I wasn't very surprised that the Ringmaster would trade us for a few dollar bills. But I hated him for it.

"I'll kill you!" I yelled, and then I ran away from the trailer — and from the circus — as fast I could.

The rest of my story it is seventy years long, but it is really very short.

I knew better than to go to the police. I was young and Italian and a carny — three strikes against me as far as the police would be concerned.

Instead, I spent the years living on my own on the streets, searching for my brother, checking the back of every neck for that crescent-shaped birthmark. I never found so much as a single clue as to where was Luciano.

Except once.

A couple days after I fled from the circus, I hitchhiked to the next town where the circus had put up its tents. My plan was to murder the Ringmaster in his sleep. How I intended to do this I do not know—I had no weapons nor any experience as a murderer.

Whatever my plan was, I was too late. Where once the circus had been there was now nothing but the ash.

I wandered around the blackened fairgrounds in a daze. Some of the larger pieces of the rubble were still smoldering and the smoke hovered above. There was also a terrible odor in the air which at the time I thought was the smell of the rotten eggs but I now know was the smell of the sulfur.

I did not know exactly what had happened, but I was certain about one thing: the fire, it had been meant for me.

In the middle of all the ashes and the debris, I spied a crumpled piece of paper. I recognized the handwriting on it even from many feet away. It was a note from my brother, written in a code we had invented for the Symphony of Smells.

It said one word: "HELP."

The note, it was like a knife inside my heart.

After the loss of my brother, the magic it no longer had any magic for me. Still, I had to make the living. So I performed in the parks and on the street corners — and on the trains when I could hop a ride with the hoboes.

Eventually, I graduated to the nightclubs and the theaters, and I believe I am a success as far as magicians go. I never socialized much, however — no friend could ever take my brother's place — and today I am an old hermit.

Yet I have never given up the hope of finding Luciano. Against all reason, I feel inside me that he is still alive.

One day, a few years ago, I was looking in a science magazine — the world of nature it has always interested me far more than the world of man — and I noticed an article about the synesthesia.

What most caught me was a reference to a prodigy child of the 1960s, a girl so talented at *the violin that she came to be an international sensation. She claimed to see the colors when she played the music—a well-known form of the synesthesia—and she wrote a magnificent piece of the music called "The Rainbow Sonata" when she was only seven years old. At age nine she was kidnapped and never heard from again.*

Another child with the synesthesia kidnapped! Just a coincidence? Perhaps. But it was the first clue I had found in seventy years. I had no choice but to investigate.

Mysteriously, all the newspaper stories about the violinist were missing from the libraries. At last, in a used bookstore in Alaska, I discovered an old magazine article that described the circumstance of her kidnapping. According to an usher at the concert hall where she had last performed, the violinist was seen talking to a woman shortly before her disappearance. The usher he said the woman was "dazzling." She had the blond hair and the gold—

"Aaargh! It's so annoying!"

Cass turned the notebook over and over in frustration, looking for more hidden pages.

"That's it?" Max-Ernest asked.

"Yeah, it just ends there."

"But we never found out what the terrible secret is."

"I know. I think maybe he wrote more but he ripped it out. Look—" Cass opened the notebook flat and pointed to a broken seam, barely visible on the inside of the spine. "Like if he had to run away really quickly and he couldn't take the whole notebook, the pages had to fit in his pocket."

"You mean like if he heard someone coming or he smelled fire or something? I guess that's possible," said Max-Ernest. "Or else maybe he was killed, and the killer took the pages. Or—"

"Exactly," Cass interrupted, grim. "You know who she is, right?"

"Who?" asked Max-Ernest.

"The Golden Lady. Couldn't you tell? The Golden Lady is Ms. Mauvais."

Max-Ernest shook his head. "No, she's not. She can't be—"

"Yeah, she is. Listen—" Cass flipped through the notebook. "She has a teeny waist, all that jewelry. She wears gloves."

"It does *sound* like her," agreed Max-Ernest. "But she's not the Golden Lady. It wouldn't make any sense."

"What—why? Name one reason you think it's not her."

"OK. Here's one reason. The lady in the story, at the circus, it was a really, really long time ago. If it was Ms. Mauvais, she would be like a hundred years old now. If she was even still alive. How 'bout that?"

Cass bit her lip. He had a point. Ms. Mauvais didn't look anywhere near that old.

"Maybe if she was a vampire, then it could be her," Max-Ernest suggested. "But that's highly doubtful. Nobody thinks there are real vampires. Except for vampire bats—they're real. And Count Dracula—he was real. But he wasn't a real vampire. He was just a mean old guy. At least, that's what people think. There's no way to know for sure. He's dead. I mean, unless he really was a—"

"OK, OK. Forget vampires. I agree, it's not her. It wouldn't make any sense," said Cass. "So what do you think we should do?"

"I think we should get rid of the notebook as fast as we can, just like he said we should at the beginning," said Max-Ernest.

"You mean stop the investigation? Don't you even want to know what the secret is?"

"It's too dangerous," said Max-Ernest. "We're only eleven. Personally, I don't want to be kidnapped—just so we can know what happens at the end of a book."

"That's not the point," said Cass heatedly. "Don't you have any sense of honor? We owe it to Pietro to find out what happened. He was such a nice man—"

"We didn't even know him!"

"I know—he didn't really know anybody. That's why if *we* don't continue his investigation, who will?"

Max-Ernest didn't have an answer.

"Besides," Cass added, "it's too late to back out. Maybe we don't know who Ms. Mauvais is, but she definitely knows who we are."

CHAPTER FIFTEEN

A Confusion of the Senses

ass and Max-Ernest emerged from behind the gym so lost in conversation that it took them several seconds to notice that the entire school yard was empty.

"I can't believe it," said Cass. "Finally they evacuate the school, and I wasn't even there."

"I think maybe it was a false alarm." Max-Ernest nodded in the direction of the auditorium: kids and teachers had started streaming out.

Amber walked toward them, her Smoochie-of-the-week dangling from her neck.

"Where were you?" she asked. "You missed the assembly!"

Amber, who aside from being the nicest girl in school was also the chattiest (if she wasn't so nice, you might have said she was the most gossipy), told them the news: Benjamin Blake was missing. That was why the police and fire department had been there.

Amber explained that Benjamin had been dropped off at school that morning, but he'd never gone to class. Nobody had seen him leave; nobody had picked him up. He didn't have a hall pass or a trip slip or a doctor's excuse or even a note from his parents. Any student who had seen Benjamin or who had any idea as to his whereabouts was supposed to tell Mrs. Johnson immediately, so the police could be alerted.

"I can't believe you didn't know," said Amber when she finished her summary of events. "I thought you loved emergencies, Cass."

"I don't love them," said Cass irritably. "I just like to be prepared. Actually, that's what we were doing just now. Preparing for an emergency."

"We're collaborators," said Max-Ernest.

Which made Cass want to throttle him.

"Oh, well, I think it's so great you two are friends," said Amber.

Which made Cass want to throttle her.

"By the way, I'm almost done with this," Amber added, holding up her Smoochie. "It's Cotton Candy. Do you want it, Cass?"

"Um, sure. Thanks, Amber," said Cass automatically.

Which made her want to throttle herself.

"It was my hundredth Smoochie," Amber boasted, as she handed it over. "They gave me this when I bought it." She gestured to the front of her T- shirt which said:

I'VE SMOOCHED A HUNDRED TIMES!

in glitter writing that sparkled in the sun. She twirled around; on the back the T-shirt said:

Honorary
Skelton Sister

"What's a Skeleton Sister?" asked Max-Ernest after Amber had rejoined her friends. "Is that a horror movie or a comic or something?"

"Not *Skeleton,* just *Skelt* — oh, never mind," said Cass. "Your name is better. That's what they look like anyways."

As she and Max-Ernest walked back to class, Cass told him about running into Benjamin that morning in the hallway. "I might have been the last person to talk to him — ever."

And I was so mean to him! she thought guiltily. But she kept that part to herself.

"Are you going to tell Mrs. Johnson?" asked Max-Ernest.

"I don't know. She'll probably just think I'm making it up," Cass said with more than a little bitterness.

Like most of the students at their school, Cass and Max-Ernest usually passed by all the artwork in the hallway without giving it any more thought than they gave the citizenship trophies in the glass case or the toy drive announcements on the bulletin board. Now, knowing Benjamin Blake was missing, they stopped and looked more closely at his paintings.

"I don't see what's so great about them," said Max-Ernest. "I mean, what are they really pictures of? They just look like screen savers."

"They're not pictures of anything, that's the point," said Cass, who suddenly felt called upon to defend Benjamin. It was the least she could do, considering how she'd treated him. "Haven't you ever heard of abstract art? Just look at the colors. And the shapes."

"What else could I be looking at? That's all there is!"

One painting consisted mainly of rippling circles, like someone had dropped something into a purple lake.

"*Rain Song?*" asked Max-Ernest, eyeing the card taped to the wall next to the painting. "Why is it a song? There's no sound, no words —"

"How'm I supposed to know? I guess it's what he thinks of when he thinks of . . . rain."

Max-Ernest said it figured that somebody as nonsensical as Benjamin Blake would disappear. He probably didn't even know where he was half the time.

"But I hope he's OK, anyway," Max-Ernest added.

"Even though he never makes any sense, he's not a bad person. At least, not bad bad. Just bad — logically. I mean, what if people were sentenced to death just cause they didn't make sense —"

He trailed off because Cass wasn't listening; she was reading the titles of the other paintings. One was called *Music of Crickets and Cars*. Another was *Song I Sing When I'm Scared*. Another was *The Radio in My Mother's Office*.

A frown took shape on Cass's face.

"What?" demanded Max-Ernest.

"Don't you see?"

"See what?"

"Benjamin Blake is like the Bergamo Brothers."

"What do you mean?"

"He has — what's it called? The confusion of the senses."

"He's synesthetic?"

Cass nodded.

"How do you know?"

"All his paintings are paintings of music —"

"So?"

"So that's a confusion of the senses. Like seeing songs."

"Huh. Maybe," said Max-Ernest, obviously not convinced.

"C'mon, we gotta tell someone!" said Cass, turning away from the paintings.

"Why? What's the big deal?"

"Don't you get it? He was the boy in the limousine. Dr. L and Ms. Mauvais—they kidnapped Benjamin."

"But I thought you said Ms. Mauvais wasn't the same lady as in the notebook."

"Well, I take it back. I don't care how old she is—they did it. Now c'mon—"

Cass started running down the hall. Max-Ernest struggled to keep up.

"You're saying all this just 'cause of a purple painting?"

Cass nodded. "They must have seen Benjamin's paintings when they were looking for us. And then she decided to take him. Just like she took the magician's brother. And that violin girl."

"You're crazy," said Max-Ernest.

"I am not!"

"This is just another one of your crazy predictions. Like with that mouse. You thought it died from toxic waste, and it was just rat poison."

"We don't know that for sure," said Cass, her ears stinging. (She hadn't known that Max-Ernest had seen the rat poison.) "Anyways, this is different. Benjamin's life is in danger, and you don't even care."

"Well, I don't think you really care, either. My new doctor says it's just 'cause of the way your dad died with the lightning and everything that you're a survivalist and you're always trying to save everybody. It doesn't have anything to do with them."

Cass stopped running and stared at Max-Ernest. "You told your doctor about my dad?"

"So? You said it wasn't a secret secret."

"It's not—"

"Then why are you so mad?"

"I'm not mad!"

"Your ears are all red."

"They're not!"

"You can't even see them."

"Anyways, it doesn't matter what you think because I don't think we should be collaborators anymore," said Cass, surreptitiously checking her reflection in a glass case.

"Really?"

"With your condition, it's not really safe. For either of us."

"Nobody even knows what my condition is!"

"That's why it's so dangerous. I just can't count

on you. No offense. It's not personal. Anyway, I gotta go to class."

"Me, too," said Max-Ernest.

Without saying good-bye, each turned away from the other and headed toward opposite ends of the hall.

I know—it's upsetting.

I wish I could report that Max-Ernest suddenly understood why Cass might have not have wanted him to tell his doctor about her father, even if it wasn't technically a secret, and that he immediately ran after Cass and apologized. Or that Cass suddenly realized that Max-Ernest hadn't meant any harm by telling his doctor, and that she immediately ran after Max-Ernest and told him they could be collaborators again. Or that they both suddenly realized that friendship was more important than petty differences and they ran back toward each other and gave each other a big hug.

But I can't report any of those things; they didn't happen. At another time, I might make up a make-up scene to make you feel better. Normally, I have no qualms about pandering to my audience. However, the way the story unfolds from here is affected by the fight between Cass and Max-Ernest. If I were to end their fight now, the rest of the story wouldn't make any sense. So forgive me — in this instance at least, I must stick with the truth.

In fact, Cass wasn't thinking that much about Max-Ernest after she left him; she was thinking about Benjamin Blake. More particularly, what Cass was thinking was that it was her fault that Benjamin Blake was kidnapped.

Her reasoning went like this:

1. Had she never taken the magician's notebook, Ms. Mauvais and Dr. L would never have come hunting for her.
2. Had Ms. Mauvais and Dr. L never come hunting for her, they would never have seen Benjamin's paintings.
3. Had they never seen Benjamin's paintings, they would never have kidnapped him.

Conclusion: it was her responsibility to make sure he got home safe before he was burned alive in a sulfurous inferno.

Cass had only one clue as to Benjamin's whereabouts: the name on the limousine in which he was taken away, *The Midnight Sun Sensorium and Spa*.

She had no idea what a sensorium was—unless it was one of those isolation tanks she'd heard about. You know, the ones in which people are submerged in water until they regress all the way back to being fetuses in their mothers' wombs? But she knew what a spa was—more or less.

Spas were places for what her mother called "me time," and they usually included a massage. Cass had even been to a spa once—if you counted the booth that Amber and her friends had built for that year's school fair. (All they did was put slimy cucumber slices on your eyes and cold oatmeal on your face, but of course everybody loved the spa anyway because it was Amber's.) The experience had done nothing to improve Cass's opinion of spas; lying around being pampered when you could be training for an emergency was the opposite of everything Cass stood for.

It figured that someone like Ms. Mauvais would have a spa.

On the plus side, if her spa existed, Cass knew just where to find information about it. She had fifty minutes to get home and back before her next class. She would have to run — and hope that no one saw her.

After a week away, she was so unused to entering her house that she forgot the alarm code; she only remembered to punch in her birth date when the alarm started to sound. The curtains were closed and the house was dark, and Cass — feeling more and more like a thief — decided to leave it that way. If the neighbors saw the house lit up, they might ask questions. For a second, she thought of Max-Ernest. Had a friend been with her, she might not have felt so uneasy. But she pushed the thought away. It was better working on her own, she reminded herself. That was the whole point of being a survivalist.

Her mother's obsession with travel guides had always mystified Cass, but she was grateful for it now. She pulled book after book from her mother's shelves, until she had a mountain of them — all about spas. Then she sat on the floor flipping through the books one after another. They had titles like *Spaaaaahhh!* and *Get Wet!*, and they were filled with pictures of sunsets, and bubbling Jacuzzis, and smiling grownups wrapped in towels and getting massages. Cass thought all the spas looked alike, but, apparently, to her mother, each spa was different from every other.

Her mother's notes were scrawled across the pages: *"Looks like a dream!" "Too much $$$!" "Where's the beach??"* Next to one resort her mother had written: *"Take Cass next X-mas as surprise?"* Quickly, Cass turned the page so she wouldn't be tempted to read the entry.

By the time she got through the pile, Cass figured she must have read about every spa in the country but she still hadn't seen a reference to the Midnight Sun. She'd already started the laborious process of re-shelving when she noticed an old, battered guide-book that had slipped behind the others. The front cover of the book had fallen off, revealing the first, yellowing page of the introduction, and . . . what was that word?

As it turned out, the word that had caught her eye was *sanitarium* (a sanitarium, she learned, is where they used to send people who had tuberculosis or were mentally ill). The introduction also mentioned *solariums* (glass rooms in which people bathed in the sun, back in the old days before their mothers worried about skin cancer) but not a single *sensorium.*

In the end, however, luck was with her. Buried inside the book Cass discovered an entry about the Midnight Sun. Here is what it said:

AH, TO BE YOUNG AGAIN!

It is the oldest quest on Earth.

The thirst that can never be satisfied.

The battle that can never be won.

Or can it?

The Midnight Sun Sensorium and Spa

promises nothing less.

Created over a hundred years ago by a select group of doctors and spiritualists, the Midnight Sun is one of the most exclusive—and most mysterious—resorts in the world.

Like the mythical Shangri-la, this magical mountaintop utopia has given rise to many rumors. Some say that guests of the Midnight Sun soak in baths of molten gold. Others that they drink the blood of newborn monkeys. Still others dismiss the Midnight Sun as a scam and a fraud.

Science? Medicine? Witchcraft? Who knows . . . Their treatments are closely guarded secrets. No one speaks about the Midnight Sun in public if he or she hopes ever to visit again.

Intrigued?

Unless you're a celebrity, or you have a royal title next to your name, it's nearly impossible to get a reservation at this secret sanctuary. But those brave enough to try can call (XXX) XXX

XXXX. Or write XXXX Xxxxxx Xxxxxx, Xxx Xxxxxxx, XX XXXXX.

Cass put the book in her backpack, mulling over what she'd read. Why did so many grown-ups want to be young, she wondered, when it took so long to grow old? It was like going on a million-mile road trip then wanting to turn around without getting out of the car.

Still, she'd seen enough commercials to know old people would do anything to look younger. OK, maybe not a bath of molten gold—it would be so hot, you'd burn up. But she didn't doubt that Ms. Mauvais would drink monkey blood, given the chance.

Now Cass had the address of the Midnight Sun. But what to do with it? That was the question she asked herself as she ran back to school.

She couldn't just give it to Mrs. Johnson. Not after their last conversation. If Max-Ernest didn't believe her theory about Benjamin's kidnapping, Mrs. Johnson never would.

Cass thought about writing an anonymous note—like a tip-off from a concerned citizen. But then she had a better idea: a ransom note. Anybody could write an anonymous note, she reasoned; a ransom note would really get Mrs. Johnson's attention. And Cass knew from detective books and television shows that the police used ransom notes to track down bad guys. With any luck, Mrs. Johnson would send them to save Benjamin as soon as she read it.

Below is Cass's note. Naturally, Cass was careful to disguise her handwriting. Also, she tried to be very polite because she was writing to Mrs. Johnson, the principal with principles:

Dear Mrs. Johnson,

Good day.

We have kidnapped the artist Benjamin Blake. Please bring one million dollars to the Midnight Sun Sensorium and Spa and leave it in a suitcase for us. Or else Benjamin Blake will be killed in a really terrible way!

Sincerely,

Dr. L and Ms. Mauvais

P.S. The address of the Midnight Sun is XXXX Xxxxxx Xxxxxx, Xxx Xxxxxxx, XX XXXXX.

It couldn't have gone worse.

Five minutes after she slipped the note through Mrs. Johnson's window Cass was summoned to her office.

Mrs. Johnson was holding the note in her hand. In all Cass's run-ins with the principal she had never seen the principal so angry.

"I am extremely upset with you, Cassandra," she said. "Did you think I wouldn't recognize your handiwork? I can't believe you would continue your childish pranks knowing one of your peers is missing and very possibly in grave danger."

"But they really did—they had a limousine with Midnight Sun on it and I saw a boy in the window!"

"And you know for certain it was Benjamin? Tell the truth."

More than anything, Cass wanted to say she did, but Mrs. Johnson saw the hesitation on her face.

"I don't know what you have against that couple, but I'm warning you, if I hear you are troubling any faculty or students—or, heaven forbid, the police—with your outlandish theories, well, I'll suspend you for the whole year! Am I understood?"

Cass nodded.

"I must admit, this is one of the most politely written ransom notes I've ever received. At least your manners are getting better. Now, out of my office!"

On the bus later that afternoon, Cass sat with her knees doubled up against the seat back in front of her, ignoring everyone and everything in her vicinity.

She *had* to rescue Benjamin Blake. But how?

Not with any help from principals or policemen.

And definitely not with any help from a certain nonstop talking boy.

The obvious step was to go to the Midnight Sun herself. But how would she get there? No way would her grandfathers take her. Not if it meant her skipping school and their risking the wrath of her mother.

Besides, even if she could get *to* the Midnight Sun, how would she get *into* the Midnight Sun? She wasn't a celebrity and she didn't have a royal title; she was just a kid. And kids didn't usually go to spas.

Except maybe for kids like Amber.

What would Amber do if *she* wanted to get in?

When Cass got off the bus, she had an inspiration.

Before she could change her mind, she pulled the old guidebook out of her backpack, and looked up the Midnight Sun's phone number. Then she dialed it on her cell phone. She could hardly believe what she was doing, and she had that giddy, dizzy feeling you get when you make a crank call—only this was much scarier.

To her relief, a machine picked up. "You have reached the Midnight Sun Sensorium and Spa," said an unmistakable, icy voice. "Please leave a message if you are ready to say good-bye to the old you, and hello to the new."

Cass shuddered, remembering what the magician had written about Ms. Mauvais making him feel as if he were drowning in the coldest water on Earth. Cass might not be synesthetic but she knew exactly what he was talking about.

"Hello. This is . . . this is one of the Skelton Sisters. I'd like to make a reservation to stay at the Midnight Sun."

She left her number. Then she dropped the phone onto the floor, wondering whether Max-Ernest wasn't right, after all. Maybe she *was* crazy.

It took her a couple seconds to realize her phone was ringing.

Holding her breath, she picked up the phone and held it several inches away from her ear as if it were a particularly lethal kind of snake.

"Hello," Ms. Mauvais tinkled on the other end. "How wonderful to hear from a Skelton Sister! To whom am I speaking, may I ask? Romi or Montana?"

"Um, neither," said Cass, thinking quickly. "I'm the other one."

"Oh, there's another? I had no idea."

"Yes, my name is Amber. I'm the youngest. They

keep me hidden. But I'm famous also," Cass explained. (She was glad she'd practiced lying on her mother.)

"Oh, you're one of those secret celebrities? My favorite kind. Being in the public eye is so tiresome, don't you think?" Ms. Mauvais inquired.

"Yes. That's why I want to stay at the Midnight Sun. I hear it's very private. And all your treatments — I hear they're all really great. I know it's hard to get a reservation. But I thought maybe since I'm a celebrity —"

"You seem to know a lot about it," said Ms. Mauvais with a light laugh.

"Yeah, I do," said Cass, not about to admit that that was all she knew.

"Well, you're in luck. It just so happens we have an opening this evening. Shall I send the limousine for you?"

"Um, yeah, I guess," Cass said, choking on her words. "That would be good."

"Terrific. I'm sure you'll love all of our treatments."

Cass shivered. The way Ms. Mauvais said the word "treatments," it sounded more like "punishments."

CHAPTER
SEVENTEEN

I've Changed My Mind

Or maybe I should say I've come to my senses.

Rather than continuing to narrate the adventures of Cass and Max-Ernest, I'm going to end this book here — while they're still safe.

More importantly, while you're still safe.

I know, you're angry with me. You've read this far — you feel you've earned the right to know how the story ends.

Go ahead: laugh, scream, cry, throw the book at the wall.

If you knew — well, there's the rub, you don't know, do you? If you knew the truth, I was going to say, if you knew everything this story entails, all those grizzly, gruesome facts, all those horrible, harrowing details, you'd thank me for sparing you.

Alas, since you don't know, you will go to your grave hating me, thinking I am your enemy — when, for the first time, I am acting like a friend.

Happily, you don't know how to find me. If you did, I've no doubt, you would try to bribe me to finish the story. I know how you are. I know how I am, too. I am very susceptible to bribes. As you've probably noticed, I have no self-control whatsoever.

I like chocolate best. But I also have a fondness for cheese.

If, for instance, you were to pass under my nose

a very ripe brie—you might think the brie was gross and stinky, but you would be wrong, oh so wrong—and you tempted me with a bite, only to tell me that the price of the bite was my continuing the story, well, I'm afraid I might start writing without a moment's thought. Now, if you were to hand me, say, a piece of chocolate, dark as night, European in origin, with a very high percentage of cocoa—don't forget that high percentage of cocoa—well, there's no saying what I would do. Or wouldn't.

As a matter of fact, it just so happens that I've been saving for a special occasion a piece of chocolate very much like the one I just described. Right now, it's sitting high up on a shelf that I can't reach without a ladder. I put it there so I wouldn't eat it without first fully considering the matter. I must admit, I've never wanted it more than I do now.

The chocolate on my shelf is of the finest quality. I won't mention the brand here; that's the kind of information that could help my enemies track me down. Trust me, though, it's not cheap. Many cacao beans have given their lives to make that chocolate. I can practically taste it now.

Hmmm, what must I do in order to eat it?

It would be wrong to eat the chocolate without offering you something in return. I'm not the kind of person who accepts a bribe and then pretends he doesn't know what the bribe means. Where's the honor in that?

In short, if I want to eat the chocolate, I must keep writing.

What an awful, awful choice! On the one side: I renounce the chocolate, stay healthy and trim, and put an end to this reckless tale-telling. On the other side: I climb up the ladder, feast on chocolate, and then, full of sugar and guilt, I continue my story, knowing I'm possibly sentencing you to a fate worse than death.

Actually, put like that, the choice is pretty easy.

I'll be right back.

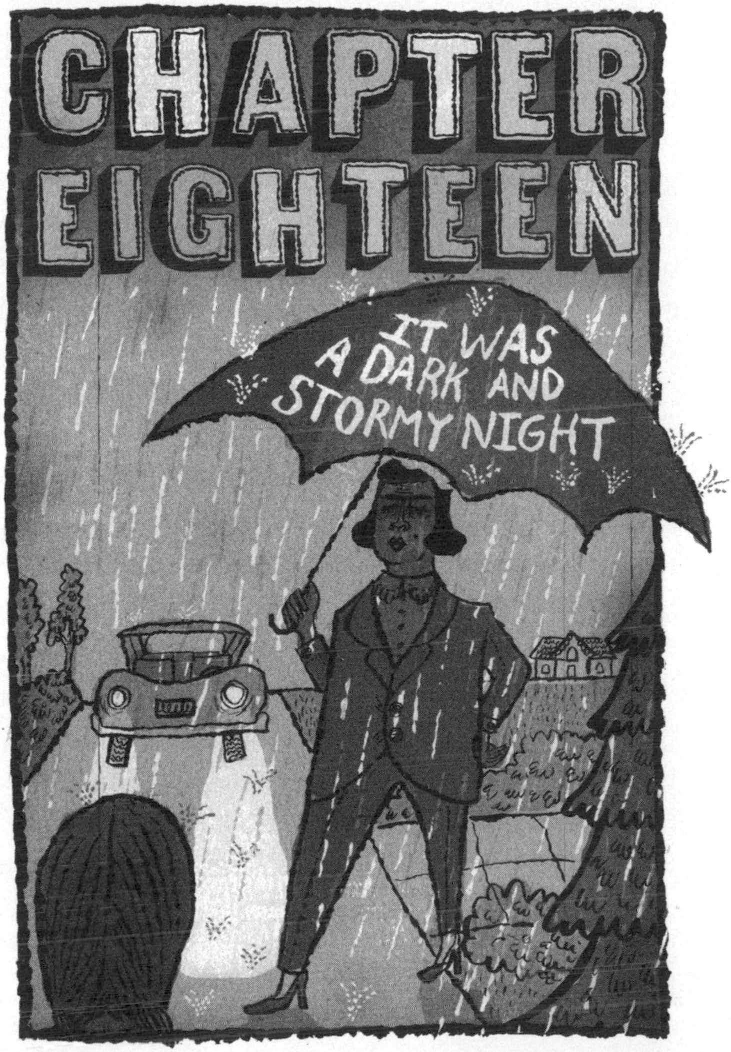
CHAPTER EIGHTEEN
IT WAS A DARK AND STORMY NIGHT

Really, it was. Dark and stormy.

As if the weather itself had conspired to turn our tale into a ghost story.

Or as if — and this seems slightly more plausible — Ms. Mauvais somehow controlled the skies and was using them to obscure the events of the evening.

In any case, the weather makes my job easier. It creates the proper mood. And it eliminates the need to hide certain facts. Like the location of the street corner on which Cass was waiting. With all the rain, you could hardly have seen her anyway.

For Cass, sadly, the weather didn't make things any easier, only wetter. And colder. Teeth chattering, she stood under a street lamp, clutching her backpack to her chest for warmth. Not that it was much help; the backpack was no drier than her clothing.

It had been difficult figuring out what to wear.

After her phone conversation with Ms. Mauvais, Cass had gone back home again, and rifled through her mother's closets; she even tried on a dress for the first time in over a year. But despite her recent growth spurt, she still looked like she was playing dress-up when she put on her mother's clothes. She'd also considered borrowing Amber's "Honorary Skelton Sister" T-shirt, but she couldn't bring herself to call and ask for it. Plus, Cass realized, a real Skelton Sister probably wouldn't wear the T-shirt anyway.

Finally, she chose to wear her usual jeans and sweatshirt, but she modified the outfit with a pair of furry boots her mother had bought for one of their never-take ski trips. They didn't look exactly like the fuzzy boots that Amber and her friends wore but they were close enough. (I know, at the beginning of this book, I told you Cass would never wear boots like those; I was forgetting she might wear them as part of a disguise.)

Now, she regretted the boots. Not only were they too big, they were soaked through. Her feet sloshed around in them, and they splattered when she walked. She felt like Bigfoot.

Her other new accessory was equally impractical for the weather: a pair of sunglasses. But even Cass knew that celebrities wore sunglasses all the time, indoors as well as out. Also, they helped disguise her face — which, presumably, is why celebrities wear them. (Had Cass asked me, I would have told her what I always tell people who are trying to go incognito: *lose the shades.* They only make you look more conspicuous.) Cass felt certain that neither Ms. Mauvais nor Dr. L would recognize her — they had seen her face for only a second — but it was best to be careful.

Her backpack, it goes without saying, she never considered leaving. Never mind whether a Skelton Sister would have worn it or not.

Cass thought wistfully about the hot pot of tea that Grandpa Larry would undoubtedly be making on a rainy night like this one. She wished she'd stopped at the fire station for a cup before heading out to meet the Midnight Sun limousine. Instead, she'd phoned her grandfathers and told them she was staying overnight at Max-Ernest's house to work on their volcano experiment (for which the due date kept being conveniently postponed). She slept there all the time, she added. And her mother had already spoken to Max-Ernest's parents, so there was no reason to ask her mother's permission.

Her grandfathers had asked a few questions and demanded Max-Ernest's phone number, but they were still feeling so guilty for making her upset about the Symphony of Smells that they hadn't given her much trouble. The hardest part was having to listen to Grandpa Larry and Grandpa Wayne argue about whether she should make her volcano erupt with Alka-Seltzer or dry ice.

"You trust me, right?" Cass had asked. (She felt a little guilty herself playing on *their* guilt, but she needed to get them off the phone.)

"Of course we do!" they assured her.

Then she had called her mother and told her pretty much the same thing—except to her mother she said it was her grandfathers who had spoken to Max-Ernest's parents, so there was no reason to phone them. "And don't call me at nine tonight, OK?" Cass added. "Max-Ernest and I are going to be working."

"Just don't stay up too late," said her mother. "All right, Cass?"

"Uh huh."

"Promise?"

"Uh huh."

"I'm sorry, I didn't catch that."

"Yes, Mom!"

"Yes, what?"

"Yes, I promise!"

"OK, I love you."

"Me, too."

"Me, too, what?"

"I love you, too! Sheesh!"

Although she and Max-Ernest weren't collaborators anymore, and it was sort of cheating to ask for his help, Cass had had no choice but to call him, too; she had to warn him that he might hear from her grandfathers, or even from her mom.

She'd been very businesslike with Max-Ernest, she thought. She told him where she'd hidden the magician's notebook and she gave him all the information she had about the Midnight Sun. And she didn't say anything about his abandoning their mission or being a coward and a traitor. (Somehow, with all the activity, she'd forgotten that she'd been the one to end their partnership.) He didn't say much at all, for a change, which was fine with her. Hopefully, he would be able play it off like she was staying with him — at least until the morning.

Then, well, everyone would start looking for her — probably. But would it be too late?

She didn't see the limousine until it splashed to a stop in front of her, glistening with raindrops.

As Cass waited, the driver got out and walked toward her, heedless of the storm. The driver was big and tall and shadowed in darkness — save for a pair of white gloves, gleaming in the night. Was it Dr. L?

Every instinct Cass had told her to run. But something that was not quite bravery and not quite fear and not quite the knowledge of Benjamin's plight kept her rooted to the spot.

"Miss Skelton?"

The voice was gruff but not as deep as Cass expected.

"Yeah, that's me," said Cass as forcefully as she could.

"I'm Daisy."

Daisy stepped into the light, revealing a decidedly un-flower-like but indisputably female face. Without another word, she opened the limousine's back door and beckoned Cass inside with a gloved hand.

Reminding herself she was a celebrity, and not the type of person to be intimidated by a limousine driver (even if that driver was the tallest woman she'd ever seen), Cass held her head high and climbed in as confidently as if she rode in limousines every day and Daisy were her own personal chauffeur.

Only after she'd settled into her plush velvet seat did Cass notice how violently her hands were shaking. She had to sit on them to get them to stop.

Hours passed in silence, Cass barely able to see out of the foggy windows. Generally, she could tell they were heading upward, but the limousine made so many turns that she lost all sense of direction. Too late, she thought of Hansel and Gretel and how you're supposed to leave a trail of crumbs when you journey into a forest.

If nobody came for her, how would she find her way back?

She told herself to stay calm, but doubts kept creeping into her head. Previously, she'd been so focused on getting into the Midnight Sun that she hadn't stopped to think what she would do once she got inside. Now that she appeared really to be on her way she wondered how she would find Benjamin — and how she would get him out.

In the back of her mind lurked other, darker questions: Why had Dr. L and Ms. Mauvais taken Benjamin? What did they want him for?

What had happened to the magician's brother, Luciano? Would she find him, too, still a prisoner after so much time? He would be an old man by now, his circus days long gone. . . .

And what about the magician, Pietro, himself? What was the terrible secret he had discovered? Was she strong enough to face it if she had to?

Suddenly, the limousine rounded a turn and broke through the clouds.

Cass wiped the fog off the window next to her and looked outside. The sky above was now clear and starry — suggestive no longer of ghost stories but rather of science fiction and space travel. A perfect sky for spotting comets or for studying the constellations if only Cass had had the time and inclination. (Unfortunately, she had neither.) Cass couldn't tell much about their location except that they were near the top of a mountain. Below them, a vast white blanket of clouds, illuminated by the moon, spread out as far she could see.

The limousine made another sharp turn, then descended into a small, hidden valley.

"Look—" Daisy commanded, breaking the silence.

Only then did Cass become aware of the warm glow suffusing the landscape around them. Craning her neck, she could just make out the source of the glow: an intense golden light peeking over the edge of the mountains. It looked like a sunrise, but it couldn't have been; the time was just before midnight.

"There it is," said Daisy. "The Midnight Sun."

hope it's not giving away too much to tell you that, only two days later, the Midnight Sun would be devoured by fire. How and why it was set on fire, and who, if anyone, was burned to a crisp, and whether or not the smell of sulfur was in the air — these are questions that will have to wait. In the meantime, the Midnight Sun's fiery fate frees me to describe it in detail. Because it is gone, you can no longer find it, no matter how good your information.

So many subjects you study in school prove unnecessary in life: for math, there is always a calculator. For English, there is always spell-check. For history, there is always the encyclopedia. Why should you hold so much knowledge in your head when it is stored right in front of you?

But there is one subject that comes in handy time after time.

I am thinking, of course, about Egyptology.

To name just one example: a thorough understanding of the mummification process is indispensable whether you are dispatching an enemy or preserving a friend or simply bandaging a head injury.

More to the point: if you are familiar with the layout of temples from Egypt's Middle Kingdom (roughly 2000–1600 BC), then you already have a sense of what the Midnight Sun looked like. In particular, the spa was an almost exact replica of a little-known temple to the Egyptian god Thoth—a temple built over the grave of an unnamed pharaoh and accessible only by a three-day camel ride through the desert.

Cass was sadly ignorant of the finer points of Egyptian architecture. She knew enough, though, to recognize a pyramid when she saw one. Passing through the Midnight Sun's massive gates, she was temporarily blinded by the blazing light, but once her eyes adjusted she could see a midsize (by Egyptian standards) pyramid standing in the precise center of the spa grounds.

Perched on top of the pyramid was something that would have astonished even the most seasoned Egyptian explorer. It was a lantern, but much more than a lantern. A perfect orb, it resembled nothing so much as a rising sun. Inside, fire danced every which way, as if fueled not by electricity or gas but rather by some unknown, supernatural source. Although the fire appeared gold at first glance, a longer look revealed a kaleidoscope of colors in the flames.

It was this lantern that Cass had seen earlier peeking over the mountains. Now, as the limousine door was opened for her, the lantern was so close she had to shield her eyes despite the fact that she was wearing sunglasses. Had she had a sudden change of heart and decided to make a run for it, the glare would have dissuaded her. Anyone in the vicinity could be seen as clearly as if a spotlight were shining directly upon her.

It's just like a prison, Cass thought.

A large gloved hand helped her out of the vehicle. She assumed the hand belonged to Daisy, until she looked up and saw Dr. L's too-handsome face smiling down at her, his silver hair glowing unnaturally in the light of the lantern.

She stifled a gasp, squeezing her backpack tight in her arms. This was the moment of truth: would he recognize her?

"Miss Skelton, welcome to the Midnight Sun. I am Dr. L," he said smoothly, just as if he were meeting her for the very first time. "Ms. Mauvais regrets she cannot greet you herself—she keeps to a very strict bedtime. But she's asked me to extend you every courtesy in her place."

Cass nodded, too overwhelmed to speak. The light was making her dizzy. Or was it nerves? Behind her, the limousine quietly pulled away; there was no going back.

"I know, it's bright here, but you'll get used to it," said Dr. L, tilting his head in the direction of the pyramid. "That lantern was brought by ship from Egypt many years ago, but the flame inside had already been burning for thousands of years before that. Legend has it, it started when a fireball fell from the sun."

"Like a meteor?" Cass managed to ask.

"Exactly. Because the flame never dies, we call it the Midnight Sun — it's like a sun that never sets. But you must be very tired."

He gestured toward a freckle-faced young man in a white tunic — and yet another pair of white gloves — standing silently next to a stone table. "This is Owen, your personal butler. He will escort you to your room."

"N-nice to m-meet you," Owen stuttered. He smiled shyly.

Cass breathed a silent sigh of relief. Owen, at least, was not very intimidating.

"But first, a small formality," said Dr. L. (His identifiably unidentifiable accent was especially strong when he pronounced the word *formality.*)

"Do you need me to pay?" asked Cass, ready to hand over the credit card her mother had given her.

Dr. L chuckled. "We'll worry about that later. It's

just that we have to look through all our guests' baggage when they arrive."

"You want to look in my backpack?" Cass asked, alarmed.

"The Midnight Sun is a place of healing, and we insist that nothing contaminate the atmosphere. Sugar. Junk food. Firearms. That sort of thing."

Cass reluctantly handed her backpack to Owen, who started removing items for Dr. L's inspection. Cass hoped desperately that nothing would reveal who she was.

"I see you've come prepared," said Dr. L drily as Owen held up Cass's flashlight and binoculars and other survivalist gear. "What's that? A space blanket? I think you'll find the bedding here is quite ample, but of course one never knows. . . . I must say, you seem a much more independent sort than your sisters."

"My sisters? I mean, you know them?" Cass corrected herself, flustered.

"Certainly. They've been here several times. Ms. Mauvais is very fond of them. But you must know that." He smiled blandly.

"Yeah, I knew that," said Cass quickly, her palms sweating. "That's why I'm here."

"Normally, we don't encourage our guests to

bring camping equipment, but we'll make an exception tonight." He nodded for Owen to return the backpack.

"However, I'm afraid I will have to ask for your cell phone," Dr. L added. "Hopefully, you'll appreciate the opportunity for silence and meditation."

Cass froze. She'd always hated silence and meditation, but that wasn't the problem. Her phone was the only thing linking her to the outside. If the worst should happen, she might at least use it to send her mother a message. Or a picture of herself waving good-bye.

Cass was about to say she hadn't brought a phone with her, but then she thought better of it. What self-respecting Skelton Sister would leave home without one? The danger of blowing her cover was too great to risk.

She reached into her pocket and handed over her phone. Good-bye, she thought. Although whether she was addressing the phone or her mother or the whole world she couldn't have said.

As Owen led her to her room, Cass tried to forget her fears and to concentrate on her surroundings. The Midnight Sun, she saw, spread out from the pyramid in a series of concentric circles: a wide reflecting pool dotted with lily pads and lotus blossoms surrounded the pyramid; a courtyard at least an acre in size and paved in sandstone surrounded the reflecting pool; and a series of low, stone buildings fronted by columns surrounded the courtyard. Flowering vines — jasmine, honeysuckle, and other more exotic varieties — crept up the columns, filling the air with their scent, and making the Midnight Sun seem all the more ancient, beautiful, and secret.*

While the lantern on the pyramid created the effect almost of daylight, the whole of the Midnight Sun seemed to be asleep; it was like coming across a remote village in the midafternoon and finding the inhabitants had all fallen under a spell. Behind one of these doors, Cass thought, Benjamin was being kept prisoner. Or would they keep him underground in some kind of labyrinth or dungeon? Perhaps he was underneath her feet at that very moment. Cass imagined a dark corridor lined with prison cells, Benjamin and Luciano and all the other children stolen by Ms. Mauvais grasping the steel bars, pleading for help.

Before she knew it, Cass was standing in her new room, and Owen was bidding her g-good night. "C-can I g-get you anything b-before I g-go?"

---

*I SAY *SEEM* ALL THE MORE ANCIENT, BEAUTIFUL, AND SECRET, BECAUSE IN REALITY THE MIDNIGHT SUN WAS NOT ANCIENT BUT MERELY OLD; THE DOINGS INSIDE, AS YOU SHALL SOON SEE, WERE ANYTHING BUT BEAUTIFUL; AND, LASTLY, NOW THAT I AM WRITING ABOUT IT, THE MIDNIGHT SUN IS SOMEWHAT LESS OF A SECRET.

Needless to say, Cass had never had a butler be-fore. She'd never even seen one before, except in the movies and on TV. Owen wasn't anything like a movie butler. First, he didn't wear a tuxedo. Second, he was too young. (Owen was that age that is older than a kid, but younger than a parent. Maybe the age of an uncle. Or of a half brother from your father's first marriage. You know, *that* age.) Third, he didn't have an English accent, or even speak properly. But that made it all the more difficult to know how to treat him.

"I don't want anything," said Cass, trying her best to sound like a bossy heiress. "Go away now."

Immediately, she'd felt like she'd overdone it. If she was too rude, she might make an enemy of Owen. "I mean, if that's OK," she added in a friendlier tone. "My shoes are still wet, and I just want to get out of them."

Owen didn't seem to notice her tone, one way or the other. "You kn-know, in the old d-days, they m-made the g-guests here sleep in w-wet socks."

"Wet socks? Why?" asked Cass, making a face.

"W-when you have c-cold f-feet, your b-blood circulates to w-warm them up. B-but they have other w-ways n-now," he said darkly.

Before Cass could ask what he meant, he was out the door.

Moorish tiles, potted palms, a bed made to look like a Bedouin tent, and an arched window facing a pyramid—her room could have been a palace bedroom in Giza. At another time, in other circumstances, Cass might have loved staying in a room like this. Now she could only regard the room with dread. It was the first hotel room she'd ever stayed in; she couldn't help fearing it would be the last.

She assured herself that her disguise was intact; if Dr. L had recognized her, he wouldn't have welcomed her so courteously. But it was no use. She lay on the bed, tensing every time she heard a sound: in her imagination, the hum of a pool filter was the churning of molten gold, and the rustle of leaves signaled the presence of angry monkeys come back for their young.

Her idea was to wait in her room until everyone at the spa had gone to sleep; then she would sneak out and look for Benjamin. As the hours passed, she kept putting off the moment. Even after the pyramid's lantern had finally begun to dim, she told herself to wait a little longer—just to be safe.

If you've ever slept anywhere other than your own

home, then you know it's often difficult to fall asleep in a strange bed; however, it's equally difficult to stay awake after you've experienced one of the longest, scariest, and most exhausting days of your life.

Cass fell asleep.

She dreamed she was traveling in Egypt, searching for a fabled trove of buried gold.

A turbaned guide, who looked strangely like her butler Owen, led her into a massive, hulking pyramid. Inside, a dark tunnel coiled around and around, getting narrower and narrower, and going deeper and deeper underground. Cass had to stoop, then crawl, then slither on her stomach. She had trouble breathing. She wanted to turn around but she couldn't. She felt claustrophobic. She was afraid she would suffocate.

Then, finally, she saw it glittering in front of her. Two spans of gold creating a giant M.

The Golden Arches.

The pyramid's innermost chamber was . . . an underground McDonald's?

She tried telling her guide, no, this wasn't right. She didn't want to go to McDonald's. In order to make their hamburgers, McDonald's raised and slaughtered so many cows that they became diseased and land was destroyed. Land that should have been used to grow grain and feed hungry people. It was an environmental emergency. There was so much cow dung that the methane gases from the dung made the air smoggy. She knew all about it from a documentary she saw with her mom.

If he'd just give her back her cell phone —

If she could just call her mom —

If only —

Please, let me out —

Please —

But Owen, I mean her butler, I mean her guide, wouldn't listen.

The magic word had lost its power.

The last doctor Max-Ernest consulted, the one who analyzed Cass's survivalist tendencies, had a theory about Max-Ernest as well: the theory was that Max-Ernest talked about things in order to avoid having feelings about them.

The doctor told Max-Ernest he should practice having feelings. (This may sound silly, but for some people it's very difficult; I myself haven't had a good, solid feeling in years.) As a beginning, the doctor suggested, Max-Ernest might try naming his feelings as soon as he noticed them. Then, instead of shooing them away, Max-Ernest might try sitting with his feelings for a while.

At first, Max-Ernest had been confused about the doctor's suggestions; all the naming and shooing made him think the doctor was talking about household pets rather than human emotions. After speaking to Cass and learning about her trip to the spa, however, he decided to take the doctor's advice.

Eyes closed, he sat on the floor trying to identify his feelings. He counted at least five (not to mention the fact that he was already *mad* at Cass to begin with, which made six):

He was *impressed* by the boldness of her plan.

He was *hurt* that she hadn't included him.

He was *annoyed* that he had to lie for her anyway.

He was *jealous* that she would get to have all the excitement.

And he was *worried* that Ms. Mauvais would discover who Cass really was.

"I know we're not collaborators anymore, but I wanted someone to know I was going to the Midnight Sun — in case they figure out who I am and I never come back," Cass had said, by way of explaining her call. "If they kill me or something, tell my mom not to get mad at my grandfathers. They don't know I'm going. So it's not their fault if I die."

Only after mulling over the conversation for several hours did it occur to Max-Ernest that *he* now knew she was going to the Midnight Sun, and therefore if something happened to her it would be *his* fault.

He couldn't tell whether that made him feel *guilty* for not doing anything to stop her or *angry* at Cass for putting him in a difficult position.

He thought about calling her back to tell her about all of his different feelings. Her phone number was right there on his phone. He could call her by hitting one button. But he didn't.

He stared at the number, suddenly realizing what it meant: Cass's number must have popped up on the spa's phone, too.

Which meant Ms. Mauvais must have known it was Cassandra and not a Skelton Sister who had called.

And she had let Cass make the reservation under the Skelton name anyway.

It was a trap—it had to be.

Quickly, he called Cass's number, but nobody answered.

He tried again.

And again.

When she still hadn't answered after ten attempts at reaching her, Max-Ernest was overtaken by another emotion altogether: *fear.*

CHAPTER TWENTY-ONE

When Cass awoke, it was dawn.

She sat bolt upright in bed, furious with herself. A whole night had passed and she hadn't even begun to search for Benjamin Blake!

Hurriedly, she slipped into her damp boots — she had slept in her clothes — and headed for the door. She only hoped she could get a good look around before the whole spa was awake.

Then she became aware of the polite but persistent tapping at the window. For a second, she had the wildly hopeful thought that it might be Benjamin himself, trying to contact her in secret.

But it was only her butler.

Owen entered, bowing slightly and carrying a tray that held a tall glass of bright green, bubbling liquid.

He wished Cass — or rather M-Miss Skelton, as he continued to call her — a g-good m-morning, and put the tray down on a table in front of her.

"What's that?" asked Cass. "A smoothie?"

"It's an e-l-lixir. M-ms. M-mauvais has one b-brewed specially for each g-guest. I d-don't know why you g-got em-m-merald. Your sisters always g-get p-pink."

This time, Cass didn't flinch at the mention of

her supposed sisters. Instead, she busied herself studying her drink. Shiny specks swirled in the bubbles. "Is that gold?" she asked.

Owen nodded. "M-ms. M-mauvais says g-gold promotes l-long l-life. It n-never t-tarnishes."

The last thing Cass wanted to do was drink something brewed specially by Ms. Mauvais, but Owen was watching. So she took a tentative sip. The elixir had a zesty, zingy, zippy sort of flavor, and it gave her a bit of a head rush. She thought she detected a faint metallic taste, but she wasn't sure it was the gold.

At any rate, the elixir didn't seem to be poison.

"W-would you l-like anything else f-for b-breakfast?"

Cass shook her head. She didn't want him returning and interrupting her again.

"W-well, if you're n-not hungry, it's t-time for your f-first t-treatment," he said. "There's a b-bathrobe and b-bathing suit for you in the c-closet. I'll w-wait r-right outside."

Cass groaned inwardly. This wasn't good at all. How could she investigate if he was waiting outside her door? Besides, she'd been hoping to avoid the treatments. Even if they didn't really involve molten gold or monkey blood.

She had to think fast. "You know what, I changed my mind — do you have waffles?"

Owen nodded. "Whole-grain, g-gluten-free, d-dairy-free, or tra-d-ditional?"

"Traditional, I guess."

"With l-lavender honey, n-natural tr-tree r-root sugar substitute, or V-vermont special r-reserve extra-v-virgin m-maple syrup?"

"Syrup. And lots of butter — already melted," Cass said to cut him off before he offered any more toppings. "And no powdered sugar — not even a lit-tle," she added automatically, because that was how she always ordered her waffles.

"No p-powdered sugar. C-coming r-ight up, M-miss Skelton."

Owen bowed and left to go get her breakfast.

Cass leaned back on her pillow wondering whether she should call him back and add some eggs to her order. Or maybe a cup of hot chocolate.

Then she remembered she wasn't really eating.

Funny how easy it is to get used to having a ser-vant. Even for a survivalist.

After waiting two minutes, Cass let herself out of the room as quietly as she could. There was nobody in sight; it was an ideal time to search for Benjamin. Where should she start—the other guest rooms?

Before she had time to consider, Owen was rounding the corner.

"Ch-change your m-mind again, M-miss Skelton? I was j-just c-coming to see if you w-wanted w-wild straw-b-berries or or-g-ganic Ore-g-gon b-blue-b-berries. But if you w-want t-to skip the w-waffle and g-go straight t-to your treatments, your G-gold B-bath is r-ready."

Her Gold Bath.

Owen said it with such nonchalance it couldn't possibly be a lethal cauldron of molten gold. Or could it? Perhaps workers at the Midnight Sun were so used to seeing children boiled alive that they were completely blasé about it. (Are you familiar with the words *nonchalant* and *blasé?* They're two of my favorite words in a crisis. If you don't know them, I'd advise you to look them up now—but make sure you don't appear too anxious when you do.)

Cass decided the wisest course was to pretend to go along with her butler, then to escape at the first opportunity.

"Yeah, I guess I'm not really hungry after all," she said, trying to sound equally nonchalant (I told you to look it up!).

*　　*　　*

On the way, Owen warned her to respect the p-privacy of any p-people she encountered. "At the M-midnight Sun, g-guests only speak t-to each other at m-meals. M-ms. M-mauvais's r-rules."

He need not have warned her because she saw only a few guests, and then only at a distance. Still, she was close enough to get a general impression. Like Dr. L and Ms. Mauvais, like all the staff at the Midnight Sun, all the guests at the spa were tan and smooth and perfect-looking. Cass hated them on sight.

Oh, one other thing: they all wore gloves. Even the man swimming in the lap pool.

"Hey, Owen," said Cass, still doing her best to act blasé (!). "What are those gloves for? Why's everyone wearing them?"

But Owen didn't hear. At least he appeared not to. And she didn't have the courage to ask a second time.

One mystery was cleared up right away: the Gold Bath was not a bath of molten gold, it was just a mud bath — with flecks of gold like Cass had found in her emerald elixir. Have you ever seen fool's gold? The kind you find shifting around the sand in a riverbed? The gold in the Gold Bath looked like that.

While we're on the subject: have you ever had a mud bath? You might find it disappointing. Cass did.

Cass had always imagined a mud bath to be smooth and creamy and chocolaty—like a bath by Willy Wonka. Instead, the mud in her mud bath was more like sludge. It was bumpy and scratchy and gloppy and full of tiny things you couldn't identify that got inside places you didn't want them to. Worse, every once in a while, a big burping bubble would float up from the bottom and fill the air with a gaseous stink. By the time she got out, she was so relieved to be done with the mud bath that she almost didn't care that Owen had showed up again, once more preventing her from hunting for Benjamin.

He promised that the next few treatments would be less messy, and considerably more pleasant. Each of them, he explained, was designed to stimulate one of the five senses.

"Is that why they call it a sensorium?"

Owen nodded. "M-ms. M-mauvais says the g-goal is to b-bring the s-senses b-back into har-m-mo-n-ny with each-ch-ch other."

"You mean like synesthesia?" Cass asked, before realizing she might be giving herself away. (After all, how many kids had heard of synesthesia?)

Owen looked at her in surprise. "Yeah, that's r-right," he said.

He led her into a large airy room with a domed ceiling of cut glass through which light refracted in an ever-changing pattern of rainbows. Cass, remembering her mother's guidebook, thought she recognized the room as a solarium. She didn't ask this time, however, not wanting to attract more suspicion than she already had.* Instead, she obediently lay facedown on a padded table, sticking her nose through a hole apparently designed for the purpose. Above, she could feel the warm sunlight streaming through the glass — although she wasn't sure whether she was feeling the real sun, or the Midnight Sun, or both. A faint breeze ruffled the long, gauzy silk banners that had been hung from the ceiling to provide privacy. She felt almost as if she were outside — yet nowhere on Earth.

A team of nearly a dozen women in white flocked silently around her, sailing in and out, disappearing behind the silk banners only to reappear seconds later holding new crystals and chimes, oils and unguents. They traipsed around the room releasing scents (Cass, who had practiced with the Symphony of Smells, identified pine, orange blossom, lavender,

*As it happens, she was right; it *was* a solarium — albeit a unique one.

and even shiitake mushroom). Then they circled, making eerie sounds with small gongs and tuning forks (someone called the sound vibrations "acupuncture without needles," and indeed Cass felt a prickling on her skin; but she wasn't sure whether the vibrations or her own anxiety had caused it).

After scent and sound came touch.

Eyes closed, Cass became aware of new sensations at all ends of her body: they scratched her scalp and they scraped the bottoms of her feet. They dug into her palms and they pulled on her fingers. They massaged her temples and patted her cheeks. They tugged on her earlobes and they wiggled her nose. They spiraled her arms and shook out her legs. They rotated her ankles and cracked her toe knuckles. They pushed and prodded and rubbed and rolled. Until she lost track of who was who and what was what and where was where.

Cass was hovering on the brink of unconsciousness when she heard Dr. L speaking from somewhere behind her.

"Hello, Miss Skelton. I hope you're enjoying your treatments," he said in his distinctively indistinctive voice. "No, please don't open your eyes. Instead, allow me to suggest some images to you. Many patients feel it helps them to relax. . . ."

Cass could feel him coming closer; it was excruciating, like an itch. She was aching to sit up, but she knew she had to lie still if she didn't want him to suspect anything.

He began murmuring in Cass's ear. "Think of the light of the Midnight Sun shining on your back. . . . It's warm . . . bright . . . welcoming. . . . Can you feel it . . . ? Good . . . Now imagine yourself floating slowly toward the light. . . . You're like a speck of dust in a sunbeam. . . . That's right, just floating . . . softly floating. . . ."

Cass told herself not to listen; the important thing was to stay alert. But there was something so lulling about Dr. L's voice. His words slipped into her consciousness without a ripple, as if they were her own thoughts.

"All those worries you carry with you," he continued, "let them all go. . . . Those fears about crimes and disasters and emergencies, they're drifting away . . . they're gone . . . gone. . . . You don't need to prepare for anything here. We're taking care of everything for you. . . . You're safe. Perfectly safe. Let's repeat that word, shall we? Safe . . . Safe . . . Safe . . ."

Cass found herself almost unwittingly repeating the word.

Safe . . . Safe . . . Safe . . .

"Good . . . Good . . . Now I'm going to ask you a question we ask all our patients, so we can better help them. And I want you to answer honestly and truthfully. Can you do that?"

Cass murmured her assent.

"Wonderful . . . The question is: Why are you really here?"

CHAPTER
TWENTY-TWO

Cass opened her eyes with a jolt. She was still on the massage table, but uncertain how much time had passed.

What happened? Had she been hypnotized?

What did she say to Dr. L? Had she told him who she was?

Alarmed, she pushed herself up and looked around. She seemed to be alone.

No, there was Owen, entering the room. How did he always know?

He greeted her as though nothing were different — she must not have given herself away, after all.

Cass was so relieved she almost laughed out loud.

By now, she had seen most of the spa — with one notable exception.

After Cass had dressed, she asked Owen what was inside the pyramid.

"N-nothing," he answered quickly. "J-just a lot of r-rocks. I w-wouldn't g-go in there."

She shrugged agreeably. But of course his answer had only increased her curiosity. And this time, she vowed, she wouldn't be so easily derailed.

Yawning, she told Owen that she was tired after all her treatments (which was true) and that she needed to rest (which was also true). She said she could find her way back to her room without him (true, too). Why didn't he take a break now and check on her later? She was going to go take a short nap (false).

"I don't know. I'm n-not really supposed to—"

"You're my butler, right? Aren't you supposed to do whatever I say?"

He nodded.

"Well, then, I'm ordering you to go relax."

"B-but if I go relax, I won't be around to follow your orders, will I?"

Cass looked at him to see if he was serious: he smiled.

They both laughed. And suddenly Cass felt she not only had a butler, she had a friend.

It was on the tip of her tongue to tell Owen why she was at the spa. Did he know about Dr. L and Ms. Mauvais? she wondered. Could he possibly be as evil as they? She didn't think so, but she decided it was better not to risk saying anything.

The way back to her room was through the hot pools. So Cass went in that direction, in case Owen was watching. She figured she'd change course as soon as she was hidden by the steam.

Just as she was about to veer off toward the

pyramid, she heard a loud sigh — and nearly slipped on the wet stone floor.

She peered down at the pool in front of her. A woman was floating on her back, her round pink face bobbing in and out of the bubbling water, as if she were simmering in a giant pot of soup.

It was Gloria Fortune, real estate agent for the dead.

What was *she* doing there?

Earlier, Cass had feared Gloria might have joined her clients in the afterlife; but, under the circumstances, stumbling upon her alive was almost more alarming than stumbling upon a corpse.

If Gloria recognized her, it would all be over.

Luckily, Gloria's eyes were closed. Cass backed away as quickly and quietly as she could.

There was no time to lose. At any moment, Gloria might pop up again — this time with her eyes open — and identify Cass. She had to find Benjamin and get out of the spa right away.

The night before, the lamp on top of the pyramid had shined so brightly that it could have been daytime. Now, late in the afternoon, the lamp was dim, its flame a bare flicker; and the spa was in shadows — so dark it could have been evening. It was as if the spa existed in its own alternative time zone, in defiance of the laws of the physical universe.

The shadows allowed Cass to cross the open courtyard in relative safety. But when she reached the reflecting pool that surrounded the pyramid she had to step out in the open. The reflecting pool, she now realized, was no pool at all; it was a moat. And the drawbridge—it was standing upright, blocking the entrance to the pyramid.

Her only hope of getting inside was to find an underground passage. Where would the passage let out, Cass wondered, if there was one? From the back of the pyramid, she traced an imaginary line to the nearest building, and she marked the spot most likely to hide an entrance to the underground.

As it turned out, the building was one of the few Cass had not yet entered. Like the others, it was designed very simply around a single, central corridor that stretched from one end to the other; but here the atmosphere was subtly more luxurious. A long, narrow, richly embroidered rug, such as you might find in a throne room, lay atop the stone floor; intimidating to step on, it nonetheless allowed Cass to walk the length of the corridor in silence. She must have passed a half-dozen doors, all closed, and all painted a deep royal blue, before she saw the one she wanted. In contrast to the other doors, it was covered in gleaming gold leaf—and had been left ever so slightly ajar.

She put her ear against the door but didn't hear anything.

Dare she? She had to. It was her only chance.

Cass cracked the door open—then stepped back in fright: the room behind the door was occupied by hundreds of people.

Or was it?

She looked again: the room was empty—save for hundreds of reflections of herself.

Nervously, she entered.

Mirrored panels covered all the walls as well as the ceiling, creating the illusion of an infinitely expanding space. Even the marble floor had been polished to a reflective sheen. A giant, octopuslike chandelier—Cass's grandfathers would have identified it as Venetian glass—hung from the ceiling and was reflected in the many mirrors, so that it seemed to be replicating in all directions. A long, backless couch upholstered in golden silk—Cass's grandfathers would have called it a daybed and noted that it was in the Napoleonic style—and a small desk plated in silver completed the picture.

Cass immediately recognized the room for it was:

the private office of Ms. Mauvais. Cold but deceptively glamorous, like the woman herself. One could easily have imagined her sitting for hours on the daybed, gazing at herself in one mirror after the next after the next after the next. . . .

Our young heroine, however, had no time for lingering. She tiptoed across the marble, examining it for telltale cracks or seams — she thought there might be a hatch door in the floor — until she found herself butting up against one of the mirrored panels, startled once more by her own reflection. Multiplied over and over, her ears seemed to grow larger and larger.

"Are you looking for me, Miss Skelton?"

A familiar chill descended on Cass as Ms. Mauvais's reflection — make that *reflections* — appeared beside hers.

She was caught: what should she do? What *could* she do?

Slowly, Cass turned around. She half hoped she wouldn't find anyone — that the blond, Barbie-esque woman in the mirror was nothing but a mirage. But she was all too real — and as fake as ever.

"I'm Ms. Mauvais. Forgive me for not introducing myself earlier. I trust the Midnight Sun is everything you hoped?"

Cass grimaced involuntarily, her heart thumping. She told herself to say something, say *anything*—but nothing came out.

"You know, I couldn't help noticing the way you were looking at yourself a moment ago," continued her hostess. "Of course, we do offer makeovers, but we thought you were more the natural type. . . . Here, let me see."

She lifted Cass's head with a gloved hand, and examined her young guest from all sides. "If you like, we can do something about it."

"About what?" Cass asked, finally finding her voice.

"About your ears. We can fix them."

"My ears?" Perhaps, Cass thought, if they talked about her ears, Ms. Mauvais wouldn't question again why she was in her office.

"Yes, I thought they were bothering you. They do rather stick out—"

"What do you mean? How would you fix them?" Cass tried gently to pull her head away, but Ms. Mauvais wouldn't let go.

"Among his many talents, Dr. L is a very gifted plastic surgeon—"

"You mean you would operate on them!?" Cass exclaimed in obvious horror, remembering too late that a Skelton Sister might have a different reaction to the prospect of plastic surgery.

"There's only so much makeup can do," observed Ms. Mauvais, at last releasing Cass's head from her hands. "Don't worry, he has a very light touch. He never leaves any scars. He's an artist. . . . Here, what do you think of mine?"

She gathered up her blond hair and tilted her neck, exposing her ears for Cass to inspect.

"Every year he works on them. They're like a sculpture that's never quite finished. He says he won't be done until I have the most exquisite ears in the world."

The way she said this, Cass could tell Ms. Mauvais thought her ears were already something special. In truth, Cass couldn't remember ever seeing any more perfect.

"Just think what he could do with a beautiful young girl like you."

Should she have her ears worked on? Cass had never even considered it. But the idea of not being teased anymore was very appealing. And Ms. Mauvais made it sound so easy.

"Your mother doesn't have ears like yours, does she? Wouldn't you like to look more like her?"

"How do you know? You haven't met her—have

you?" Cass asked, momentarily unsure whether they were talking about the Skelton Sisters' mother or her own.

"No, of course not," Ms. Mauvais laughed. "I just thought — well she got married, didn't she? And what man would marry a woman with ears like yours?"

Suddenly, Cass could feel herself burning with shame and anger and a deep sort of hatred. She was certain her ears had never been so red. But Ms. Mauvias appeared not to notice.

"Well, you don't have to decide now. Come —" She grasped Cass by the arm, making it impossible for her to even think about looking for Benjamin. "It's almost time for dinner. And we have a surprise guest this evening."

Who was Ms. Mauvais's surprise guest? Take a guess.

I'll give you a hint: it wasn't Gloria. As a surprise she'd already been spoiled, anyway.

Here's another idea: what if the surprise guest was *a real Skelton Sister*? It's just plausible enough. After all, the Skelton Sisters had been to the Midnight Sun several times before. Or so Dr. L said.

The complications that ensued would no doubt be very entertaining. I can just imagine it now: Ms. Mauvais saying to Cass, "Look who's here, it's your sister!" Cass starting to say that she didn't have a sister, then remembering who she was supposed to be. The real Skelton Sister acting confused, asking what this was all about.

Cass would have to think very fast to avoid being exposed as a fraud. She might claim that she was actually a half sister of the Skelton Sisters, and that she was kept secret even from them. Or she might claim that her sister really did know her, but that the sister had had an accident, and now suffered from amnesia.

Perhaps Cass would be so successful in her ruse that she would convince the Skelton Sister that they really were sisters. Now, that would be something!

Alas, Ms. Mauvais's surprise guest was not a

Skelton Sister. It was someone far less surprising—at least if you've been following the story.

Less surprising. But more gratifying, I hope.

An elaborate, castle-shaped tent had been erected for dinner. It held three rooms altogether; and not until Cass followed Ms. Mauvais all the way into the third did she see the spiky-haired boy sitting on a cushion in the corner.

Yes, you were right, the surprise guest was none other than Max-Ernest—and Cass, for one, felt extremely grateful when she saw him.

No longer angry at him, she was aware only of how lonely and scared she'd been since their partnership had ended. Had Ms. Mauvais not been standing nearby, Cass might have run and thrown her arms around her long-lost friend. (Well, knowing Cass, she wouldn't throw her arms around Max-Ernest under any circumstances, but that was sort of how she felt.) As it was, she was afraid even to say hello. She didn't want Ms. Mauvais to know she recognized him.

Max-Ernest, also, was uncharacteristically silent. As Cass settled onto the cushion next to his, he gave her one of those quick, intentionally fake smiles that look like they are made by fingers pulling on the sides of your mouth. He seemed nervous, but that was only to be expected, thought Cass.

What was he doing there, anyway? How did he get in?

Suddenly, Cass felt panic rising in her stomach like sickness.

"Surprised, Miss Skelton? — or should I say, *Cassandra?*" asked Ms. Mauvais.

"Who — who's Cassandra?" she stammered.

"Oh, don't be silly. Did you really think we were so easily fooled?" Ms. Mauvais said cheerfully. "I know, I should have said something when you called. But I didn't want to scare you off. I'm afraid we got off on the wrong foot the first time we met. Please will you let me make it up to you now?"

Cass forced herself to nod. She could hardly sit up straight, she was so dizzy.

Ms. Mauvais smiled in delight — if you could call it a smile. (Her face barely moved but she showed a little more of her too-white teeth.) "Thank you for giving me a second chance! I so want us to be friends."

Cass tried to smile back but she couldn't. She was wondering whether she was going to puke.

"Good! Now, I'm going to go find the others," said Ms. Mauvais. "I'm sure you two have a lot of catching up to do."

She placed her hand on Max-Ernest's head, and ruffled his hair. "Have you ever seen such a handsome young man?" she asked. Then she leaned over and kissed Max-Ernest on the forehead. "I'll be back in a second, darling, I promise."

She walked away, leaving a lipstick mark on his face. And a look of total shock on Cass's.

Before Cass could absorb the full awfulness of what she'd just witnessed, Max-Ernest started speaking in a rush. She'd never seen him so wound up.

"Don't worry, she's not my girlfriend or anything, that's just the way she is — all kissy and stuff. It's kind of embarrassing, but she's really nice, once you get to know her. Seriously, I know you're going to like her — she's even nicer than Amber! Dr. L's pretty nice, too. He says he's going to cure my condition. They use an ancient Egyptian method. Technically, it's a lobotomy but it's nonsurgical. Instead of cutting your head open, they enter through your nose with a long straw. And since there's no feeling in your brain, it's practically painless! How 'bout that? Afterward, Ms. Mauvais's going to take me to Paris — that's where she's from. I'm sure you could come, too, if I asked her — she'll do anything I want. What do you think, do you want to go to Paris?"

Cass stared at him, not blinking. She thought perhaps she'd been drugged, and she was having an hallucination. That would explain the nausea.

Max-Ernest looked at her expectantly. "Well, aren't you going to say anything?"

"Did they hypnotize you? Is that why you're acting like this?" Cass asked, finally realizing that she was, alas, perfectly clearheaded. "'Cause I hope so, for your sake."

"What do you mean? Acting like what?"

"Never mind," Cass sighed. "How did you get here?"

"I made a reservation. Just like you."

"You made a reservation?" Cass repeated. "And they just let you come? What did you tell them?"

Max-Ernest squirmed in his seat. "Well, nothing really, just—"

A horrible thought struck Cass. "Did you tell them you had the notebook?!"

"I still have it! I haven't given it to them yet," said Max-Ernest defensively. "But it doesn't matter anyway. They're not how you think they—"

"It doesn't matter?! Have you totally forgotten about Pietro? About Luciano? About Benjamin?"

"C'mon, Cass. I know what you think, but think

about it, have they done anything bad to you? I mean, since you've been here."

"Well, no, not yet, but—"

"And they knew who you were all along, right?"

"Yeah, I guess—"

"See. How 'bout that? They're not evil then, after all. . . . You know, it's OK to be wrong sometimes. Everybody is. Even me."

Cass shook her head. "Now, I *know* you were hypnotized!"

Before the matter could be resolved one way or the other, Gloria sailed into the tent, her round face beaming. (Notice I didn't say she wouldn't be at dinner—just that she wasn't the surprise guest.)

"Cass!" cried the real estate agent. "Aren't you going to say hello to your old friend, Gloria? Or don't you recognize me? I know, I look twenty years younger, don't I? And twenty pounds lighter!"

Gloria twirled around so she could be seen from all sides.

Cass nodded mutely. No doubt about it, Gloria was half the size she was before. More remarkable still was how friendly the real estate agent was acting. Cass wasn't sure she hadn't liked Gloria better in her earlier, meaner incarnation. Now she was harder to ignore.

"Isn't this place just too, too fabu?" Gloria continued. "True, the Egyptian theme might be a little exotic for some. But the setting! As they say in my business—location, location, location! And the treatments! Heavenly! And don't get me started on those elixirs. Have you ever tasted anything more delicious?"

She paused briefly for Cass to nod in agreement. Then went on:

"Remember that lucky day when we all met? Well, Dr. L gave me this itty-bitty one to drink afterward. And I was hooked. I wanted more the very next day. More, more, more! He said it was too early, but I wouldn't take no for an answer. I followed him all the way to the spa to get it. And am I glad I did! They work miracles here—!"

"Miracles have very little to do with it, Ms. Fortune."

It was Dr. L himself, joining them under the tent. He looked as cool and composed as ever—if a tad irritated by Gloria.

Gloria pouted like a chastened schoolgirl. "I'm sorry, Doctor. Your little Gloria is just so grateful for everything you've done. Everything you do—"

"Everything we do is here is based on science," said Dr. L curtly. "Not perhaps what you think of as science. But the True Science. The One Science."

"What kind of science is that?" asked Max-Ernest, who was under the impression that he already knew all the kinds of sciences that there were.

"The science of the essence. The science of which all others are part," said Dr. L. "Everything on Earth springs from the same essential substance. Once you find it, anything is possible. Turning lead to gold. Old to young. Even turning frumpy real estate agents into beautiful women."

Cass looked involuntarily at Gloria, but Gloria didn't seem to register the insult—she was so smitten with Dr. L.

"How wonderful!" she said. "What's this science called? Is it Egyptian?"

Ms. Mauvais, who had just reentered the tent, cleared her throat. "I believe our dinner is here," she said.

ven Cass, who was feeling slightly less sick, but all the more upset about the situation in which she found herself, had to admit the dinner table looked magnificent. It was covered with a cloth sewn entirely of crimson flower petals, each petal lush and perfect and not a bit bruised or ripped. On this luxurious crimson bed sat a dozen crystal candlesticks of varying heights as well as numerous glittering urns and platters of exotic, Oriental design. Each place setting came with a pair of gleaming golden chopsticks and ornate sets of silverware — tiny forks, oddly curved spoons, needle-like knives — that had the look of ancient surgical instruments.

On the whole, the table looked less like a dinner table than a shrine to some jealous and demanding god. This effect was only heightened when the kitchen staff began to bring in the food — so solemnly and silently they might have been making offerings in a temple rather than serving dinner.

Indeed, whenever a new dish appeared, Ms. Mauvais described it with an almost religious reverence.

"The base of this custard is the rendered cartilage of a tiny marsupial that lives under rocks on an island in the South Pacific," she said of the first course, which arrived in individual thimble-size serving cups. "Excellent source of calcium. Also prized by fisherman for its waterproofing properties . . . I do hope you aren't vegetarians."

"The pale blue dust you see is pollen from a flower that blooms only at the elevation of eleven thousand feet and only after a very long winter," she said about the topping on a roll that looked like a powdered donut but which was anything but sweet. "Some indigenous peoples believe it sharpens the intellect. Certainly, it is very helpful in clearing the sinuses."

"Bear liver sautéed in codfish oil," she announced when a particularly unattractive lump arrived in front of each diner. "A dish beloved by the Vikings. The reason they could survive so long in the cold. You may find it a little gamey."

Before they ate any given dish, Cass and Max-Ernest were instructed to close their eyes and smell it. "Remember, what you experience as taste is mostly scent," said Ms. Mauvais. "By itself, the tongue can only identify four flavors — or is it five?"

"Five," replied Dr. L. "I believe scientists recently discovered a taste for fat."

After smelling their food, they were to examine it closely from all angles, so as to appreciate any subtleties of color and shape.

"Should we listen to it, too?" asked Max-Ernest,

who was clearly hanging on Ms. Mauvais's every word.

"Well, that depends on whether your dish is making any noise, doesn't it, sweetheart?" she responded. "Why don't you give it a try?"

Obediently, Max-Ernest tilted his head toward his plate. Across the table, Cass rolled her eyes in disgust.

Despite her rapturous descriptions, Ms. Mauvais, Cass noticed, didn't eat for most of the meal. She merely sipped from a tall glass of red wine — at least Cass assumed it was wine. It was the right color but it looked disturbingly thick.

The one dish Ms. Mauvais ate was the last. It consisted of a small quivering mass that pulsed intermittently like a heart. It was served only to her and she did not describe it like she had the others. Instead, she speared it suddenly and violently with a chopstick — then swallowed it whole.

As Ms. Mauvais sighed in satisfaction, Cass thought she detected a new vibrancy in her hostess's pale white cheeks.

"I have a sensitive stomach," Ms. Mauvais explained. "There are very few things I can eat. And they have to be very, very fresh."

*   *   *

After their plates had been cleared, Ms. Mauvais focused her attention on her guests. "Now, my darling young people, I wonder if you know what you have in that notebook. Did you peek inside at all?"

"No, we didn't," said Cass before Max-Ernest could say otherwise.

"I don't know exactly what's in it myself, but I fear the worst," said Ms. Mauvais. "You see, Pietro was a dear, dear friend. But I'm afraid he was quite ill — mentally, I mean."

"Mentally? You mean he was crazy? It didn't seem like it," said Cass defensively. She felt somehow as though she was being personally insulted.

"Oh, so then you did read it?"

Cass reddened, not saying anything more.

"Your ears, my dear — think about my offer!" said Ms. Mauvais in a singsong tone. "But yes, to answer your question, I'm sad to say he was totally delusional. He had this imaginary friend — a twin brother — whom he invented as a child. He made up this incredible story about this brother being snatched away from the circus when they were boys."

At this, Cass and Max-Ernest couldn't help glancing at each other.

"I see you're familiar with this story — that's

what I was afraid of. It was very vivid for him, but for most of his life he knew it was a fantasy. Only in his later years did he begin really to believe it. . . . Are you quite well, Doctor?" asked Ms. Mauvais, addressing Dr. L, who had remained remarkably quiet ever since she had brought up the notebook.

His face looked tight, as though he might be choking on something, but he waved off her concern. "I'm fine," he said, covering his mouth with a napkin.

"Well then," Ms. Mauvais continued, "when I suggested to Pietro that his brother didn't exist outside his imagination, he became violent—he actually accused me of being the one to steal his brother, if you can believe that. It didn't seem to occur to him that I was much too young to have been alive when he was a child."

Ms. Mauvais chuckled and touched her forehead. "Much too young," she repeated.

Could that be true? wondered Cass.

Was Max-Ernest right about Ms. Mauvais? Had she judged her too harshly? Just because Ms. Mauvais was a bit chilly and strange? Or because—Cass remembered this now for some reason—Max-Ernest had once said Ms. Mauvais was the prettiest woman he'd ever seen?

Was she jealous? Was *that* all it was all along?

"Then why do you want the notebook so badly?" Cass asked, scrambling to climb out of the mental rabbit hole into which she was falling. "If it's all made up."

"Because we don't want it to get into the wrong hands. Because we loved Pietro, and we want the world to remember him at his best—not as some crazy person."

The more Cass thought about it, the surer she became that she wasn't sure of anything.

She had no proof that what the magician had written had really happened.

No proof that Ms. Mauvais was involved in Luciano's disappearance.

No proof even that Ms. Mauvais was involved in Benjamin Blake's disappearance.

For all Cass knew, Benjamin Blake was already back home, safe and sound—and there'd been no reason at all for her to come save him.

In her agitation, Cass banged the table—and accidentally knocked the wineglass out of Ms. Mauvais's hand. The glass flew into the air and — s-p-i-l-l-l-l-l-l-l-l-l-l-l-l-l-l-l-l-l-l-l-l-l-l-l-l-l-l-l-l-l-l-l-l-l-l-l-l-l-l-e-d —

You know those frozen-in-time moments when life suddenly turns into a kung fu movie and you see everything in slow motion? The glass was in the air for less than a second, but that second was long enough for Cass to think a thousand things — and to realize why the sight of Ms. Mauvais's wine had disturbed her earlier.

Two words: *monkey blood.*

Was it monkey blood? To be frank, I don't know — some rumors are just rumors. In any event, Cass was about to be greeted by a sight far more disturbing than a glass of blood.

Here, let me put you back in the scene — in real time, this time:

The glass flew into the air, and spilled — wine, blood, elixir, who knows, I won't delay it any longer — out in an arc, splattering all over one of Ms. Mauvais's long creamy white gloves.

"You clumsy girl!"

Fury passed in a blush over Ms. Mauvais's face as she yanked off her glove. "This was my favorite pair. I bought them at the Paris flea market over ninety years a—"

She stopped speaking, following her guests' eyes with her own.

Gloria stifled a gasp.

Everyone was staring at Ms. Mauvais's hand, un-gloved for the first time.

It was the hand of someone — of some*thing* — else. With fingers so thin and frail you could almost snap them off. With nails so yellow and cracked they were claws. With skin so translucent you could see every bone, every ligament, every vein.

It was the hand of an old woman.

A very old woman.

An older woman than Cass had ever seen.

CHAPTER TWENTY-FIVE

They say that eyes never lie. But I think it's much truer to say that hands never do.

It was inevitable, in a life as long as Ms. Mauvais's, that she expose her hand now and then. Still, she hadn't lived as long as she had to let a little spill rattle her. Seconds later, she'd already slipped on a new pair of gloves.

As if nothing had happened, she turned to Gloria, who was sitting in a kind of stunned stupor. "Do you mind giving us a moment?"

"Not at all," said Gloria, not moving.

"Thank you," said Ms. Mauvais, nodding to a spa staff person who'd been standing discretely nearby. Silently, he helped Gloria out of her seat, and led her away as if she were an invalid — or perhaps an inmate in an asylum.

Ms. Mauvais turned back to Cass and Max-Ernest.

"So. Where is the notebook?" she asked, her chilly voice now an ice storm.

Before telling you how Cass and Max-Ernest responded, let me remind you of something that Max-Ernest mentioned at an earlier point in our narrative: they were only eleven.

They were surrounded on all sides by spa staff. They had no idea how, or if, they were ever going to get home. They had no weapons in their pockets, nor any knowledge how to use a weapon should they have had one. They were not superheroes, in short, they were kids. And they had just seen one of the scariest sights of their young lives (although I think Ms. Mauvais's hand would have spooked anyone who happened to see it, no matter what age). So please have sympathy when I tell you that they didn't hesitate very long before giving Ms. Mauvais what she wanted.

First, however, Max-Ernest looked over at Cass. He didn't say anything out loud but his expression said something like, *okay, you were right, I made a terrible mistake, and now we're in the worst trouble of our lives, and I'm really scared, and what should I do?*

And then Cass nodded back in a way that said something like, *yeah, yeah, I understand all that, I'm really scared, too, just hurry up and give Ms. Mauvais the notebook before she kills us.* (Really, what was the alternative?)

And then, and only then, did Max-Ernest pull the notebook out of his bag.

Ms. Mauvais took it, her re-gloved hands trembling. "At last! How many years have I waited!"

"Well, now you have it, so I think we'll just go," said Cass, motioning for Max-Ernest to get up.

"You're not going anywhere yet," said Ms. Mauvais sharply.

She opened the notebook and looked briefly at the inscription. Then she flipped through the blank pages with increasing irritation, much as the kids had when they first looked through them.

"This is all? What kind of trick is this?"

"Here, let me look," said Dr. L.

He took the open notebook and glanced briefly at the inscription, the bare ghost of a smile crossing his face.

Then he handed the notebook back to Ms. Mauvais. "I think you'll find the notebook's quite full. If you look on the undersides of the pages."

Ms. Mauvais looked searchingly at Dr. L. "A code?"

He nodded.

"So then it's his. It's real," she said with palpable excitement.

Ms. Mauvais fiddled with the notebook impatiently, until its accordion-like pages opened up in front of her. Quickly, she scanned the pages, as if searching for a particular word or phrase that she expected to pop out. When she got to the last page, she looked up, enraged.

"Where's the rest? What did you do with it?"

"We don't know where it is," said Max-Ernest nervously. "We thought maybe he ripped out the pages—"

"Liar!" Ms. Mauvais screamed. "You read it. And now you're keeping it from me!"

Max-Ernest cowered, a far cry from the excited boy of an hour earlier.

Cass tried to defend him. "He's telling the truth. That's all there was."

But Ms. Mauvais appeared for once to have lost control and she was hardly listening. "The Secret. I know he found the Secret. He was so close, he must have. He kept it from us. But he can't anymore! And neither will you! I won't let you!"

She gripped Cass and Max-Ernest each by their forearms, showing surprising strength in her frail fingers.

"Tell me what it is," she hissed. "Tell me the secret!"

At the sound of Ms. Mauvais's words, Daisy (who Cass had not seen since she arrived at the spa, but who Cass now realized must always have been lurking) appeared at the entrance of the tent, blocking the way out with her tall frame.

Several spa staff stepped closer to the table, closing in on Cass and Max-Ernest. In the eerie light of the tent, their beautiful tanned skins looked like hard shells. And their once-sympathetic smiles turned to stony stares.

Cass's first impression of the spa had been correct; it was a prison after all.

Have you ever been locked in a room hours away from home by people you have every reason to believe are capable of murder or worse?

Neither have I.

Maybe that's why I can write about it without shedding a tear.

Tragically, Cass and Max-Ernest did not have the same luxury. They had to experience imprisonment firsthand.

Ten minutes after we last saw them, Max-Ernest was pacing back and forth in a state of agitation extreme even for him. "Stupid . . . stupid . . . stupid . . ." he was saying to himself. "How could I be so —"

"Will you stop muttering, please?" said Cass. "It's really annoying."

"You hate me, don't you? I mean, I don't blame you. I hate me, too —"

"I don't hate you," said Cass in a not very friendly tone. (Max-Ernest might be admitting his mistakes, but the image of Ms. Mauvais kissing his forehead was still fresh in Cass's mind.) "I'm just trying to think how to get past those guys — you know, so we can get out of here alive."

She gestured toward the window where Daisy and Owen could be seen standing guard outside the door. From our more comfortable perspective, they were a funny-looking couple: the tall, dour limousine driver and the shorter, freckled butler. But no doubt they were more than capable of keeping a pair of eleven-year-old kids from escaping.

"I knew I shouldn't have brought the notebook!" said Max-Ernest, still speaking to himself as much as to Cass. "But they said it was the only way I could get a reservation. How else was I going to get in?"

"Forget about it. You didn't have a choice," said Cass. "But since we're on the subject—what I don't understand is why you had to come here in the first place. I thought you were done investigating."

"Because I figured out they knew who you were—that's why."

"So?"

Max-Ernest looked at her like she was nuts. "So—so, you were here."

"So?"

"So, I didn't want them to kill you."

"Oh . . . you didn't?" said Cass, trying to get used to the idea.

"Duh. I swear, sometimes you don't make any sense," said Max-Ernest.

"Huh," said Cass, "I guess sometimes I don't."

And she started to smile.

As for the rest of their conversation — well, if some conversations are too upsetting to record, others are too sappy and sentimental. Have you ever heard two people make up after they've been fighting? It's not very interesting unless you happen to be one of those people yourself. I prefer listening in on insults and curses; let everyone else listen to the apologies and declarations of friendship.

I'm sure I don't have to tell you how glad Max-Ernest was that he and Cass were collaborators again. However, at the risk of getting mushy, I'll point out that as glad as he was, Cass was more so. You see, as many times as she had tried to save the world, nobody had ever tried to save *her* before. She was so touched that Max-Ernest had come to rescue her that it almost made up for the fact he had no plan of escape.

Almost.

Just as the rosy glow of their reunion was beginning to fade, and the direness of their situation was again coming into focus, the door opened and Dr. L strode in.

No longer the silky-smooth doctor who welcomed Cass to the spa, he wore an expression of fierce concentration, as if he was struggling to contain a deep, volcanic rage. Cass and Max-Ernest instinctively backed away from him.

"Ms. Mauvais is not happy. And neither am I," he said with ominous understatement. "We were hoping to find certain . . . information."

"You mean the Secret," said Max-Ernest, a little hoarsely.

"Yes, I–mean–the–Secret," Dr. L said through gritted teeth. "If you know anything about it, if you saw anything, if you even *think* anything—I advise you to tell me now."

"Or what—you're going to torture us?" asked Cass, much more boldly than she felt.

"Perhaps," said Dr. L dismissively. He pointed an accusing finger at the kids: "But it's what the Secret will do to you that you should be scared of."

"What do you mean? Secrets don't *do* anything," said Max-Ernest, stepping next to Cass.

"Besides, you don't even know what the Secret is," said Cass, taking Max-Ernest's hand protectively.

"We know certain things," said Dr. L, coming so close to them that they were backed into a corner.

He started listing facts like a man obsessed: "We know when the Secret was discovered: 1212 BC. We know where: Luxor, Egypt. We know by whom: a court physician. We also know that three days after his discovery, he was executed. What we don't know is why!"

He looked penetratingly at the kids, as though he suspected they knew the answer—as though they might even be responsible for killing the physician themselves.

"Was it because the physician refused to tell the pharaoh the secret?" Dr. L asked in a menacing tone. "Or did the physician tell the pharaoh his secret?—and the secret so enraged the pharaoh that he demanded the physician's head!"

"W-why would the secret make him so mad?" asked Max-Ernest.

"Precisely! And there's more—" said Dr. L, almost feverish now. "Before he died, the physician wrote his secret on a scrap of papyrus, intending the secret to be buried with him. And so it was. Until years later, when the papyrus was taken by tomb robbers. They had no idea of its value—they may not even have read it—but they died violent deaths soon after, and incited a forty-year war."

He searched the kids' faces to make sure they were properly scared. They tried not to show any reaction. But of course they were scared—at least of Dr. L.

He nodded with grim satisfaction and started pacing around the room. The subject of the Secret lit his face with an expression so vampiric one could almost have imagined a cape billowing behind him.

"In the early 19th century," he continued, "the papyrus surfaced in Prague, where it was purchased as a curiosity by an antiquities dealer. He gave it to an Egyptologist for translation. The Egyptologist went mad, and the papyrus was never seen again. As for the antiquities dealer, he spent the remainder of his life in a fruitless search for the Secret, until he died alone and destitute, prey to a terrible, flesh-eating virus."

Dr. L spun around and faced his young audience, his eyes gleaming.

"Now, I ask you — does this sound like a secret you want to keep?"

"So the Secret is a curse?" asked Max-Ernest, his head full of nightmarish visions.

"It's a formula. It's many things."

"A formula for what?" asked Cass.

"Never mind that," said Dr. L quickly. "Ms. Mauvais and I have prepared all our lives to learn the Secret. You are children. It will destroy you."

"We keep telling you, we don't know anything about it," said Max-Ernest, pleadingly.

"It's true," said Cass. "There weren't any more pages in the notebook — I swear!"

Dr. L stared at them, weighing their words — and their fates.

"If nobody ever saw the papyrus again, how do you know so much about it?" asked Cass, curiosity overcoming caution. "Did Pietro find it?"

"Pietro had very different ideas about the Secret," said Dr. L evasively. "We did not see eye to eye on the subject."

"He did — he found it, huh?" said Cass, feeling suddenly very reckless. "And you guys tried to get it from him. And when he wouldn't give it to you, you burned down his house. And you killed him!"

She hadn't necessarily intended to say so much — but now that she had she felt oddly victorious, as if she'd been waiting to make the accusation all along, and had finally succeeded.

"Killed him, did we?" Dr. L asked, half smiling. "Then who has the missing pages from his notebook? If *he* didn't take them —"

His eyes turned to steel. "Empty your pockets — both of you!"

Max-Ernest immediately complied, pulling out of his pants odd bits of paper, gum wrappers, a crumpled trading card, a chewed-up straw, and placing them on the table beside him.

As Cass put her hands in her pockets, her mind whirled:

Earlier, when Dr. L was looking at Pietro's notebook, something had half occurred to her, just the smallest seed of an unformed thought. Later, listening to the way he pronounced Pietro's name, the seed had come back to her as a half-formed suspicion. Now her suspicion was growing into a full-blown prediction.

But how to test it?

Dr. L looked at her angrily. "Didn't you hear me?! I said empty your pockets — now!"

"OK, OK."

Cass dug deeper and felt something sticky . . . Could it be? Yes, it was . . .

Cass pulled the Smoochie out of her pocket.

Making sure Dr. L was watching, she brazenly smeared it across her lips. Then she held up the Smoochie like a prize.

Max-Ernest looked at her like she was out of her mind. "What are you doing?" he mouthed.

"Do I smell . . . cotton candy?" asked Dr. L, frowning.

"Yeah, it's my lip gloss," said Cass with studied casualness.

"Lip gloss? Let me see it," he commanded.

Cass handed it to him. "It's made by the Skelton Sisters," she said. "It's just regular lip gloss, but people buy it 'cause of them. Kind of dumb, if you ask me."

Dr. L examined the Smoochie quizzically, as if it were some unusual artifact, if not an Egyptian antiquity. Then he held it to his nose.

He closed his eyes and inhaled, holding his breath as if he couldn't bear to let the scent go.

Max-Ernest looked at Cass — *what's going on?* But she just shook her head — *wait.*

Completely lost in the moment, Dr. L let the Smoochie drop right out of his hand.

When he opened his eyes, there were tears in them.

"Did it hurt your eyes? Sometimes the really smelly ones do that," said Cass, knowing perfectly well that wasn't what happened.

"No — it was nothing! Just something from the past . . . ridiculous!"

He leaned down to pick up the Smoochie. "This is mine now," he said, pocketing it.

He'd only bent his head for a second, but it had been long enough for Cass to get a glimpse of the back of his neck — and to get the proof she was looking for.

There was a knock on the door. Daisy entered

the room, ducking slightly to avoid hitting her head in the doorway.

"Excuse me, Doctor. It's the boy. He has a high fever. They think he might not make it. Ms. Mauvais says it has to be tonight."

"Benjamin Blake!" exclaimed Max-Ernest, before Cass could dart him a look. "What are you doing to him?"

Dr. L stared at them, grim. "Ms. Mauvais is right. You kids know too much — and maybe not enough. You have twelve hours to decide whether you remember anything helpful. After that —" He left the threat hanging. "Of course, if all goes well tonight, we may not need you anymore. And that will be your bad luck."

After he left, Cass turned to Max-Ernest. "Well, did you see it?"

"What?"

"The birthmark on his neck. It was shaped like a crescent moon."

Max-Ernest opened his mouth — speechless, for once, at the thought that that horrible, horrible man was Luciano Bergamo.

CHAPTER
TWENTY-SIX

benjamin blake

prize-winning
Artist

For most of his life, Benjamin Blake thought he was bad at art—mostly because he didn't understand it.

When other kids drew a triangle on top of a square, he didn't see a house, he heard the shrill whistle of a train over the dull thud of a rock landing in dirt.

When they drew a circle around two dots and a curling line, he didn't see a smiley face, he smelled baking cookies punctuated by two beeps and a low whine.

To Benjamin, everyone and everything was a unique combination of sound and color, smell and taste. When he drew, he tried to capture all these different dimensions of his subjects. But when other kids looked at his drawings all they saw was a jumbled mess. So Benjamin assumed he wasn't any better at art than he was at math or science or Foosball.

Then he took an after-school enrichment class called "Art Out of Bounds." In the class, he saw a picture of rocks that someone had stuck in a lake to form a spiral; the rocks were an example of a kind of art called Earthworks. He also heard about people who got up on stage and did silly things; they were called Performance Artists. And he heard about people who just wrote lists of ideas for art they never made; they were called Conceptual Artists.

It seemed like it would be pretty easy to be an artist if you could do any of those things.

In Art Out of Bounds, students had to do things like create imaginary languages and invent alternatives to gravity. When students wanted to draw or paint or sculpt or do any normal art things, their teacher — who had long dreadlocks that bounced up and down when he spoke and made everything he said seem really important — encouraged the students to make abstract art rather than try to copy the world around them. "Copies are what Xerox machines are for," he said, which was funny because he had just showed them some Xerox art that didn't look like a copy of anything.

Benjamin tried explaining that his paintings weren't abstract, they were copies of the world as he saw it. But the teacher said that was close to the same thing and not to worry. After that, Benjamin started painting everything he saw, especially music, which was Benjamin's favorite thing to look at.

Without telling Benjamin, the teacher submitted his work to the Young Leonardos Contest. Nobody could believe it when Benjamin won first prize, least of all himself. Not only had he never won a prize before, he'd never even entered a contest before.

Benjamin liked winning. But it wasn't easy being a winner.

All of a sudden, everybody wanted to talk to him, and talking was very difficult for Benjamin. Usually, when he talked, people thought he was crazy. Or else that he was reciting poetry.

Like those two impressive-looking strangers in the school yard—the Golden Lady and the Silver Man.

"You have such a wonderful eye. Or should I say, such a wonderful *ear?*" said the Golden Lady. "I haven't seen such a talented young man since, well, since this man here was a young boy."

"Oh, but I never painted like that," said the Silver Man with a self-deprecating laugh. "This boy is one of a kind. Aren't you, son?"

But Benjamin couldn't even muster a proper thank-you. He knew whatever he'd said must have come out wrong because instead of their smiles feeling warm, their smiles didn't feel like anything at all.

Benjamin didn't like these strangers.

They both had gray voices. Gray was the color of computer voices and recorded messages. In Benjamin's experience, when people had gray voices they were usually lying. But his mother had told him that it wasn't fair to judge people by the color of their voices; especially since nobody could see the color except him.

It was hard to believe that other people didn't see the strangers' words curling like smoke out of their mouths — or was it more like breath on a really frosty day? — but he tried not to look. Besides, if he just listened to *what* the strangers were saying, and not *how* they were saying it, he had to admit they were being very friendly.

They told him they had come to take him to an art camp.

"It's going to be really fun," said the Golden Lady. "We have all kinds of unusual art supplies and there'll be plenty of other young artists for you to play with."

Benjamin was relieved they weren't taking his prize away; for some reason he thought they might. Nonetheless, this art camp sounded peculiar. Even Benjamin, who had never been to camp, and who had very little sense of time or dates or seasons, knew people went to camp during summertime, not during the school year, and definitely not during school hours. But the strangers were grown-ups, and therefore he had to listen to them, and they said they had special permission from Mrs. Johnson, and they promised to bring him back to school at the end of the day.

As he mulled over what they were saying, he barely noticed that the strangers were escorting him out of the school's back gate.

It was only after the limousine pulled away from the school that he remembered his mother's other instructions: never get into a car with strangers.

Realizing he'd made a drastic mistake, he looked back at the lost safety of his school. The gate was still open, and a girl was looking out. It was Cassandra, the girl with the big pointy ears who for some reason always reminded him of mint-chip ice cream, kind of chocolaty but mostly minty. Their eyes locked for a moment and in his thoughts he yelled for help. Unfortunately, as weird as his brain was, he didn't seem to be capable of mental telepathy.

One of the strangers put a handkerchief to his face, and then everything went black.

Benjamin woke still tasting mint-chip ice cream.

He was wearing some kind of white tunic and he was in bed in a small, unfamiliar room. The room was almost completely bare, with white walls, a stone floor, and a tiny window high up near the ceiling.

There was something indescribably strange about the room—what was it? It was the silence, he realized after a moment. He had never before experienced the total absence of sound.

He scratched his head and discovered it was completely smooth. Like an egg. He was bald.

Where was he?

Only then did he notice the Golden Lady standing nearby, studying him.

"Am I dreaming?" he asked, struggling to speak clearly.

She shook her head.

"Is this a hospital? What happened?"

"You're in a purification chamber," she said in a hushed tone. "Now, be quiet and close your eyes. You're not supposed to have any stimulation."

"What about art camp?"

"Later, Benjamin. Later."

When he opened his eyes again, he was alone and he was afraid. Either he wasn't dreaming or he was dreaming and unable to wake, which was worse.

When the Golden Lady reappeared, she didn't say anything.

He told her he was hungry and she gave him some kind of whitish drink that looked and felt like milk but had no taste or smell.

As time passed, the lack of stimulation started to affect him. He began imagining things: sounds, colors, smells, tastes. These sensations weren't in the front of his mind but in the far back—like when you have a hearing test and the beeps are so high- or low-pitched that they're almost outside the range of human ears.

When a real sound at last penetrated the room he was so lost in his own head that at first he didn't realize what it was. When he finally recognized it as the sound of a car engine, he stood up in his bed; by standing on top of his pillow, he could peer out the room's window. It was night outside, and he could just make out a road through the trees. The limousine was passing by.

A girl was pressing her nose against the limousine's rear window, and suddenly Benjamin's mouth was full of the taste of mint-chip ice cream. It was Cassandra, the girl who had stood outside the school watching when he was driven away; and now he was watching her. It was like the same scene in reverse. He considered waving or yelling but then he decided he must be imagining her. What were the chances that she would be there?

He must have been dreaming after all.

CHAPTER
TWENTY-SEVEN

INTO THE PYRAMID

L.
L, DR. L.
L FOR LUCIANO.
L FOR LONG-LOST BROTHER.
L FOR LOATHSOME LUNATIC DOCTOR.
L FOR LYING TO THEIR FACES THE WHOLE TIME.

How obvious in retrospect. And how awful.

Cass hadn't told Max-Ernest because she knew he'd say it didn't make any sense, but—secretly—she'd been hoping to save Luciano at the same time she saved Benjamin. She'd imagined the magician's brother as a frail old man with long gray hair, trapped in a jail cell. Her plan was to free him. To tell him how much Pietro loved him. To make his last days happy ones.

And all along this make-believe prisoner had been their real-life captor?

Ms. Mauvais, Cass knew, must have turned him somehow when he was a boy.

Turned him against his brother. Turned him into what he was today.

But that didn't excuse him. That didn't excuse kidnapping—or murder.

To think Pietro had spent his life searching for a brother who was nothing but a traitor!

Cass felt betrayed. Personally betrayed.

*　　*　　*

Max-Ernest agreed that Dr. L deserved the worst kind of punishment. But he offered so many different ideas for what that punishment should be that Cass had to beg him to stop thinking of punishments, and to start thinking of ways to escape.

Unfortunately, the latter was much more difficult than the former.

In the two and a half hours since Dr. L had been informed that "it had to be tonight" (whatever *it* was), the spa had come alive with activity.

The lantern on top of the pyramid, previously dimmed, now blinked on and off, intermittently flooding the spa with light, and clearly broadcasting some kind of message—although, Cass and Max-Ernest were quite sure, the message was not Morse code.

Through the window of Cass's room, they had a view of the spa's tall front gates. They watched the gates open every few minutes, each time admitting new guests drawn to the Midnight Sun lantern like so many moths to a flame. By now there had been at least forty such arrivals, roughly doubling the population of the spa, and filling the courtyard surrounding the pyramid with a strange and not very joyous sort of party.

From a distance, it was difficult to tell what if anything the spa's new guests had in common—save the appearance of coming from far-off places or far-off times or both. One man wore a top hat and waistcoat, and another wore an Arab kaffiyeh. One woman came in an antique kimono, and another came in a sari. Some of the guests arrived in cars so old they resembled horse-drawn carriages. A few rode in on horseback.

The one thing Cass and Max-Ernest could tell was: whatever was happening tonight, these people had been waiting for it a long time. Some of them were so desperate to get inside the pyramid they stood at the edge of the moat as if ready to wade across.

Ms. Mauvais, more glittering than ever, mingled among them like a perfect party hostess—waving, greeting, gesticulating. She seemed at once to be begging their forbearance and stirring their impatience into a frenzy.

Finally, the large bronze doors at the pyramid's base swung open, and the narrow drawbridge was lowered over the water. As the crowd surged toward the drawbridge, Cass had a better view of the guests, and she was able to confirm that they all shared one more familiar, unnerving feature:

"Hey, you see that—" she said to Max-Ernest.

"What?"

"They're all wearing gloves."

On the other side of the window, their backs to Cass and Max-Ernest, Daisy and Owen were watching the same scene. Cass had been trying to get Owen's attention for hours, hoping that he might have some sympathy for her plight—that she hadn't just imagined that spark of friendship between them.

Now that Daisy's attention was focused on the pyramid, Cass tried motioning to Owen again. But Owen refused to acknowledge her in any way—even though, she was sure, he could see her out of the corner of his eye.

"He's just as bad as the rest of them," Cass grumbled. "I don't know why I thought he was nice."

She stopped talking in order to listen to the conversation that was taking place outside.

"Most important night of the year," Daisy was saying, "maybe the most important night of our lives—and we're stuck out here."

"G-go ahead, I'll watch the k-kids," said Owen.

"Really?"

"Sure. One of us should g-get to see w-what's happening."

"I don't know . . ."

"Oh, g-go on. Stay in the b-back. No one will see you. And I won't t-tell anyone."

"All right. Just for a second. But I'll come back before they're through. And thanks—"

As soon as Daisy left, Owen slipped into the room. Cass refused to acknowledge him.

"Dudes. Time to bail," he said. "There's a phone at an old ranger station three miles down. But you gotta steer clear of the road 'til then. Soon as Daisy's back, they'll be all over you."

Cass eyed Owen in confusion. It was like a whole new person had walked into the room. Her butler had gone from stutterer to surfer in sixty seconds.

"Who are you?" she asked. "Are you like a spy or something?"

"Or something. Here, tie me with this—so they don't think I helped spring you guys."

He held out a length of phone cord. (Cass was glad to see that his hand, now bare, was the hand of a young person.)

"Wow, I've never met a spy before," said Max-Ernest. "I knew spies were real, though. Well, I didn't know know—"

"Just tie me up, and haul," said Owen. "As it is, I put your chances at about ten percent. Wait any longer, your little butts are history."

Cass and Max-Ernest held up their bags. They'd already packed in preparation for an escape.

But Cass wasn't exactly prepared to follow Owen's plan.

"We can't leave yet," she said as she and Max-Ernest started winding the cord around Owen. "You know the kid, Benjamin Blake—he's in the pyramid, isn't he? They're going to kill him, right?"

Owen didn't say anything. He didn't have to.

"He goes to our school," said Cass.

"So? That leaves more milk cartons for you two."

Cass couldn't tell if he was serious. "He's why we came," she said.

"Well, he's why *she* came. And she's why *I* came," Max-Ernest amended, looking at Cass. "Anyway, she's right, we have to save him," he added quickly.

Owen scoffed. "Reality check. You're children and there's a hundred people in there. And these guys—they're so full-on spooksville you can't even imagine."

"I think we can, actually," said Max-Ernest. "We know all about the lobotomies and everything."

"Man, they get through with you, you'll wish you had a lobotomy."

Cass held up a scarf. "Are we supposed to gag you with this?"

Owen nodded. And before he could say anything else she tied it around his mouth.

"Thanks, Owen."

"Yeah, thanks . . . man," said Max-Ernest.

Owen grunted in frustration. The kids had done such a good job tying him up that he was helpless to stop them.

"By the way," said Cass, walking out, "your surf talk needs work. Your stutter sounded more realistic."

The spa was empty; everyone was inside the pyramid.

Even so, Cass and Max-Ernest tried not to make any noise as they entered the hall of mirrors that was Ms. Mauvais's office. Better to be safe.

"There has to be a secret door in here," whispered Cass. "I've been everywhere else — it's the only place it could be."

Max-Ernest nodded — and a hundred reflections nodded with him. He and Cass both started walking around the periphery of the room — he clockwise, she counterclockwise — examining the edges of all the mirrors. Until they met in the middle of the wall opposite the office door.

Max-Ernest stared at the mirror in front of them.

"Will you stop looking at my ears," said Cass,

who was having trouble avoiding them herself. "I'm not cutting them off, I don't care what anybody says!"

"I wasn't even looking at your ears. I was just thinking—isn't the pyramid this way?"

"Yeah, I think so."

"Well, wouldn't you want a window here, to see it? I mean, unless there was something behind the mirror—"

Cass pushed on the mirror—it opened immediately.

There was a flash of blond hair—

They both gasped—*Ms. Mauvais!*

No, they saw when they looked again, it was just a wig, sitting on a mannequin head.

"Must be an extra," said Cass, breathing hard.

"She wears a wig?" said Max-Ernest, sounding almost disappointed.

"Yeah, and probably a fake nose, too," said Cass, sounding almost like she was gloating.

Cass closed the panel door and tried the next one. Behind it stood an old wooden filing cabinet such as you might have found in a doctor's office in a previous century.

Sitting on top of the filing cabinet was—

"I *knew* they took it," said Cass.

— the Symphony of Smells. Max-Ernest started to pull it down, but Cass stopped him.

"It's too heavy. Let's get it on the way out."

"OK, but don't you at least want to peek in here—?" he said, indicating the file cabinet.

Before she could close the second panel door, Max-Ernest pulled open a drawer and started flipping through files.

"Look—the Bergamo Brothers."

He picked out the file and opened it in his hands. Old faded newspaper clippings fell out, showing Pietro and Luciano performing in the circus as children.

Quickly, Cass and Max-Ernest looked through the rest of the files in the drawer. There were about a dozen, each containing information on a different child. All the children were prodigies of some sort: musicians, artists, poets, mathematicians, some of them born as much as a hundred and fifty years ago. One file had a picture of a beautiful Chinese girl playing the violin. Cass and Max-Ernest looked at it sadly, remembering the girl described in Pietro's notebook.

Attached to the photos and newspaper clippings, detailed charts described the children's medical conditions; almost all of them ended with the word *deceased* next to a date.

"You think she killed all of them?" asked Max-Ernest. "I wonder why she didn't kill Luciano."

"I don't know, maybe she liked him too much. And then he got too old or something. Or maybe she wanted a collaborator. . . . C'mon, we don't have time," said Cass shutting the drawer. "Who knows what they're doing to Benjamin in there!"

The next panel was a door.

Stepping through it, Cass and Max-Ernest found themselves in a small, vault-like library crammed with books — piles and piles of books — all of them, you could tell at a glance, rare and priceless. Some were gilded and encrusted with jewels. Others were studded with brass and bound with leather straps. Some looked so old that they would turn to dust if you touched them. It was like walking into a treasure trove of books, hoarded by pirate librarians.

As Cass searched for hidden doors and passageways, Max-Ernest couldn't take his eyes off the books; he started thumbing through them almost against his will. While many of them had bindings of great beauty, their insides held nothing but horrors. Even the most casual inspection revealed etchings of nightmarish creatures like two-headed men and three-headed dragons, women with bat wings and monsters born in glass bowls. There were fiery planets and stormy oceans. There were ancient maps to places you should never go. Instructions for experiments you should never try. And memory keys for secret codes best forgotten.

"Hey, Cass," Max-Ernest whispered over his shoulder. "Have you ever heard of alchemy?"

"Sure, it's like wizard stuff," she answered from the other side of the room.

"Yeah, but there are real alchemists, too. At least, there were people who really tried it. Listen to this —" said Max-Ernest. "*Alchemy holds that all life is made of One Thing. Traditionally, this thing is called the Philosopher's Stone — although it is not so much a stone as a secret formula. If they could only find it, alchemists believed that they could turn lead into gold, and that they could make themselves immortal.*' Doesn't that sound like what Dr. L was talking about? Remember — 'the True Science' where everything is one?"

"Yeah, maybe," said Cass, not really listening. "But come look at this —"

Okay, I have a confession to make.

Max-Ernest didn't really read that passage aloud. He saw a reference to alchemy in a book, asked Cass if she knew what it was, then put the book down. Those words describing alchemy — I wrote them myself. You won't find them anywhere else, certainly not in a jewel-encrusted book in a library next to a pyramid.

The thing is, I didn't know how else to slip in the information, and you're going to need it in order to understand the pages ahead.

Also, I have to admit, I've begun to care about you to some small — very small — degree. And what is that expression — forewarned is forearmed? After all, being able to grasp what is going on in a book is one thing, being able to survive it is another.

You see, Ms. Mauvais's spa wasn't really a spa — or not only a spa. It was home to one of the oldest and most powerful, and by far the most sinister group of alchemists in the world — they who call themselves the Masters of the Midnight Sun.* And while they had not yet discovered the Secret, they had plenty of secrets already — and dangerous ones at that.

If only Cass and Max-Ernest had had the same advantage I'm giving you! Then they might have taken Owen's advice and run home while they could. Instead, they acted like heroes — that is to say, foolishly, without regard to safety or common sense.

You, I trust, will not make the same mistake.

Now, back to the story:

---

*That said, not all alchemists are quacks or criminals. Chemistry began with alchemy. Psychology, too. Sir Isaac Newton — the man who discovered gravity — was an alchemist. So was the man who invented modern medicine. Next time you go for a checkup, ask your doctor if he or she believes in alchemy. If the answer is no, tell your doctor to go into another business!

"I'm sure it leads to the pyramid; it's got to," said Cass as Max-Ernest joined her in the back of the library.

She was standing in front of a bronze door embossed with Egyptian hieroglyphs—

On second thought, let's have a chapter break. I don't know about you, but I could sure use it.

CHAPTER TWENTY-EIGHT

INTO THE PYRAMID

Part two

'm sure it leads to the pyramid; it's got to," said Cass as Max-Ernest joined her in the back of the library.

She was standing in front of a bronze door embossed with Egyptian hieroglyphs. The door was hardly hidden or secret, but it was much smaller than average, and partly blocked by books. It looked like the door to a safe, or perhaps to a tomb — a door designed to keep people out, not to let people in.

In the exact center of the door there was a large dial surrounded by the letters of the alphabet: a combination lock.

"There must be a secret password," she said. "But how do we figure it out?"

"Maybe there's a clue somewhere . . ."

"Sure, if we knew how to read hieroglyphics." Cass was already feeling discouraged.

"Can you read English?"

Max-Ernest pointed —

Surrounding the hieroglyphics, intermingled with lotus blossoms and scarabs and all sorts of unidentifiable Egyptian designs, were words written not in an ancient Egyptian language but rather in plain English.

When you put them together, this is how they read:

WHAT WORD BEGINS THE BEGINNING?
WHAT IF YOU ERASED THE END OF LIFE, AND
REPLACED IT WITH THE CENTER OF JOY?
NOW END AS YOU BEGAN.
FOR YOUR NAME IS A MIRROR. AND YOU
ARE THE REFLECTION OF US ALL.

"It's some kind of riddle, right?" asked Cass, tilting her head to make sure she'd read all of it. "Like the Riddle of the Sphinx?"

Max-Ernest didn't say anything. His brow was furrowed in concentration.

"You think if we solve it, we'll have the combination?"

"Yes! Let me think," said Max-Ernest, annoyed.

"Well, you better hurry, because Benjamin Blake —"

"I know!"

"*What word begins the beginning?*" Cass read aloud. "The beginning of what?"

"Will you please just —"

"See what it's like when the other person keeps — Well, did you get it?"

Suddenly, Max-Ernest was smiling. "Just the beginning part — it's the oldest one in the book."

"OK, what is it?"

"*The.*"

"The? The what?"

"Just *the*. The first word of the words *'the begin-ning'* is *the*."

"It can't be that simple."

"A lot of riddles are like that. I should know — I've read over ten thousand of them."

"OK, if you say so," said Cass doubtfully. "What's the next part? The *end of life* is death, right? But how do you replace death with joy? Does that mean you're happy that someone's dead? I guess if you're like Ms. Mauvais or Dr. L—"

"I don't know — if it's like the first part, then it's just about the words, not what they mean."

"So what is it then? Benjamin could be dying right now! And I don't think anybody's going to re-place him with joy!"

"I know, I know. I have to think—"

"Well, think fast."

Max-Ernest covered his ears so he wouldn't hear her — then removed them immediately.

"Wait, I've got it—at least, I think I do. I think — it's *E*."

"What do you mean?"

"The *end of life* is the last letter of 'life' —*E*. And *the center of joy* is *O*—the middle letter of 'joy.'"

"It's the letters? How'd you figure that out?"

"There's lots of letter riddles. Like, why is C the coldest letter? 'Cause it's in the middle of *ice*. Get it? C is—"

"OK, OK, I get it. That's a really dumb riddle. Don't lose your concentration! So you make T—H—E into T—H—O?"

Max-Ernest nodded. "'*Now end as you began . . .*'" he read.

"Maybe you start over with *the*?"

"Will you just let me—actually, that sounds right," said Max-Ernest.

"It does? So then we get—T—H—O—T—H—E? That's not a word."

"Let's try it anyway."

They tried the combination twice, first starting by dialing to the right, then starting by dialing to the left. Neither way worked.

"Oh, wait—duh," said Max-Ernest. "We forgot the last line. '*For your name is a mirror, and you are the reflection of us all.*'"

He went back to his thinking pose, covering his ears with his hands again. Cass tapped her toes anxiously. She was trying to let him think, but it was very difficult.

"Hey, Max-Ernest, what was that called? Remember that mirror writing you talked about?"

"Palindromes," he said, not uncovering his ears.

"Yeah, what about that?"

"Could be," said Max-Ernest, muttering to himself. "Let's see, if it was a palindrome, it wouldn't have the *E*, which would still make sense with the start over part . . . I guess then it would be T—H—O—H—T, which sounds weird, but . . ."

But that combination didn't work either.

Cass groaned. "We're never gonna figure it out. I wonder if there's some other way into the pyramid . . . What!? Tell me! Tell me! Did you think of something else?"

Max-Ernest was staring at the door.

"You see that hieroglyph in the middle? That guy with the head of a bird? I was just thinking that I saw it in one of the alchemy books."

"And this helps us how?" asked Cass, disappointed.

While Cass waited impatiently, Max-Ernest hurriedly picked up one of the books he'd looked at earlier.

"Yeah, he's right here," said Max-Ernest, reading fast. (This time, he really was reading!) "It says he's the

Egyptian god of wisdom and magic and the inventor of writing. Also the record keeper of the dead. Often pictured with the head of an ibis—that must be the bird head on the door. Believed by alchemists to have been reincarnated as Hermes Tris-me-g—never mind, can't pronounce it, but he was the father of alchemy. How 'bout that?"

"Fascinating," said Cass.

Max-Ernest grinned. "Guess what the god's name is—Thoth! That's our combination—T—H—O—T—H. Thoth."

"Thoth?" Cass repeated, getting excited.

"Thoth."

"Thoth?"

"Thoth!"

"Thoth Thoth Thoth Thoth Thoth!" Cass imitated him, laughing. It was impossible to say without lisping.

The door opened with a satisfying *click*.

They were at the top of a stairwell. Cass put her finger to her lips, and Max-Ernest managed, for the moment, not to say anything.

Silently, they descended the stairway, until they found themselves in a dimly lit passage—so narrow our two friends had to walk one behind the other.

"We must be under the moat," whispered Max-Ernest.

Cass nodded, thinking nervously of her pyramid dream. She felt a wave of claustrophobia come over her.

The passageway was not, however, as long or windy as the one in her dream. Instead, it ended abruptly — at a stone wall.

"Oh, great," whispered Max-Ernest. "Now what?"

He was about to turn around when he saw that Cass was standing close against the wall, looking through a spy hole in a small, hidden door. He nudged her and she stepped to the side — by half an inch — so he could look as well.

On the other side of the door was a vast room: the interior of the pyramid.

CHAPTER TWENTY-NINE

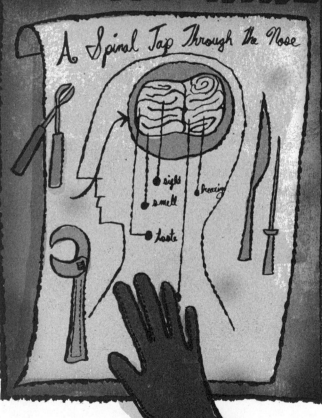

The spy hole didn't allow them to see the entire room at once, but by shifting angles they could piece it together in their heads like a collage.

The floor was tiled with a translucent stone the color of a tropical ocean, and it extended farther in all directions than you would have thought possible from the outside. The walls, which were covered in gold leaf, stretched all the way up to the pyramid's top, where an open skylight allowed in light from the Midnight Sun's glowing lantern. A raised altar stood in the middle of the room, and on top of the altar stood a large iron bowl (smaller than a Volkswagen Bug but bigger than a witch's cauldron) in which a fire burned with the same iridescent flame as the lantern above.

The audience surrounded the altar on all sides, creating a kind of theater-in-the-round. Straining in their seats, they stared at the fire with a sort of thirst, like desert animals stalking an oasis. Among them sat a handful of people Cass recognized as having been spa guests — all members, it seemed, of this ancient, alchemical cult.

Although they couldn't see her, Cass and Max-Ernest could hear Ms. Mauvais's icy voice echoing all the way into the passageway where they stood. The pyramid had the acoustics of a world-class concert hall. Ms. Mauvais was not, however, hosting a concert. Far from it.

"I know how eager we all are to begin," she was saying. "But I believe we have a couple birthdays to celebrate this evening."

By standing on tiptoe, Cass and Max-Ernest discovered they could catch glimpses of Ms. Mauvais standing on the altar beside the fire. She was dressed as always in gold, but she was wearing now what looked like some kind of Egyptian headdress, and her eyes were lined with black kohl. She could have been Cleopatra addressing her subjects.

"Roxana, sweetheart, stand, will you—so we can all see your lovely face . . . ?"

A young woman—she looked, anyway, not much older than a girl—stood up, and smiled shyly at the crowd.

"How old are you today—ninety-seven? Still so young! Look at her, everyone—no more than a teenager!"

They applauded politely—and she blushed prettily. Then sat down.

"Now, Itamar, darling, where are you?" asked Ms. Mauvais, looking out at her audience. "Will you please indulge your old student and stand up?"

An old man raised himself up on his cane. He was ghost-pale and almost expressionless, as if human emotion cost him too much effort. But his eyes were alive and watchful; and he wore a sleek black suit so impeccably tailored it seemed by itself to hold up his skeletal frame.

"Today, Itamar turned four hundred and eighty-nine! Four hundred and eighty-nine years old! Can you believe it? Our very own Renaissance man. Take a bow, Itamar."

The room applauded more vigorously this time. Itamar bowed his head — ever so slightly — then lowered himself back into his seat.

"All of you here — all of you brave souls — you are all testimony to our success. Every year our elixirs grow stronger, and our lives grow longer. And yet—" Ms. Mauvais's tone turned somber. "And yet — we must face it — the ultimate triumph has eluded us. We call ourselves the Masters of the Midnight Sun — but still we chase the sun! We have not won —" Here her eyes lit up and she proclaimed with a flourish of the arm, "Until now!"

Back in the passageway, Max-Ernest was shaking his head. "It isn't possible. It just isn't. I mean, a hundred and fifty maybe —"

"You saw her hand!" whispered Cass.

"Yeah, but, people would know. It would be in books."

"Shh—"

The audience had fallen quiet—Dr. L was taking his place on the other side of the fire. This was what they'd all been waiting for.

"To a baby, there are not five senses but one," Dr. L announced in a tone that was part doctor and part priest. "The world is a blur of sight, sound, smell, taste, touch—and maybe of senses we don't even know about. As the baby grows older, the senses separate from each other and forget that they all once sang the same song."

As he spoke, Dr. L looked searchingly at his audience, measuring their reactions, making sure he had everyone's full attention; it was as if he were still the circus performer he'd been as a boy. And yet the white smock he wore was more appropriate for a ritual sacrifice than a magic trick.

"We think of this new adult world as 'reality.' But what if it is reality that is lost? What if the real world were the baby's world, a world where everything and everyone were interconnected?" Dr. L paused dramatically, then gestured to a spot behind the fire. "There are a few, like this boy here, who hold on to that world, the *real* real world, well into adulthood."

Max-Ernest gasped—and Cass covered his lips with her hand.

Dr. L had stepped to the side, allowing the fire to illuminate his young patient. Benjamin was strapped inside a strange and intricate contraption that combined the most sadistic features of a dentist's chair with the most lethal elements of an electric chair. His bald head was restrained at an unnatural angle, and his closed eyes twitched continuously. A jumbled maze of glass tubing surrounded him like a long and twisted IV.

He appeared to be asleep—but hardly restful.

"These lucky people experience life as a rainbow of sensation called synethesia," Dr. L continued. "Their brains are living treasures. For they hold the key to the Secret we have sought so long."

As if to illustrate Dr. L's words, Benjamin trembled violently in his seat. In the passageway, Cass and Max-Ernest watched, transfixed: it was easy to imagine that Benjamin's brain was seeing indescribable things.

"For centuries, we—we followers of the True Science—we have searched for our so-called

Philosopher's Stone by melting metals or mixing chemicals or digging in the dirt. We have looked everywhere except the one place we might have found it—in the mind of the philosopher himself."

Dr. L held up a stick. It was long and slender and bent at the end. It appeared very old.

"With this reed the Egyptians vacuumed the internal organs of the dead. We will use it in much the same way—although tonight we won't be making a mummy. Well, not exactly."

His audience chuckled leeringly, as if he were describing an amusing but tasty dish.

"First, we will enter through the sinuses, here— Then we travel upwards to extract cerebrospinal fluid from the patient's ventricular system, here—"

Dr. L touched the reed to the bridge of Benjamin's nose, then traced a line upward and around to the back of Benjamin's head. Unconsciously, Max-Ernest touched his own head; Dr. L, he remembered, had had similar plans for him.

"In essence—a spinal tap through the nose," Dr. L summarized. "For this boy, I'm afraid brain death is a near certainty. But a price worth paying, I think. Because what *we* get in return is nothing less than life itself. Everlasting life."

As he said these words, he pulled a small vial out

of his pocket, and poured its contents into the fire beside him. The fire flared up high, its flames bright yellow—and suddenly the pyramid filled with the smell of sulfur.

"Everlasting life," Dr. L repeated.

"Cass," whispered Max-Ernest.

"Shh. I'm thinking."

"But—"

"I'm trying to think of a way to save Benjamin. They're gonna suck his brains out any second!"

"I know—"

"Then let me think! Remember how I let you—"

"I was just going to say—that vial, it looks like he got it from the Symphony of Smells."

"That's it!"

"What?"

"That's how we save him. C'mon, we're going up there—" She pointed to the open skylight at the top of the pyramid.

Max-Ernest stared. "Up there? How?"

"From the outside—now follow me!" said Cass, already starting to retrace their steps.

When they got to Ms. Mauvais's office, Cass stopped to take the Symphony of Smells out of the closet.

"I thought you said it was too heavy," said Max-Ernest.

"It's for my idea—"

They were about to exit the office when they heard footsteps coming their way.

Putting her finger to her lip, Cass silently re-closed the office door.

"Hello? Is someone there?" Daisy's voice called out.

They crouched down behind Ms. Mauvais's desk, their hearts thumping in their ears. If Daisy entered, they would be caught—for certain.

"Ms. Mauvais? Doctor?" Daisy addressed the office door. "I'm just—I had to get some food for those kids. I'm on my way back right now. Won't be a second—"

The big woman hesitated. Then, hearing nothing, she continued on her way.

Cass and Max-Ernest exhaled.

"I think she was scared she was going to get in trouble," Cass whispered, stifling what would have been a giggle in more relaxed circumstances.

A moment later, they stood in front of the moat. The drawbridge had been pulled up.

"Oh no," said Max-Ernest. "What are we supposed to do now?"

"This—" said Cass, pushing him into the moat.

"But I can't swim—!"

"You don't have to—see, you're standing!"

"I am?"

The water was only about waist deep. But that didn't prevent Max-Ernest from complaining that he was drowning as they waded across.

"C'mon, hurry!" said Cass. "He's gonna be brain-dead any second!"

When they got to the other side, they started scrambling up the pyramid without pausing to dry off.

The stone block steps were big and slippery, and sometimes Cass and Max-Ernest had to use their hands to pull themselves up. But somehow they managed to climb the pyramid in less time than it would take most of us to climb a staircase at home.

"So, what's the plan?" asked Max-Ernest, panting, when they got to the top.

CHAPTER THIRTY

A MESSAGE FROM ABOVE

As you've seen — or heard, depending on how you want to put it — the acoustics inside the pyramid were especially good. This was one of those places in which you don't want to make any embarrassing sounds. Forget sneezes and coughs — even the smallest, was-that-breakfast-or-lunch belch, or the softest, nobody-will-know-it's-me fart, could be heard on the other side of the room.

Which brings me — by a somewhat unpleasant route — to my point.

The interior of the pyramid was not only a space where *sounds* reverberated, it was also a space where *smells* reverberated. With so many people in a single room, ventilated only at the top, the air became a little, well, humid.

The smell of sulfur — that old stink of *huevos podridos* — was still lingering as Ms. Mauvais stepped in front of the fire and raised her arms in the air, her long sleeves hanging like golden wings. She seemed to address the sky itself as she cried:

"Thrice Great Hermes — hear me!"

With the entire assemblage fixing their attention on Ms. Mauvais, very few people noticed the small object — actually a glass vial — that dropped out of nowhere as if in response to her words. And only a slightly larger number noticed the small violet flare that erupted when the vial landed in the bowl of fire.

But nearly everyone noticed the sweet, flowery smell that flooded the room. Most eyed their neighbors accusingly, as if someone was wearing a particularly odiferous perfume.

Dr. L—who was bent over Benjamin, prepping the boy's nostrils for the operation—raised his head briefly, and sniffed. Then he returned his focus to Benjamin, presumably coming to the same conclusion.

Ms. Mauvais didn't seem to notice the smell at all.

"The Egyptians called you Thoth. The Greeks called you Hermes. The Romans called you Mercury," she intoned, her arms still raised in supplication.

The next vial to drop out of the sky—several more people saw this one—caused a pale green, sparkling flare when it fell into the fire. It filled the room with a light, herbal, faintly medicinal scent that, if you'd had a lot of colds, you might have recognized as echinacea.

Again, Dr. L raised his head, but this time he held it up a little longer and inhaled thoughtfully. Then, he shook his head as if to shake off some dark fantasy, and started to prod Benjamin's nose with the reed. He was about to begin the operation.

Ms. Mauvais faltered only briefly before continuing, "Hermes Trismegistus, we call upon you now. Give up at last your Secret!"

As the third vial dropped, several people pointed to it—their attention wholly diverted from the altar. When a dark blue-black flame jumped up from the fire, the entire room gasped. And, as the curling black smoke filled the room with the scent of licorice, everyone sniffed in unison.

Then they broke into loud applause. It was all part of Dr. L's show. Or so they assumed.

Dr. L, too, had turned his attention away from the imminent operation. But he wasn't clapping. He looked stunned, almost sick, as if he had just heard some terrible news.

"What's happening?" Ms. Mauvais asked him anxiously. "Who's doing this?"

Up on top of the pyramid, Max-Ernest turned excitedly to Cass. "It's working! How 'bout that? Now do *P*!"

"I don't see it—"

"It was peanut butter, remember. H – E – L – P. Heliotrope. Echinacea. Licorice. Peanut butter."

"I know it was peanut butter. It's just not here. It's supposed to be in number twenty."

She showed him the open Symphony of Smells

case and pointed to the empty slot. Max-Ernest quickly started overturning vials, reading labels.

"It has to be here. It has to—"

"Oh wait!" said Cass. She tore into her backpack, reaching down to the very depths, and pulled out a zip-lock bag full of old, smashed-up trail mix. Inside, there were five ancient, shapeless peanut-butter chips. Cass showed them to Max-Ernest.

"Think these will work?"

"I don't know—it doesn't really look like enough. How 'bout if you mix them with one of the others?" He looked through the vials and pulled one out. "Here. Butter-flavor."

"Try it."

"Me?"

Cass nodded.

Max-Ernest pushed the peanut butter chips into the vial, then held it over the open skylight.

"Here goes— Oh no!"

In his nervousness, he let it drop a little sooner than he meant to.

The vial veered off to the side and looked like it would miss the fire altogether.

At the last second, it hit the rim of the bowl and fell into the fire.

Cass and Max-Ernest waited breathlessly until a small yellowish flame flared up. Soon, the smell of peanut butter was released, not as strong as the other scents, but strong enough to waft all the way up to them.

Our two friends sighed in relief.

Down below, Dr. L staggered as if he'd been shot.

"Pietro! Fratello mio! Venga qua!" he cried. *"Quanto tempo devo aspettare?* Where are you? Speak to me!"

Completely overwrought, he spun around the altar, then looked up toward the skylight.

Cass and Max-Ernest jerked their heads out of view.

"You think he saw us?" asked Max-Ernest, panicking.

"No. He thinks we're his brother. For sure."

As if to underline her point, Dr. L shouted his brother's name again. *"Pietro! Pietro!"*

"Is it really him? Are you sure?" asked Ms. Mauvais, almost as distraught as Dr. L. "Could he have survived?"

Dr. L didn't answer. He ran off the altar—and out of the room.

"Everyone, please. Stay calm. Everything's fine.

We'll be right back," said Ms. Mauvais to their audience. Then she raced after him.

"C'mon. We gotta get down now," said Max-Ernest, about to climb down the side of the pyramid.

"Yeah. But not like that."

Cass reached into her backpack again and pulled out a coil of rope. Working quickly and professionally, she wrapped the rope around one of the lantern's steel supports, and tied it with two half hitches the way Grandpa Larry had once shown her.

Then she dropped the free end of the rope through the skylight. It dangled over the fire, just out of reach of the flames. She tried not to look.

Max-Ernest stared, frozen.

"It's the only way we'll get down there before they reach us," said Cass, more calmly than she felt.

Max-Ernest just shook his head.

"It'll be easy. You just swing a little bit when you get to the fire. Then jump when it's out of your way."

Max-Ernest shook his head again.

"OK, you get caught if you want. I'm going by myself."

"You mean without me?!"

Without answering, Cass lowered herself through

the skylight. She knew if she hesitated she'd never do it.

Deliberating about whether or not to follow her, Max-Ernest looked down the length of rope—

"Cass—stop! Look!"

Cass looked down: the end of the rope had caught on fire and, like a fuse, the flames were advancing toward her. At any moment, they would reach her, and she'd fall to a fiery death.

The strange thing was she didn't panic. Or rather, she did panic, but the part of her that was panicking was like another person—a child screaming next to her—while she figured out what to do. She was a survivalist, she reminded herself; this is what she'd been training for.

Cass tried to remember what she'd learned in gym about wrapping the rope around her leg as a brace—but she succeeded only in slipping down another foot.

So she abandoned technique and used her instincts.

If you've ever climbed up a rope, you know it's a lot harder than climbing down one. But the possibility of being burned alive is a powerful incentive. Just as her feet started to feel the heat, she pulled herself back up to the top — and rolled away from the skylight.

"Wow. We almost added you to the Symphony of Smells," said Max-Ernest, who looked like he'd barely escaped being burned alive himself.

"Very funny," said Cass, on her back and still breathing hard.

Then she laughed. "Actually, that really was kind of funny. Mean. But funny."

"Really? It was?"

"Uh huh."

"So then — I made a joke?" asked Max-Ernest, beginning to smile. "How 'bout that?"

"Yeah, and it took me almost dying," said Cass, sitting up.*

She smiled back at him to show she wasn't mad. "By the way, thanks for saving my life."

"You're welcome," said Max-Ernest, like it was no big deal. But of course it was. Cass didn't say thank you very often.

"I didn't really want to go down there without you — I thought you would follow me," Cass added. "But I shouldn't have gone anyway. I mean, since we're collaborators and everything. Sorry."

---

*SERIOUSLY — IS THAT WHAT MAKES SOMETHING FUNNY? THE THREAT OF DEATH? MAYBE. BUT HERE I THINK IT HAS MORE TO DO WITH THE SPECIAL UNDERSTANDING THAT EXISTS WHEN TWO PEOPLE HAVE LIVED THROUGH THE SAME EXPERIENCE — AN EXPERIENCE THAT IN THIS CASE WAS VERY DANGEROUS AND QUITE UNIQUE. *NOT ENOUGH FOR ONE, JUST RIGHT FOR TWO, AND TOO MUCH FOR THREE* — SOMETIMES SHARING A JOKE IS JUST LIKE SHARING A SECRET.

"Don't worry about it," said Max-Ernest, like this wasn't a big deal either. But of course it was. Cass apologized even less often than she said thank you.

Down below, fire had spread to the pyramid walls. People were screaming and running for the exits. It was pandemonium.

"Okay, let's get down there," said Cass. "Your way."

"Wait—what if Dr. L is on his way up?"

They peeked over the side of the pyramid.

Sure enough, Dr. L was running up the stone steps, with Ms. Mauvais just a few steps behind.

"Pietro! Pietro!" he kept shouting.

There was only one thing to do: go down the other side.

When they reached the bottom, Dr. L's silhouette was visible atop the pyramid. Behind him, smoke and fire spewed out of the skylight.

"Hey — it looks we made a volcano after all," said Max-Ernest, pointing to the pyramid. "Maybe we can turn it in for extra credit. How 'bout that?" He looked at Cass to see if she would laugh at this joke, too. But she hadn't heard him.

She was staring at Dr. L, who was holding something in his hands — "My backpack!"

"You can't worry about that now, we have to run," said Max-Ernest — which, when you think about it, was quite reasonable under the circumstances.

"But the Symphony of Smells is in there!"

"C'mon, we have to run," repeated Max-Ernest with a little more urgency.

"I know, it's just — he'll know it's us!"

"C'mon!" Max-Ernest, repeated again, yelling this time.

"OK, OK. They're gonna hear you —"

Cass and Max-Ernest ran along the edge of the moat until they got to the pyramid's front entrance. The last stragglers were still coming out and Cass and Max-Ernest had to push past them to get inside.

By the time they stepped onto the altar, the room was empty.

Flames had crawled all the way up Cass's rope as if it were a giant candlewick. The fire was now threatening to engulf the entire pyramid. The smell of sulfur was so strong it was almost unbearable.

The ruckus had finally wakened Benjamin Blake. He stared at the flames in front of him, confusion and terror evident in his face.

"Hey, Ben. Try to relax, OK? We're going to get you out of here," said Cass in a surprisingly gentle voice.

In reply, he mumbled something that sounded like a question, but was totally undecipherable.

Or would have been to anybody but Max-Ernest.

"You're inside a pyramid," Max-Ernest answered while Cass started unbuckling the straps that bound Benjamin to the chair. "Not a real pyramid — well, kind of a real pyramid. It has a real pyramid shape. But it's not really in Egypt. And not in any other place they have pyramids, like Mexico or Peru. Anyway, the pyramid's on fire, as you can see, and there's people outside that want to suck your brains. But don't worry about that — you're going to be fine!" Max-Ernest concluded in as reassuring a tone as he could muster.

The last of the straps fell off — and Benjamin fell to the floor. Whatever Dr. L had done to him had left him very weak.

Cass and Max-Ernest pulled him up with difficulty. When they succeeded in getting him to stand, he mumbled again.

"What's he saying now?" asked Cass.

"I don't know. Something about mint-chip ice cream?"

"We'll get ice cream later — lots," Cass said to Benjamin. "But right now we have to walk, OK? — fast."

Cass and Max-Ernest half pushed, half pulled, and half carried Benjamin across the tile floor. (I know, that's three halves, which is an impossibility — but so was getting him out of there.)

When they got close to the entrance, Benjamin started mumbling again and shaking his head.

"He says we have to stop. There's smoke — we can't go through the door," said Max-Ernest.

"But the fire's in here, not outside."

"He says not *that* kind of smoke. Gray smoke. The smoke is . . . Ms. Mauvais? Is that right, Ben?"

Benjamin nodded as vigorously as he could given his condition.

Then they heard Ms. Mauvais shouting outside

the pyramid. "How could you be such an idiot? To fall for a trick like that!"

"Shut up! Or I'll kill you, too — right after those wretched kids!" Dr. L shouted back.

The kids made a beeline for the pyramid's back door.

They slammed it shut behind them just as Dr. L and Ms. Mauvais entered the pyramid.

Benjamin said something under his breath.

"He says 'phew,'" said Max-Ernest.

"Yeah, I know. I got it that time," said Cass.

Through the spy hole, they watched Ms. Mauvais scanning the room for them. Behind her, Dr. L gripped Cass's backpack as if he was about to tear it apart.

"C'mon —" said Cass. "Before they see us!"

Coughing, the kids ran through the smoke-filled passageway. Lights flickered on and off.

"Stay low. That way you don't breathe in so much smoke," Cass instructed.

In the library, books were already starting to burn: tiny pieces of text floated upward as they turned to ash. Portraits of medieval monsters were devoured in flames. And bits of engraved bat wings flew through the smoke. It had been the best library of its kind this side of Budapest. Now it would be gone forever—and no one even stopped to look.

By the time they managed to get Benjamin outside, Cass and Max-Ernest were almost as exhausted as he was.

Around them: chaos.

The whole complex was on fire, and panicked guests were running every which way, ignoring the efforts of staff to herd them in a single direction. Two horses, now riderless, reared back, then bolted into the smoke.

"This way—" said Cass in an urgent whisper. "Here, take my hands so we don't get separated—" She offered a hand each to Max-Ernest and Benjamin, and they all took off together in the direction of the spa's front entrance.

With all the commotion, no one seemed particularly concerned to see them zigzagging through the crowd.

As they passed her room, Cass pointed to the body lying on the ground beside the door. It was Daisy, gagged and tied up in Owen's place.

"I bet she was surprised!" Cass said admiringly. "Wonder how Owen got out. We tied him up so tight."

Cass waved. Daisy glared in mute rage as she struggled to free herself.

* * *

The open gate loomed in front of them. They were seconds away from escape.

Then they heard Daisy yelling, "Stop them! They've got the boy! Close the gate!"

Somewhere, someone obeyed her—the gate closed.

Dozens of angry staff and guests started converging on them.

They looked back toward the pyramid. Fire raged. There was no retreat.

The frenzied crowd shouted "Get them!" and "Don't let them go!" and "Throw them into the fire!"

And then they heard the sound of a car engine.

The kids braced themselves for the worst: the Midnight Sun limousine was barreling toward them.

"What did the Bergamo Brothers say again?" asked Max-Ernest. "I mean, when they thought the lion was going to eat them?"

"*Arrivederci.*" Cass squeezed his hand.

The limousine screeched to a stop, missing them by inches.

"Cass! Max-lad! Get in, ye all!"

It took the kids a second to realize it was Owen leaning out the window, now speaking with an Irish brogue.

And another second to realize they hadn't been caught, they were being offered a ride.

Cass and Max-Ernest were barely able to get Benjamin into the limousine before Owen started backing up.

"Nice timing," said Cass.

"Aye. So 'twas," said Owen, with what might pass for a mischievous Irish grin.

Cass and Max-Ernest looked back through the limousine's back window and saw Dr. L and Ms. Mauvais coming around the side of the pyramid.

"Stop that limousine!" shouted Ms. Mauvais. "Now!"

But by then the fire had jumped from the bridge to the outer buildings—and staff and guests alike were fleeing in all directions.

"If you don't run after them, I'll cut you all off! No elixirs for any of you!"

Nobody heeded her.

As the limousine crashed through the spa gates, Ms. Mauvais clenched her fist in frustration. Her perfect skin was stretched so tight it looked like her face might rip in half.

Disgusted, Dr. L hurled Cass's backpack into the flames.

Inside the limo, Cass winced as if it were part of her that had been tossed into the fire.

Owen careened down the dark mountain roads at a maniacal speed, certain they were being followed.

But, gradually, he and his passengers started to relax. And the drive began to feel more like a road trip and less like a prison break.

"So are you going to keep talking like you're Irish?" asked Cass. "I just want to know, 'cause if I meet somebody who's like speaking German or Rastafarian or something, I want to know if maybe it's you."

"So I'm acting, am I? You think I'm not being the real Irishman?"

"Yeah, pretty much."

"She's a right clever lass, isn't she?" said Owen, turning to look back to the others. Max-Ernest nodded, grinning.

Owen eyed Benjamin. "So that's Ben, is it? What's the story, Ben? You look mad out of it. What drugs would they be giving you back in there?"

Benjamin groaned incoherently.

"He says they didn't give him anything," Max-Ernest translated. "It's just your driving,"

"Said that, did he?"

"No. I was just joking," said Max-Ernest.

"Not funny," said Owen.

"Well, I thought it was," said Cass, laughing.

"Really?" asked Max-Ernest.

Cass nodded.

Max-Ernest grinned happily. "How 'bout that?"

Cass turned to Benjamin. "You know what—mint-chip is my favorite ice cream. We'll get some soon, I promise."

Benjamin smiled — and nodded off.

Even Cass and Max-Ernest started to get woozy as the adrenaline of the evening's events wore off.

Noting that it had been months since he'd been able to listen to any "real music," Owen turned on the radio — blasting hip-hop with lyrics that the kids were glad their parents weren't around to hear.

With the road as curvy as it was, there was no way they could have seen a vehicle that was more than a few feet ahead of them; with the music at such a high decibel level they couldn't have heard the vehicle either.

So it was almost a miracle when Benjamin sat up in his sleep and screamed in his clearest voice, "Stop!"

Owen slammed on the brakes. The limousine skidded to a stop.

A few feet in front of them, a pickup truck was parked lengthwise across the narrow road and honking loudly.

"Who's that? Are they from the spa?" asked Max-Ernest, now wide awake.

"Well, we're not waiting long enough to find out, are we?" said Owen. "Hold on, ye all — let's hope this limousine likes the bumps!"

He started backing up.

Then the honking was joined by a familiar and extremely loud bark.

"Wait!" said Cass. "That's Sebastian!"

Owen braked again and everyone looked back at the pickup truck. Standing beside the truck were Grandpa Larry and Grandpa Wayne, waving like madmen.

CHAPTER THIRTY-TWO

DO-IT- YOURSELF ENDING

Only bad books have good endings.

If a book is any good, its ending is always bad — because you don't want the book to end.

More importantly — more importantly to me, anyway — endings are hard to write.

You try wrapping up your story, showing how your characters have grown, sewing up any holes in your plot, and underlining your theme — all in a single chapter!

No, really. Try.

Because I'm not going to do it.

(I'll give you a hint about the theme of this book — it has nothing to do with the value of hard work. It isn't "If at first you don't succeed, try again," or anything honorable and inspiring like that.)

Oh, I won't leave you hanging entirely. There are levels of cruelty that even I am not capable of.*

As writing material, I will give you a few key incidents: things that happened after Cass and Max-Ernest were rescued, and that would have to be included in the ending of this book, if it had an ending.

To make it easier for both of us, I'm going to organize the material according to the characters in-

---

*WHEN YOU TAKE OVER THIS CHAPTER, YOU SHOULD PROBABLY REWRITE THAT LAST SENTENCE TO READ, "THERE ARE LEVELS OF CRUELTY *OF WHICH* EVEN I AM NOT CAPABLE." TEACHERS DON'T LIKE IT WHEN YOU END SENTENCES WITH PREPOSITIONS LIKE *OF* OR *IN*. THEN AGAIN, YOU SHOULDN'T BE SHOWING THIS BOOK TO YOUR TEACHER ANYWAY.

volved. When these pages land in your hands, you can rearrange events as you see fit.

Owen

Let's get rid of him first.

What I would imagine for Owen is a touching little good-bye scene in which he teases the kids about tying him up and says they better be careful because he's going to get them back when they least expect it. Then he would leave with a tip of the hat, promising more adventures to come.

All this, don't forget, in an amusing new accent—East Indian, say, or Korean.

You like that scene? Please use it.

But it didn't happen.

What really happened is that Owen drove away as soon as he knew the kids were safe with Cass's grandfathers. He was so quiet about it that nobody noticed until the limousine was gone. I can't say why he didn't say good-bye—it wasn't very polite, and it hurt Cass's feelings more than she would have cared to admit. Maybe he didn't want to intrude on Cass's moment with her grandfathers. Or maybe he couldn't choose the right accent for a good-bye. Or maybe spies are just like that.

The Grandfathers

If you don't mind, I'll skip the part of the ending where Sebastian jumps out of Wayne's truck and runs over to Cass and starts licking her face.

And where Cass hugs both her grandfathers in turn, and then both at once, and then both in turn again.

And where she says she knew, just *knew*, they'd come, and she guesses (correctly) that Max-Ernest's parents told them where to look.

And, if you don't mind, I'll skip the part where the kids all climb into the back of Grandpa Wayne's truck and they start driving down the mountain and everybody is really tired but really happy.

You knew all that stuff was going to happen as soon Cass heard Sebastian's bark.

But there is one event that occurred on their way home — well, really it was more of a conversation — that I'd like to tell you about.

Picture an old, roadside gas station. Grandpa Wayne was sitting in the driver's seat of his truck, studying a map, while Grandpa Larry was filling the truck with gas. Cass and Max-Ernest sat in the back of the truck with Benjamin, who was sleeping next to them on a blanket so ratty it must have belonged to Sebastian. Sebastian, meanwhile, was standing by the truck's tailgate, sniffing the gasoline in the air like it was a delectable treat.

They'd already gone over the events that had transpired at the Midnight Sun five or six times when Max-Ernest looked at Cass and said, "So, I guess my doctor was wrong."

"About what?" asked Cass.

"About how you're just a survivalist 'cause of your dad being hit by lightning, and you don't really care about saving people. 'Cause you actually did, you saved someone." He pointed to the sleeping Benjamin.

"Yeah, I guess so," said Cass, sounding oddly uncertain.

"Lightning, huh?" asked Grandpa Larry with a raised eyebrow. Apparently, he'd been listening from the gas pump.

"You don't know anything about it!" said Cass, her ears turning red.

"Well, I know about good stories, and I'm all for them," said Larry diplomatically, climbing back into the truck's front cab.

Inside the cab, he whispered something into Wayne's ear. Wayne nodded somberly and started driving the truck back onto the road.

"I guess I should tell you, I mean, now that we're alive and everything," said Cass, speaking to

Max-Ernest but looking at her grandfathers, "I didn't really tell you the whole story — about my dad."

"You mean there's more, besides him being hit by lightning?" asked Max-Ernest, eyes wide.

"Well, I don't really *know* that he got hit by lightning." Cass hesitated. "Actually, I don't even know if he's dead."

"You mean you made up the story?" asked Max-Ernest, incredulous.

"I heard it on TV. . . ."

Max-Ernest stared at her, then broke into a big smile.

"So, basically, you lied," he said as if this were great news. "That cancels out my telling my doctor! We're even! How 'bout that?"

"You don't have to be so happy about it."

"So who was your real dad?" asked Max-Ernest after a moment.

"I don't know," said Cass matter-of-factly.

"You don't? Didn't your mother tell you?" Max-Ernest couldn't hide his astonishment.

Cass shook her head.

"Well, didn't you ever ask?"

"Yeah, when I was little. But she used to just say she would tell me when I got older. And ever since, it's like, I don't know, I'm afraid to ask. Like it would hurt her feelings or something."

"Well, I think you should ask again—"

"Leave her alone," said Grandpa Larry, leaning out the back window. "She'll ask when she's ready."

"OK," said Max-Ernest. "I was just saying—"

But he didn't say anything more.

Cass's Mother

As you can imagine, Cass's mother entered a state of extreme anxiety as soon as Cass failed to answer her cell phone at the usual hour. Proud of her self-control, her mother waited a whole minute before she called Cass's grandfathers to ask where Cass was. When she couldn't get through, she calmly and rationally drove to the airport—and screamed at the top of her lungs until she got on the first flight home.

Late that night, as Grandpa Wayne's pickup truck pulled up in front of the firehouse, a taxi was pulling out. Cass's mother stood in the doorway. Her eyes grew stern when she saw Cass hop out of the back of the truck.

"Cassandra! What were you doing in the back of that thing—do you know how dangerous that is? Not to mention against the law. And you two—"

she said, pointing at Cass's grandfathers. "You promised!"

Now, to my mind, Cass's mother getting mad about Cass riding in the back of a truck — when Cass had been doing far more dangerous things only a short time before — is both funny and realistic. But you may want to leave it out and go immediately to the following:

And then Cass's mother — she couldn't keep it up any longer — she took her daughter in her arms and wouldn't let go for one and a half minutes. (I know that doesn't sound long, but count it out — one and a half minutes is a long hug.)

"I missed you so much," she said.

"Me, too," said Cass.

And then Cass — she couldn't stop herself — she cried for the first time since these adventures began, as if she'd been saving up her tears and now she was spending them all at once.

Max-Ernest's Parents

Max-Ernest's parents are minor characters who serve mainly as comic relief. (Relief for us, I mean. For Max-Ernest, no doubt, they weren't funny at all.) Nonetheless, they deserve a mention:

When he returned late that night, Max-Ernest

naturally expected his parents to be full of questions. He started to explain, but his parents stopped him.

"No, don't say anything," said his father.

"No, not a word," said his mother.

A strange thing had happened while Max-Ernest was away: his disappearance had brought his parents together. Their concern for their son had made them overcome their differences — and agree to split up.

Henceforward, they promised, they were going to be proper divorced parents. They would each have a house — separate from the other.

"You ran away to send us a message," said his father.

"And we heard it loud and clear," said his mother.

Max-Ernest thought it best not to correct them.

Amber

There's absolutely no reason to go back to Amber at this late point in our story. But she would get really mad if we didn't.

Not that she would say so. As the nicest girl in school, she would probably say it was "totally fine — I mean, I wouldn't put you in my book, either."

I take it back. There is a reason to go back to Amber. If only to report what Cass said the next time Amber offered her a Smoochie.

Cass said, "No."

A little word, it's true — but, for Cass, a big deal.

Mrs. Johnson

If Dr. L and Ms. Mauvais are the true villains in this book, then what is Mrs. Johnson? If I had to pick, I would say Mrs. Johnson represents *the law*. She's like the policeperson in the world of our book — the one who makes the rules, and who punishes you when you break them.

Which gets us that much closer to the ending of our ending.

By now, readers will be wondering how much Cass and Max-Ernest confessed about their trip to the Midnight Sun.

The answer is: everything and nothing.

Oh, they tried.

But whenever they described their experience, reactions ranged from polite skepticism to outright disbelief.

You'd think that Benjamin Blake might have been some help. Why would he have a shaved head, Cass asked, if no one had wanted to suck his brains? But other people didn't see it that way. There were plenty of reasons, they said. Like maybe he wanted to look like he was in a rock band. Or maybe he had lice.

Frustratingly, Benjamin himself had only the vaguest memories of his ordeal. As far as anyone could tell from his mumbled account, Cass and Max-Ernest had taken him on a trip to Egypt, where he sat around a campfire and ate mint-chip ice cream.

The day after Cass and Max-Ernest returned, a team of firemen and police investigators went to examine the site of the Midnight Sun, and the kids waited hopefully for their report. But the fire had decimated the entire spa. Incredibly, there were no survivors other than the kids. Or no survivors willing to identify themselves anyway. It was as if the Midnight Sun had never existed. The investigators would say only that they suspected arson.

After hearing the police report, people were no longer skeptical about Cass and Max-Ernest's story; they were downright suspicious.

In a more emotionally satisfying book than this one, the principal would have wept when Cass returned. She would have apologized for ever doubting Cass, and she would have begged Cass's forgiveness. There would have been some sort of celebratory assembly and Cass and Max-Ernest might even have received medals—for "best survivalist" and "best code breaker," say.

Well—by now you know this book better than that.

(And, no, I'm not giving any ground on this one.)

Mrs. Johnson couldn't prove it, but she was certain that Cass and Max-Ernest were responsible for Benjamin Blake's disappearance, rather than for his rescue.

I won't go into detail about their hours of detention and hard labor because the subject is too infuriating to my sense of justice (yes, I have a sense of justice, although not always an active one, I admit). If you're a sadistic sort, you can flesh out that part for yourself. Otherwise, join me in turning a blind eye to their suffering.

Thankfully, after what Cass and Max-Ernest had been through, any punishment their principal could dish out was comparatively easy to endure.

What was harder to endure was that no one in the world believed them.

Dr. L and Ms. Mauvais

You didn't honestly think they'd gone up in flames—did you?

I can't tell you much about our villains' actions

after our heroes escaped. I don't know how many of their guests they let burn to death (probably most of them) or what awful price they extracted from those they saved (probably a high one). I don't know what sinister alchemical materials they managed to salvage before they ran. Still less can I tell you about their nefarious plans for the future, although I would bet my life they had them; creatures like Dr. L and Ms. Mauvais do not, as a rule, give up after a setback—they vow revenge.

What I can tell you with certainty is that they were last seen silhouetted on top of a mountain ridge not far from what was once the Midnight Sun. They were on horseback (remember those horses running loose during the fire?), and they had paused to take in the view and to say good-bye to their old fortress of a spa. Then, with a cry that echoed for miles, they whipped their horses into a gallop and disappeared over the ridge.

Wherever they were heading, it was too close. Whenever they return, it will be too soon.

*PLEASE WRITE IN BLACK OR BLUE INK ONLY. ATTACH EXTRA PAGES AS NEEDED.

THE END

WELL, NOT REALLY.

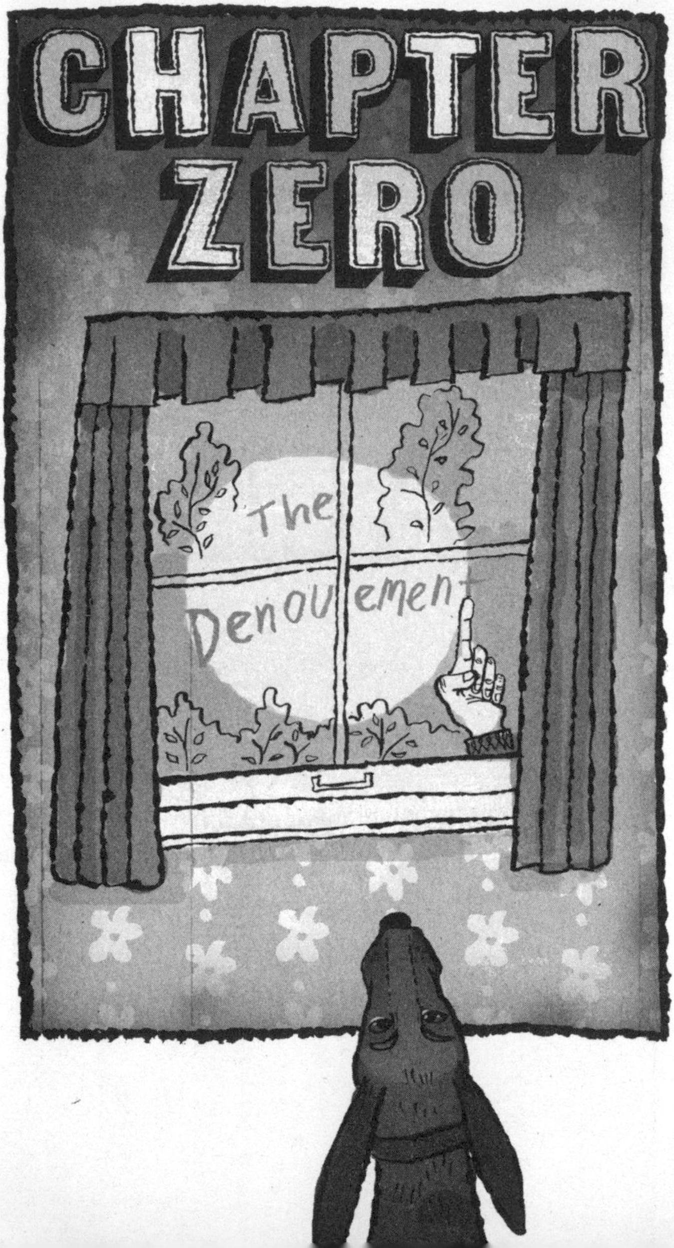
CHAPTER ZERO
The Denouement

No, that last chapter wasn't really *the* last chapter.

Don't feel bad if you put a lot of work into it; the work wasn't wasted. Many important things happened in that chapter — at least I think so.

I'll tell you what, if you're *that* angry, just push the book aside and forget all about this chapter — and all about Cass and Max-Ernest, and all about the Secret, and all about me, too.

Good riddance, right?

No, you want to keep reading?

OK, how's this for a compromise: why not think of your chapter — Chapter Thirty-two — as the last chapter? As for this chapter — we'll make it Chapter Zero. If anyone asks, it doesn't exist. It's the nothing chapter. The un-chapter. It simply doesn't count.

And we won't call it *the ending,* either. That grand title we'll leave for your chapter. This chapter we'll call *the denouement.*

One dictionary defines denouement as "a final part in which everything is made clear and no questions or surprises remain." By that definition, it is exactly the wrong word to describe this chapter. This chapter will make nothing clear; it will raise many questions; and it may even contain a surprise or two. But I say we call it the denouement anyway because the word sounds so sophisticated and French.

You see, there was one more occurrence in the lives of our two heroes that I must relay before we are finished. And this occurrence—I doubt it will give you what people call "a sense of closure." If you're anything like me—and I fear you are, if you've read this far—you'll find it more maddening than anything else.

My intent is not to torture you. I want merely to show you that there is a larger picture—that our story doesn't begin and end with this book.

Or with Cass and Max-Ernest.

Or even with you and me.

One rainy Wednesday afternoon, not very long after her experience at the Midnight Sun, but long enough so that she'd already grown extremely tired of trying to convince people that her experience was real, Cass was sitting upstairs at the firehouse having tea with Grandpa Larry—just as she had done every Wednesday for years.

This time, however, they were not alone. Much to the delight of Grandpa Larry, who loved nothing more than a fresh audience for his stories, their

Wednesday ritual had recently grown to include Cass's new friend, Max-Ernest, and as a special guest today, Benjamin Blake.

This week's tea was Earl Grey—a tea that Benjamin insisted was incorrectly named because it tasted pale blue. (Benjamin had a similar complaint about orange pekoe, a tea that he said tasted olive green; green tea, on the other hand, was not green but bright yellow.) Grandpa Larry tried to explain that Earl Grey was named not for its color, but for Charles Grey, the Second Earl Grey, also known as Viscount Howick. However, his young listeners didn't appear to care much about the Viscount. So Grandpa Larry gamely switched topics, and started to relate an old and gratifyingly bloody Chinese legend about the origin of tea.*

It was then that they heard Sebastian barking downstairs: a customer had arrived.

"It's Gloria—I'll be in back!" Grandpa Wayne shouted from below.

As always, Gloria had arrived at the fire station with a big box of stuff. The kids waited impatiently as Grandpa Larry carried it in for her.

"Gloria, this is Max-Ernest and Benjamin. And

---

*THE LEGEND CONCERNED A BUDDHIST MONK WHO KEPT FALLING ASLEEP WHENEVER HE TRIED TO MEDITATE. THIS MONK GOT SO FRUSTRATED THAT HE EVENTUALLY CUT OUT HIS OWN EYELIDS. (I KNOW — *OWWW!*) ACCORDING TO THE LEGEND, THE WORLD'S FIRST TEA BUSHES GREW IN THE SPOT WHERE HIS EYELIDS FELL. AND THAT IS WHY, TO THIS VERY DAY, DRINKING TEA HELPS PEOPLE KEEP THEIR EYES OPEN WHEN THEY'RE TIRED.

you remember Cass —" said Grandpa Larry, after he'd finally found space to put the box down.

"I think so," Gloria said. "Wasn't she here last time?"

Cass waited for more, but Gloria only smiled in a vague sort of way, as if Gloria barely remembered her.

"Yeah, and we saw each other at the Midnight Sun, too," Cass prompted, in case Gloria thought Cass didn't want her to mention it.

"The Midnight Sun? You mean the spa?"

Gloria seemed genuinely surprised. "You must be thinking of someone else," she said. "I took a terrible fall right before I was supposed to go. Ask Larry, he'll tell you. Spent a week in the hospital. They thought I might have amnesia — it was just like *Days of Our Lives*! But how was it? I'm dying to hear! I didn't know they allowed children. . . ."

Cass looked closely at Gloria, expecting some secret communication — a threatening glance or a sly wink. But Gloria's face was blank. Either she thought she was telling the truth or she was a very good actor.

"Um . . . it was . . . OK," said Cass slowly. "But it's not really there . . . now . . ."

"It isn't?" Gloria asked, confused. "What do you mean?"

"Cass, will you please put Sebastian outside? He's about to chew this box apart," Grandpa Larry broke in before Cass could answer.

"It's so weird," said Cass as she tied Sebastian to a post in back of the fire station. "It's like I dreamed the whole thing. The spa. Ms. Mauvais. Everything."

"Well, you didn't—and even if you did, how come I dreamed it, too?" Max-Ernest protested. "Unless we had some kind of Vulcan mind meld. Or wait, I know, maybe we're two split personalities in one schizophrenic brain! That would explain everything—"

"I didn't mean I really thought I dreamed it—just that it felt like that," said Cass, cutting him off. (Even though Max-Ernest had supposedly been cured, he still had a tendency to go on and on if you didn't stop him.)

Benjamin, who'd been silently struggling to follow the conversation, mumbled something and pointed back toward the fire station.

"He says to be quiet and listen. He thinks it might be important," Max-Ernest translated.

Inside, Gloria was telling Larry a story. As loud as she was, they could only make out about half of her words:

". . . Never so surprised . . . in all my life . . . the gardener . . . and here I was trying to show the house . . ."

As she listened, Cass grew increasingly excited. "She's talking about the magician's house! You think she discovered something?"

They weren't able to pose this question to Gloria immediately, because Benjamin Blake's mother had arrived to pick him up. But as soon as he'd gone, Cass and Max-Ernest begged Gloria to start her story again from the beginning. She didn't understand why they cared so much, but she was happy to oblige. (Gloria had lost her memory, not her love for attention.) The story went like this:

Gloria had been showing the magician's house to some prospective buyers when, as sometimes happens at awkward moments, "nature called" and she had to excuse herself to go "freshen up." Just as she was about to enter the bathroom, the bathroom door opened and an old man in a straw hat stepped out, carrying a box.

Needless to say, Gloria "had a heart attack."

Very calmly, as if he'd been expecting her, he explained that he was the gardener — the one who first reported the magician's disappearance — and that he was just cleaning up the magician's study. He pointed out that she had missed some things when she packed up the house.

He asked Gloria if she would mind taking the box he was holding to the fire station — the *estacion de bomberos*, he called it. Gloria was so flustered she agreed right away.

Only after she'd left the house did Gloria start to wonder how he knew about the *estacion de bomberos* in the first place.

"And there you have it," said Gloria, patting the big box she had brought in. "That's the whole she-bang."

"Well, I have to say, you're none the worse for the experience — you look fabulous," said Grandpa Larry, looking at the newly svelte real estate agent. "Doesn't she, Wayne?!" he called out to Grandpa Wayne, who was standing in the back of the store tinkering furiously with an old record player.

"Fabulous!" Wayne agreed, not looking up.

"That's what everybody's saying!" said Gloria wonderingly. "Ever since that fall. You know, I can't help thinking that someone must have hypnotized me while I was unconscious. It's almost like I really went to that spa — instead of the hospital!"

*　　　*　　　*

After Gloria left, Grandpa Larry let Sebastian back in. Grandpa Wayne reemerged—it turned out the record player wasn't so desperately in need of fixing, after all—and everyone, dog included, went upstairs to have more tea, and to look through the box the gardener had sent.

Immediately taking charge, Cass opened the box with a kitchen knife, insisting that she get to handle everything in the box before anyone else. (She could tell her grandfathers thought her behavior a little selfish, but they didn't say anything—probably because they didn't want to reprimand her in front of Max-Ernest.) The box was filled to capacity with small items covered in newspaper. Cass eagerly unwrapped them, inspecting each one for clues and secret messages. But the more things she inspected, the clearer it became that there were no clues to be found. The box contained only dishware—plates and bowls and cups.

Cass was crushed. She'd been predicting, or at least hoping something. Something she hadn't mentioned to her grandfathers, or even to Max-Ernest. Something about the magician's gardener. But now, it appeared, she'd been wrong. The gardener was exactly who he said was. The box of stuff no more than a box of stuff.

Her grandfathers, on the other hand, couldn't get over their good luck. "Can you believe somebody's getting rid of this?" asked Grandpa Larry holding up a pastel plate. "Do you know what Russel Wright goes for these days?"

Taking a few sample dishes, Larry and Wayne ran downstairs to check them against pictures in books they had. Cass knew they would be at this for hours. The gardener couldn't have chosen better things to send if he'd intentionally set out to give her grandfathers the most distracting items possible.

"So what do you want to do now? 'Cause I sort of have homework," said Cass to Max-Ernest. She didn't really want to do homework, but she wasn't much in the mood for company anymore.

"I dunno . . . Hey, what's he smelling?" asked Max-Ernest. "There's nothing left in there."

Cass followed Max-Ernest's eyes over to Sebastian, who was sniffing the empty box, and wagging his tail.

"There's probably just some kibble under it or something," said Cass, refusing to be very interested.

Still, she picked up the box and peeked underneath — nothing.

Nonetheless, there was something unusual about the box.

"What's this made of? Why's it so heavy?" she asked, shaking it in her hands.

She put the box back down and looked inside. Then she looked at the outside. Then she looked at the inside again.

This time she reached down — and started pulling up the cardboard.

The box had a false bottom.

Hidden beneath the cardboard were two packages wrapped in paper and tied with string. The larger package was addressed to Cass, the smaller to Max-Ernest.

In a more sober moment, Cass might have reflected on the dangers of opening an unexpected package from a total stranger. This was not a sober moment, however.

She and Max-Ernest both tore open their packages at once.

Fortunately, the packages did not contain explosives; they were not even booby-trapped.

Cass's contained a backpack.

I wish I could describe the way the backpack looked. But there's a very good chance she's still carrying it to this day, and I don't want to give you any more ways to identify her than I already have. At any rate, it wasn't the backpack's appearance that made it special. In fact, when Cass first saw it, she was almost disappointed that it looked so normal.

Inside—that was another story. The backpack was filled from top to bottom with state-of-the-art survival gear—all very compact and lightweight and built to withstand the hardest use and the harshest conditions.

The backpack's best features she didn't notice until the backpack was empty. These were the things the backpack *did*—as opposed to the things it contained. For instance, if you pulled one cord, a parachute popped out. If you pulled another cord, the shoulder straps inflated and the backpack became a flotation vest. If you turned the backpack inside out, and unzipped it all the way around, it expanded into a full-size tent.

Cass knew her mother would be unhappy to see Cass wearing a backpack again (lately, her mother had been trying to get her to carry a shoulder bag) but Cass had a feeling this was a backpack she would never want to take off.

Max-Ernest's package was also disappointing when first opened. It contained what looked like a familiar, handheld device—a kind of device you see every day, and not even a very special version. But it only took Max-Ernest a few seconds to discover that the device wasn't what it looked like—at all. It didn't even accept any game cartridges. (Oops. I almost gave away what it was disguised as.)

It had a false front that lifted up at the touch of a hidden button. Underneath was a small, tablet-style computer/scanner specially designed for cracking secret codes—the ULTRA-Decoder II. As Max-Ernest would learn after experimenting for a while, the Decoder included keys for decrypting all known code systems, and tools for deciphering unknown ones. Its memory contained full dictionaries and character recognition software for over a thousand languages including Aramaic, Sanskrit, and Navajo. It could even read Egyptian hieroglyphics.

One thing the Decoder did not do was tell jokes.

Max-Ernest loved it anyway.

"Are you guys OK up there?" called Grandpa Larry.

"We're fine!" Cass yelled back.

They were ready to hide their packages if Larry came upstairs. But, apparently, he and Wayne had yet to finish researching their new dishes.

A moment later, Max-Ernest was busy translating the word *fart* into every language he could think of (someone had told him that fart jokes were funny), and Cass was taking a second look at her flashlight—not only a flashlight, it turned out, but a warning siren, tracking device, and two-way radio.

Between the rain and the steam from all the tea, the kitchen window had fogged to the point where you could no longer see through it. Whenever the light passed across the glass, thousands of tiny droplets would briefly illuminate then disappear. This must have happened a half-dozen times before Max-Ernest looked up from studying the Decoder and saw it—

"Look!" he said, but by then the light had passed again.

He had trouble getting Cass to aim her flashlight again at the just the right point, but eventually she hit the spot.

And now Cass could see it, too.

Someone had written a message on the glass—just as anyone might, say, sitting on a bus next to a foggy window. But this message was not scribbled with a finger. Rather, it looked like someone had used some kind of fine writing instrument. And it didn't say anything like "Joe was here" or "Terry + Samantha = Love." Actually, it didn't look like it was even written in English.

It was written in code.

By the time they started deciphering the message, the fog was disappearing from the window, and the message was disappearing with it.

Max-Ernest grabbed a notepad and pencil from the kitchen counter. He scribbled in a kind of delirium — the kind that only comes when you've eaten too much Halloween candy or when you're trying to transcribe a secret message before it vanishes forever.

Max-Ernest held up the page as soon as he'd finished copying the message.

Here is the first line exactly as it appeared on the window:

CSTO RTPPTKCOT TKC JTX-SOKSPQ:

For several minutes, the kids studied the mixed-up letters with increasing frustration.

Then Max-Ernest looked up and smiled. "What does J—T—X dash S—O—K—S—P—Q look like?"

Cass shrugged. She had no idea.

"Well, what if X was X, like really the letter X, even in the code—"

"It's your name — Max Ernest!" said Cass.

"Right — how 'bout that?"

"Which means J equals M, and T equals A."

"And S is E, and O is R, and K is N, and P is S, and Q is T."

Using one of Grandpa Larry's red pens (Larry still had a lot of them from the days he taught high school), Max-Ernest rewrote the first line of the message, substituting letters according to the formula they had just worked out. This is what he came up with:

CEAR RASSANCA ANC MAX-ERNEST:

"'*Dear Cassandra and Max-Ernest,*'" read Cass, filling in the blanks. "It's a letter to us! . . . Hey, shouldn't you be using your Decoder?"

It was almost too simple a code for the Decoder. Having gotten so far, Max-Ernest could have decoded the rest of the message himself, but it would have taken him much longer. The Decoder did the job in less than a second.

It also told them that the code's keyword was "TERCES."*

"*Terces?* What's that mean?" asked Max-Ernest. "I don't even think it's a word."

*IF YOU WANT TO LEARN HOW TO DECIPHER A KEYWORD CODE YOURSELF, CHECK THE APPENDIX.

"I don't know—maybe we'll find out if we read the letter," said Cass, who felt as if she'd been waiting years to read it, rather than a few minutes.

It's difficult to describe the feelings that our two friends experienced as Max-Ernest read the letter aloud from the screen of his Decoder. Even if you were good at having feelings—and I, as you know, am not—I think you would have trouble finding names for this particular mix of emotions.

There were a few easier, old-fashioned feelings, like: Happiness. Excitement. Pride. Anxiety. Fear. But there were other, vaguer, harder-to-pin-down feelings, like: A pit in the stomach that means something is either really good or really bad or both. A feeling of being old and young at once. A sense of beginnings and endings happening at the same time. A certainty that your life is changing, but an uncertainty about how it's changing and whether you want it to.

There was also a feeling that combined confusion, recognition, and amusement all at once.

That feeling came from the way the letter was written.

The funny thing was: even after the letter was decoded, it still didn't sound exactly like English. It sounded foreign.

Foreign in a familiar way.

Foreign in a way that felt to Cass and Max-Ernest like an old friend.

I've included the letter below with one minor but necessary excision. The letter, I think, speaks for itself.

So this is good-bye. For now.*

Dear Cassandra and Max-Ernest:
Congratulations for escaping yourselves from the Midnight Sun.

By rescuing the boy, Benjamin Blake, you have not only saved the life, you have performed for the whole world the service — keeping the evildoers from the great power.

Unfortunately, Ms. Mauvais and Dr. L, they have escaped themselves also. At this very moment, they collect for themselves their army. And every day they come closer to the Secret. The Secret is not what they think it is, but that is all the more reason we must protect it from them.

We have very little of the time. Many lives, they are at stake.

*See, I warned you about endings.

In recognition of your bravery and unique talents, I hereby invite you to become members of the Terces Society — and to enlist in our fight against the Masters of the Midnight Sun.

Understand this: once you swear to the Oath of Terces, your lives, they will never be the same. You will face the hazards and the hardships. And you must obey all the orders without the questions.

If you accept to join our noble cause, leave a *xxxxx xxxx* in this window next Wednesday.

The man you call Owen, he will find you and take you to us.

In the meantime, please watch carefully the boy, Benjamin. He is more valuable than even you know.

I beg for you to join us. Without you, I fear, we will not succeed.

I am sure I do not have to tell you — speak to no one about this letter. For you have now entered yourselves in the circle of the Secret. And anyone who knows of the Secret — their life is in the grave danger.

With the greatest admiration and respect,

P. B.

APPENDIX*

Grandpa Larry's Compass Recipe
To make a compass in a bowl of water, you need a magnet, a cork, and a stickpin (or thin needle). Hold the pin by one end, and brush the magnet down the pin from one end to the other — in one direction only. Never brush the magnet back up the pin. Repeat twenty times or more until the pin is fully magnetized. Then push the pin through the cork. Gently place the cork in the bowl of water. The floating cork will rotate until the pin points north. This is how sailors navigated before the invention of the modern compass. Feel free to share this information; it's not a secret. Just don't tell anyone where you heard it.

Cass's "Super-Chip" Trail Mix
Author's note: I've never tried this recipe myself, but Cass swears by it.

---

*APPENDIX USUALLY MEANS "SMALL OUTGROWTH FROM LARGE INTESTINE," BUT IN THIS CASE IT MEANS "ADDITIONAL INFORMATION ACCOMPANYING MAIN TEXT." OR ARE THOSE REALLY THE SAME THINGS? THINK CAREFULLY BEFORE YOU INSULT THIS BOOK.

Ingredients:
$\frac{1}{4}$ cup chocolate chips
$\frac{1}{4}$ cup peanut-butter chips
$\frac{1}{4}$ cup banana chips
$\frac{1}{4}$ cup potato chips
. . . and no raisins, ever!

Instructions:
"Pre-break" banana chips and potato chips by dumping them into a big bowl, then crushing with a cup. (Try to make all pieces the same size — about $\frac{1}{4}$ inch around.) Mix in chocolate chips and peanut-butter chips. Pour into ziplock bag. Seal. Eat in emergencies. Or when you don't like what's being served for dinner.

Circus Glossary
Here is some of the lingo the Bergamo Brothers learned when they were in the circus. But be careful. If you use these words incorrectly, a real carny will know you're just a rube!

All Out and Over — Means the show has ended. (Or in our case, the book.)

Bally — The platform a circus or carnival performer stands on when he's trying to attract a crowd for the sideshow. It gets its name from the *ballyhoo:* "Step right up! Prepare to be excited and amazed!"

Like everything else in the circus, the bally and the ballyhoo are designed for one purpose: to trap the audience into paying as much money as possible.

Big Top — The main circus tent. Where the Bergamo Brothers first caught sight of the Ringmaster who would later sell them for a few dollars.

Blowdown — When a storm knocks over the Big Top — and suddenly everyone in the tent looks like a clown.

Blowoff — A special, curtained-off show at the end of a circus tent. The idea is to get people to buy another show ticket on their way out.

Carny — A carnival worker. Sometimes toothless. Always conniving. Of course, a circus and a carnival are not exactly the same thing. (A circus worker is sometimes called a *cirky*.) But the circus that the Bergamo Brothers joined had elements of both — you could say it was the worst of both worlds!

Clem — A fight with the locals.

Jump — The jump is the distance a circus or carnival travels between performances.

Mark — An audience member — i.e., a sucker.

Mentalist act — A mind-reading routine like the Bergamo Brothers'.

Midway — The area between — midway, get it? — the circus exit and the entrance to the Big Top. This is where the sideshow stalls and concessions are lined up.

Roustabout — A laborer in the circus. Also a fun word to say.

Rube — A rube is exactly what you are if you don't know the word *rube*. In other words, a dupe. A townie or other circus newbie.

Shill — Shills work for the circus but they pretend to be ordinary customers impressed by the sideshow acts — so that other customers get excited enough to cough up their money. Think of parents at a school performance. You know how they always clap really loudly, even when their kids sing out of key or flub their lines? Parents are terrible shills.

Slum — The useless stuff you buy from a circus vendor, like teddy bears and plaster statuettes. Otherwise known as toys and prizes.

Swag — See slum.

Tip — Audience or crowd. "*Turning the tip*" means getting the crowd to pay to enter a show.

With it — Hip to the carnival scene. A carny. You're either with it — or you're not.

Keyword Codes

The secret letter Cass and Max-Ernest received from the Terces Society was encrypted with a keyword code. If you want to try encrypting or decrypting a letter with a keyword code yourself, here's how:

In a keyword code, the first letters of the alphabet are replaced by a secret word. For instance, if TERCES is your keyword, A is replaced by T, B by E, C by R, D by C, and E by S. (You skip the second E in TERCES because you can't repeat letters.) After the letters of the keyword, the alphabet proceeds normally—minus the letters that have already been established. Therefore, in this case, F is replaced by A, and G by B. H, however, is not replaced by C, because you've already used C for D; instead, H is replaced by D.

In the end, your code looks like this . . . Or rather, YLUO RLCS ILLHP IFHS QDFP:

T	E	R	C	S	A	B	D	F	G	H	I	J	K	L	M	N	O	P	Q	U	V	W	X	Y	Z
A	B	C	D	E	F	G	H	I	J	K	L	M	N	O	P	Q	R	S	T	U	V	W	X	Y	Z

A Personal Recommendation

Those readers whose knowledge of Egyptology is as shamefully deficient as Cassandra's could do worse than to pick up a copy of *The Egyptian Book of the Dead,* also known as *The Papyrus of Ani.* A guide to the next world, it includes many important spells and instructions for success in the afterlife—a useful introduction to ancient Egyptian life aboveground as well!

The Bergamo Brothers' Card Trick

This is one of the card tricks that the Bergamo Brothers performed when they were first learning magic. Of course, they performed it on the deck of a ship, and with a real deck of cards, but you'll get the idea.

Choose one of the six cards below and think about it really hard.

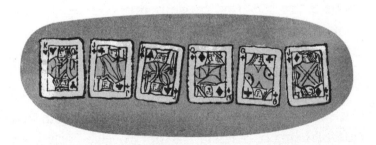

Now, keep thinking about it as you flip to the next page. All the cards will appear again—except the one you're thinking about.

Your card isn't here, is it?

Think it was just a coincidence? Try again. Go back to the last page, choose a different card, and think about that card. Then return to this page and see if it's here. . . .

Want to try the trick on someone else? Hand this book to them and make them choose a card. Better yet, forget the book. Grab a deck of cards and put on a show.

If you haven't yet figured out the secret, I'll tell you how the trick is done. But remember, the first rule of being a magician is not to give away your tricks. So don't let anyone else in on it, no matter how much they beg or plead or threaten you.

What you'll need: a deck of cards and a top hat. (A cowboy hat also works. A baseball hat? — not so much. Think *style*.)

Before your audience arrives:

Separate all the face cards from the deck.

Then divide the face cards into two groups of six cards each.

Each group of six should include: one black king and one red king, one black queen and one red queen, one red jack and one black jack.

Remove a card from one of the groups and return it to the original deck. You now have one group of five cards and one group of six cards.

Hide the group of five cards in your hat. If there is a ribbon around the inside of the hat, try sticking them under the ribbon. That way you can wear the hat without disturbing the cards.

Spread the other six cards faceup on a table.

You're now ready to begin.

Tell someone in your audience, preferably a sibling whom you want to annoy, to choose one of the cards on the table. Tell this person not to say the name of the card aloud. Instead, he or she should simply think about the card — really hard.

If you're wearing your hat, take it off — being very careful not to let the hidden cards fall out. Then pick up the cards off the table and put them in your hat, too. Be sure to keep the two sets of cards separate.

After a suitable magical interlude in which you

pretend to concentrate on the cards, and perhaps even put the hat back on, remove the hidden group of cards (the group with only five cards) and arrange them in front of you.

Ask your victim, that is, your audience member, if his or her card is on the table.

None of the original cards will be there — because they're in your hat. But your audience will think that only the one card is missing.

Et voilà!

THE END

THE END

REALLY.

Now that you've survived the first book
—if you think you're brave enough—
flip the page for a SECRET sneak peek at
Book #2.

But be warned:

IF YOU'RE
READING
THIS, IT'S
TOO
LATE

Coming October 2008 from
Little, Brown and Company

PROLOGUE

~~The flashlight pierced the darkness~~
~~The flashlight *slashed through* the darkness~~
~~The flashlight *beam sliced* through the darkness *like a sword*~~

The flashlight beam darted — *yes!* — across the dark hall, illuminating a wondrous collection of antique curiosities:

Finely illustrated tarot cards of wizened kings and laughing fools . . . glistening Chinese lacquer boxes concealing spring traps and secret compartments . . . intricately carved cups of wood and ivory designed for making coins and marbles and even fingers disappear . . . shining silver rings that a knowing hand could link and unlink as if they were made of air . . .

A museum of magic.

The circle of light lingered on a luminous crystal ball, as if waiting for some swirling image to appear on the surface. Then it stopped, hesitating on a large bronze lantern — once home, perhaps, to a powerful genie.

Finally, the flashlight beam found its way to a glass display case sitting alone in the middle of the room.

"Ha! At last!" said a woman with a voice like ice.

The man behind the flashlight snickered. "Who

was it that said the best place to hide something was in plain sight? What an idiot." His accent was odd, ominous.

"Just do it!" hissed the woman.

Grasping the heavy flashlight tight in his gloved hand, the man brought it down like an ax. Glass shattered in a cascade, revealing a milky white orb — a giant pearl? — sitting on a bed of black velvet.

Ignoring the sharp, glittering shards, the woman reached with a delicately thin hand — in a delicately thin white glove — and pulled out the orb.

About the size of an ostrich egg, it was translucent and seemed almost to glow from within. The surface had a honeycomb sort of texture comprised of many holes of varying sizes. A thin band of silver circled the orb, dividing it into two equal hemispheres.

The woman pushed aside her white-blonde hair and held the mysterious object to her perfectly shaped ear. As she turned it over, it whispered like an open bottle in the wind.

"I can almost hear him," she gloated. "That horrid monster!"

"You're so sure he's alive? It's been four, five hundred years . . ."

"A creature like that — so impossible to make —

is all the more impossible to kill," she replied, still listening to the ball in her hand.

A small red bloodstain now marked her white glove where one of the glass shards had cut through; she didn't seem to notice. "But now he can escape us no longer. The Secret will be mine!"

The flashlight beam fell.

"I mean *ours*, darling."

Beneath the shattered display a small brass plaque gleamed. *The Sound Prism, origin unknown,* it read —

AAAAAAAA
AAAAAAAA

AAAAAAAAA
AAAARRGH!

CONTINUED IN BOOK 2—
IF YOU DARE!